P9-CBB-976

# Nightstruck

# Nightstruck

## JENNA BLACK

**TOR°**
**TEEN**

A TOM DOHERTY ASSOCIATES BOOK

*New York*

This is a work of fiction. All of the characters, organiza-
tions, and events portrayed in this novel are either products
of the author's imagination or are used fictitiously.

NIGHTSTRUCK

Copyright © 2016 by Jenna Black

A Tor Teen Book
Published by Tom Doherty Associates, LLC
175 Fifth Avenue
New York, NY 10010

www.tor-forge.com

Tor® is a registered trademark of Tom Doherty Associates,
LLC.

The Library of Congress Cataloging-in-Publication Data is
available upon request.

ISBN 978-0-7653-8004-3 (hardcover)
ISBN 978-1-4668-7176-2 (e-book)

Our books may be purchased in bulk for promotional,
educational, or business use. Please contact your local
bookseller or the Macmillan Corporate and Premium
Sales Department at 1-800-221-7945, extension 5442, or by
e-mail at MacmillanSpecialMarkets@macmillan.com.

First Edition: April 2016

Printed in the United States of America

0  9  8  7  6  5  4  3  2  1

TO THE BALDWIN SCHOOL, UPON WHICH THE SCHOOL IN THIS BOOK IS VERY LOOSELY BASED. AND A SPECIAL THANK-YOU TO MR. SHAKESPEARE (YES, THAT REALLY WAS MY ENGLISH TEACHER'S NAME), WHO INTRODUCED ME TO CREATIVE WRITING AND STARTED ME DOWN THE LONG ROAD TO BECOMING A FULL-TIME WRITER.

# Nightstruck

# PROLOGUE

whisper of movement in the darkness, not visible to the mortal eye. A hush falls over the deserted alley, the sound of nearby cars fading into an impossible distance. The street holds its breath, and the heavy stone wall of the church on the corner shies away from a newly formed cold spot, a pinprick flaw in the barrier that keeps the Night Makers from entering the mortal world.

It has happened before, this brief failure of the barrier. The flaw is tiny. Inconsequential. Certainly too small for the Night Makers to fit through. But it is large enough to admit a thin tendril of magic, magic that has no place in the world of mortal creatures.

It is a lure, a baited hook that awaits unwary prey.

Six times has this hook been cast between the worlds, and six times has the barrier sealed up the opening before the bait was taken. But seven is a special number, a *lucky* number—or an unlucky one, depending on one's point of view.

This time, the hook would sink deep into mortal flesh, each taste of mortal blood widening the hole in the barrier, allowing more and more magic—and other things—through.

The magic settles into the shadowed corner of the church's

stoop. The Night Makers enjoy this irony of location. Like the thick, inky smoke of an oil fire, the magic forms a blacker shadow, one that slowly begins to take shape. The shape is small and imperfect. It would not pass inspection in the bright light of day. But for the purpose of this night, it would do. Yes, it would do nicely.

The shape solidifies. Moments later, it lets out a long, unearthly wail.

And the trap is set.

# CHAPTER ONE

$\mathcal{W}$alking the dog when it's twenty degrees outside isn't my favorite thing in the world, but, as usual, my dad was working late, and if I didn't take Bob Barker (don't blame me; my dad named him) out for a walk, I'd have an even more unpleasant chore in front of me. Bob is a seventy-five-pound German shepherd, and I know from experience he can make one hell of a big mess.

I bundled up in my down coat, pulling on a wool hat even though it would make my hair into an electrified puffball. Bob waited impatiently, eyes focused on me with the unnerving intensity only a dog can manage, his tail wagging in anticipation. He'd be just as eager to go out if it were *minus* twenty.

"Don't say I never do anything for you," I muttered at him as I clipped on his leash and stepped outside into the arctic blast.

My dad and I live on a narrow side street in Center City, Philadelphia. As Center City neighborhoods go, it's pretty good, but I was always glad to have Bob at my side when I had to go out at night. He wasn't a police dog, but he'd had some of the same training, and no one remotely sane would mess with him. I walked him down to Walnut Street, shivering and cursing the icy wind as Bob went through his usual routine of sniffing everything in the neighborhood to confirm that it smelled the same as it did six hours ago.

"Hurry up!" I ordered him, but he was having too much fun sniffing to pay much attention to me. My dad, with his deep, stern voice, could probably get Bob to stand on his head with nothing but a simple voice command, but me, not so much.

We made our torturous way around the block, Bob squirting a drop or two of pee on every immovable object we passed. The moment he finally took care of business, I made a beeline for home. We were on Chestnut Street, and the fastest way back to my front door was to cut down an alley that I would ordinarily avoid. Even so close to home and in a safe neighborhood, my city-girl instincts balked at walking down a narrow, deserted alley at night. But I was freezing, and I had Bob, so I made an exception just this once.

There was nothing in the alley except for the back side of a few businesses, all of which were closed for the night, their windows dark. There was a church at the far end, but its windows were dark too, and as Bob and I walked away from the busy street, I felt like I was somehow leaving civilization behind. It didn't help that one of the streetlamps had burned out, creating pockets of shadow around recessed doorways and hulking Dumpsters.

A strange shiver ran down my spine, and my footsteps slowed.

*It's not strange to shiver when it's twenty degrees out,* I told myself.

But something felt . . . off. I looked all around, searching for a logical explanation for why I was suddenly creeped out. I saw nothing, though there were a couple of shadowy areas that were probably big enough to hide the maniacal serial killer my lizard brain seemed to think was lurking.

I was chilled to the bone and could no longer feel my nose. If I stopped being a wuss about the alley, I could be home in less than five minutes. I wanted a giant mug of hot cocoa and my electric blanket.

But then I noticed that the hair on the back of Bob's neck had risen, and his ears had gone flat. I wasn't the only one who sensed danger in the darkness. Bob was staring intently at the pool of shadow at the base of the stone steps leading up to the church, and his lips peeled away from his teeth. The shadow wasn't big enough to hide a knife-wielding psycho, and I wondered if maybe Bob had spotted a cat. Or maybe even a rat.

Whatever it was, I wanted no part of it. One of the self-defense lessons my dad the police commissioner had taught me was to always listen to my instincts, and they were telling me in no uncertain terms that it was time to get out of that alley. I felt a little silly being spooked when there was no visible threat, like a little girl who was afraid of the dark, but there are worse things in life than feeling silly.

That was when I heard the wailing cry that turned my blood to ice and set my heart racing. Bob let out a furious bark and lunged toward the shadow, practically yanking my arm out of its socket. He was seventy-five pounds of pure muscle, and in a tug of war, I was bound to come out the loser.

"Bob, heel!" I yelled at him in my most commanding tone.

I must have sounded like I meant it, because Bob stopped straining against the leash, although he was still snarling, and his every muscle was quivering with his desire to attack. I didn't know what had made that bloodcurdling noise, but it wasn't a rat or a cat.

"Come on," I urged Bob, giving his leash a little tug. At that point, I'd have happily walked a mile out of my way, if that's what I needed to do to avoid that pool of shadow.

The cry came again, sounding as unearthly, as alien as before. I felt like I should cross myself, or maybe make a sign to ward off the evil eye. The sound was utterly and completely *wrong*. I took a step backward, tugging on Bob's leash. Every instinct was screaming at me to run, but I couldn't make myself turn my back on that shadow.

I don't know if it was a trick of acoustics or if my imagination had been running wild with me, but the sound seemed to change. The unearthly wail became something much more ordinary, and I realized what it was: a baby crying.

The hair on the back of my neck and arms prickled, and I froze. I wanted the safety of my house, the security of a closed and locked door. Finally identifying the sound as a crying baby rather than a bloodthirsty monster didn't chase away the sense of wrongness that gripped me. It didn't seem to be calming Bob down any, either. My instincts were still telling me to get the hell out of there, and I kept hearing my dad's voice in my head, telling me to listen to my instincts.

But what kind of person hears the cries of an abandoned infant—on a subfreezing night, no less—and runs away? It was a *baby*, for God's sake! There was nothing to be scared of, and leaving a helpless baby to freeze to death in an alley just wasn't an option.

The problem was Bob. He'd obeyed my command to heel, but he was still bristling and snarling. There was no way I could get close to that baby with him on the end of the leash. He was well trained and usually pretty obedient, but I'd never had to control him when he went into attack-dog mode, and I was afraid he was too strong for me.

I looked around, hoping to spot someone else running to the rescue, but there was no one in sight. It was all up to me.

I tied Bob's leash to a lamppost, making three knots in the leather and praying it would hold. He barely seemed aware of my presence, his entire attention focused on the baby and his overwhelming desire to attack it.

"What is the matter with you?" I asked him, wishing he could actually answer. I'd been creeped out the moment I stepped into the alley. I could tell myself I'd watched too many horror movies and it was all in my mind, but that didn't explain how Bob was acting.

"Bob, stay," I ordered him firmly, but the moment I stepped away, he was straining against his leash, unconcerned with the fact that he was strangling himself in the process. I shook my head at him and hoped the knots in the leash would hold.

The baby's cries were growing weaker, to the point where Bob's snarls almost drowned them out. I began walking toward the church, trying to act sure and confident, as if I could somehow convince myself to shake off the weirdness. I still couldn't pick out the baby's shape in the pool of darkness, but there was a sense of movement, as if maybe the baby was kicking its arms and legs in its desperate attempt to get help.

How could anyone leave a baby out in the cold? I knew churches were popular spots for abandoning unwanted babies, but anyone with half a brain would know that this particular church was closed for the night. Which made me think whoever had left the baby had intended for it to die. Thanks to my dad's job, I was more aware than most of how much evil there is in the world, and how cruel human beings can be. And how important it is for ordinary people—like me—to show compassion and responsibility.

Even knowing all that, I found my feet reluctant to move me forward. Maybe, if I just called 9-1-1, they'd get here in time to save the poor kid without me having to get any closer.

And if an innocent baby died because I was too chickenshit to help it, how would I ever live with myself? How could I ever look my dad—who'd risked his life countless times as a police officer—in the face? I was already something of a family disappointment, and I couldn't bear to make it worse.

Calling 9-1-1 seemed like a good idea anyway, so I got out my phone and made the call as I continued to force myself forward. Behind me, Bob was still barking and snarling, but the baby's cries had faded to weak-sounding whimpers.

"Nine-one-one. What's your emergency?"

I had reached the edge of the pool of shadow, and I could finally make out the baby's shape, though it was still hard to see. It seemed to be wrapped in a black blanket, as if whoever had left it there had put extra effort into making sure no one would find it and rescue it.

"My name is Becket Walker," I said, hoping the dispatcher would be extra attentive to a call coming from the commissioner's daughter. "I've found an abandoned baby."

I squatted in the darkness beside the bundled baby, who was no longer even whimpering. The blanket was tucked so firmly around it that all I could see was a baby-shaped lump. A fold of the blanket was draped over its face. I stammered out the address to the dispatcher, then decided the only sensible, humane thing to do was to pick up the baby and share what body heat I could. The dispatcher was asking me questions and trying to give me instructions, but I wasn't listening.

"Hold on a moment," I said. I put the phone down on the church steps, then gently picked up the black-wrapped bundle with both hands.

I almost dropped it, because it didn't feel like I expected it to. The body within the blanket felt strangely loose and pliable. My stomach turned over, the sense of wrongness once again coming back full force.

The 9-1-1 dispatcher was still talking to me, but I had no attention to spare. Something within me rebelled at the feeling of that body in my arms, but I fought my revulsion. Maybe the baby had some kind of birth defect and that was why it had been abandoned. That didn't make it any less worth saving.

I cradled the baby against my body with one arm, then reached for the fold of blanket that covered its face. Maybe when I looked into the baby's innocent eyes, I'd finally stop feeling so . . . weird.

There was a pin sticking out of the section of blanket over the baby's face. Thanks to the pressing darkness, I didn't see it until I pricked my finger on it. I cursed as a drop of blood welled on the tip of my finger. I still couldn't see the baby's face, though I had a vague notion of eyes watching me from the blanket's interior. I reached for the edge of the blanket again, this time being careful to avoid the pin, and brushed it away from the baby's face.

There *was* a face in there somewhere—I could see a pair of green eyes staring out at me—but I couldn't make out a single feature. It was if the baby had somehow absorbed all the light, leaving nothing but a black hole where its face should have been.

My chest tightened, making it hard to breathe, and the air around me suddenly seemed even colder. Once again, I was struck by the sense that something was very, very wrong, though my conscious mind couldn't seem to figure out what.

Maybe it was the expression in those eyes. I'd never seen a baby stare at anyone with such intensity, especially not a baby who'd recently been bawling.

I froze, my hand still hovering near the baby's face, unable to look away, unable to move, as I tried to focus my gaze enough to pick out a nose or lips or chin. The drop of blood on the tip of my finger dripped down onto the baby's face—or at least onto where the baby's face should be.

Something flared in those green eyes, and the baby smiled at me. I let out a little scream and dropped it, scrambling back away from it on my butt. I didn't know what it was, but it was *not* human. That smile had revealed double rows of razor-sharp teeth.

My heart was pounding, and my body was suddenly drenched in sweat. I could hear Bob barking and snarling in the distance, and the dispatcher's voice was an indecipherable hum from my phone on the steps.

The baby—or whatever it was—moved out of the shadow, the black-wrapped bundle undulating like an inchworm. It rose up and looked at me, showing me those malevolent green eyes and the neat little rows of fangs around its smile.

And then the whole thing, baby, blanket, and all, broke apart like it was made of ash, crumbling and then being caught on a sudden burst of wind. The wind carried a cloud of what looked like dust toward me. I ducked and held my breath, but not fast enough to totally avoid the cloud. The wind swirled, then gusted again, blowing the cloud away and dispersing it into the night.

. . .

I was still shaking when I finally got home, and though I was freezing, my case of the shakes had nothing to do with the cold. I wrapped myself up in a blanket and curled up on the couch, trying to process what had just happened. Bob seemed as freaked out as I felt, jumping onto the couch beside me and putting his head in my lap. He wasn't allowed on the couch, but house rules were the least of my concerns. Besides, he was a warm body, and he made me feel safe. Well, safer, at least.

What the hell had happened out there?

I shuddered and clutched the blanket more tightly around me. I heard again that first sound, the inhuman wail that had triggered some primal instinct to run. And then the cry of an innocent baby, terrified and alone in the cold.

Had either one of them been real? Had I somehow imagined the whole thing? Because what I thought I saw was impossible.

If I'd been even a little less freaked out, I wouldn't have been surprised when the police showed up on my doorstep. I'd made that 9-1-1 call, and I'd identified myself quite clearly. There was no way telling the dispatcher to "forget it" was going to work.

The patrolmen who stopped by to talk to me were perfectly nice, going out of their way to be polite, no doubt because they knew who I was. I was glad I couldn't read minds, because I don't think I would have liked what I saw in theirs.

Naturally, I couldn't tell them the truth about what had happened. They'd either lock me in a nuthouse or assume I was on drugs. So I told them that what I'd thought was a baby had turned out to be an alley cat. Cats can sound kind of like babies sometimes, right? And it was dark out. I'd called the police before investigating because I thought the baby might need immediate care, and then I hung up on the dispatcher in abject embarrassment when the "baby" had jumped out of a pile of rags and turned out to be a cat.

It made me sound like an airhead, but that was better than psycho or druggie. I don't know if the cops bought it, but they didn't call me a liar. Not to my face, at least.

If only I could make myself believe my own story. But my mind insisted on reliving those last few moments, when the baby had inched out of the shadow and bared those awful teeth at me. And when it had vaporized—for want of a better word—right in front of my eyes.

Which reminded me suddenly that the cloud of . . . whatever had passed right over my head. I ran a shaking hand through my hair and practically threw up when I saw the oily black streak that was left on my palm. It wasn't much. Not so much a streak as a smudge. And there were probably a million things it could be, other than baby residue. I'd been wearing a hat, after all. But I bolted for the bathroom anyway.

I washed my hair about eighteen times, my skin crawling. The mark came off my hand easily enough, and if there was any more of it in my hair, I didn't see it amid the suds I rinsed off. Yet I felt sure I was tainted somehow. I didn't know what that "baby" had been, couldn't even think of some convenient folkloric label to pin on it, but I was convinced, body and soul, that it had been evil. And I wished I'd listened to my instincts instead of being a Good Samaritan.

My night went from bad to worse a couple hours later, when my dad got home. He'd heard about the 9-1-1 call, of course, and he didn't buy my story of mistaken identity.

"I can't believe you would do something so selfish and childish!" he said. He didn't yell, but with that deep, commanding voice of his, he didn't have to. He glared down at me with steely eyes, so furious his cheeks flushed.

"It was an honest mistake," I replied, making my eyes go big and wounded. When he and Mom were still together, doe eyes had often worked on him, but ever since the divorce this past summer, he was in a perpetual state of pissed off, and he seemed to like it there.

"Not another word!" he snapped. "You didn't call the police because you saw a damn cat. What was this supposed to be? A protest about me working so late?" His scowl deepened. "Did that friend of yours put you up to this?"

This was just what I needed after my already traumatic, terrifying, and embarrassing night. How could my dad think I would make a crank call to the police? And why would he suddenly drag Piper into this just because he didn't like her?

"No one put me up to anything," I said, my own pulse quickening with anger. Sure, I'd gotten in trouble a few times lately, and most of the time it had been with Piper by my side, but I'd given Dad no reason to think I'd call 9-1-1 just for shits and giggles. It stung pretty hard to think he gave me that little credit. "This wasn't a prank, and it wasn't some stupid cry for attention. It was an honest mistake, like I said."

"Don't make it worse by lying."

I crossed my arms over my chest and tried to look defiant instead of hurt. "So what you're telling me is that you've already decided what happened and why, and you don't give a shit about my side of the story."

For a fraction of a second I thought I'd scored a point, that Dad finally realized how unfair he was being. His eyes briefly softened, and there was a hint of doubt in them. But he hadn't gotten where he was today by allowing himself to feel uncertain of anything. And getting him to change his mind was like trying to turn the *Titanic*.

"You are grounded for two weeks," he told me. "You will not leave this house except to go to school and run errands. No Internet, and no phone."

He held out his hand in a silent demand that I hand over my phone. When my dad says I'm grounded, he doesn't fool around. I guess he was used to dealing with scumbags who made taking advantage of loopholes into an art form. I'd be lucky if he didn't periodically toss my room just to make sure I hadn't borrowed a phone from anyone.

"This isn't fair," I told him with a hitch in my voice. "I've done nothing wrong." That, at least, was perfectly true.

He just stood there with his hand extended, his face cold and devoid of anything resembling fatherly compassion.

He didn't used to be this way. He'd never exactly been warm and fuzzy, but he'd been fair, and he had a soft side that only my mother, my older sister, and I saw. There had never been any doubt in my mind that he loved me. But he'd been a different man since the divorce went through, harder and angrier and unyielding. I wanted my pre-divorce father back, but I didn't think that was going to happen, at least not until after I graduated high school and left home.

When they'd split up, my parents had let me choose who I wanted to live with, and I'd chosen Dad because Mom was moving to Boston and I didn't want to start a new school for my senior year. Right now, that wasn't looking like the world's greatest decision.

"I should have gone with Mom," I told him as I slapped my phone into his hand.

# CHAPTER TWO

There's a part of me that's always been jealous of Piper Grant, even though she's my best friend. For one thing, she's beautiful, whereas the most flattering way I can describe myself is "somewhat attractive," and that's only on my good days. She's tall and lean, with lustrous red-gold hair that never seems to get frizzy or oily or tangled. As far as I can tell, she's never had a zit in her life, and if we didn't go to an all-girls school, she'd surely have every straight boy in school trailing after her in adoration.

Someone who looked like she did could easily become a bitchy mean girl, but Piper wasn't like that. I'd had enough of bitchy mean girls in middle school, thank you very much. Piper was popular, but she never let it go to her head. She seemed to like just about everyone, and just about everyone liked her right back. Except my dad, who thought she was a spoiled, entitled rich kid who got off on manipulating her "worshipers," which is what he said I was.

Although Piper and I went to the same school, we weren't in any of the same classes. She wasn't stupid—the Edith Goldman School for Girls doesn't admit stupid people—but she wasn't bound for academic glory, either. I'm in A.P. everything, and she was just scraping by "normal" classes with indifferent grades. We didn't even have the same lunch break, so the only time I got to talk to her was when we passed each other in the hall, or after school.

I'd been thinking all day about what I was going to tell her about last night's nightmare encounter. On the one hand, she was my best friend, and if I couldn't tell *her* the truth about what happened, then I couldn't tell anyone. On the other hand, why should she believe my crazy story when I barely believed it myself?

Every time I passed her in the hall, I expected her to stop and ask me what was wrong. I wasn't *trying* to act all weird, but I'd barely gotten any sleep, and I was so distracted by my own thoughts that twice I almost walked by without seeing her. Two of my teachers had taken me aside and asked if everything was okay, so I knew I was being pretty obvious. But Piper isn't the most observant person I've ever met—my dad would say because she's too self-absorbed to notice other people—and if she thought I was acting funny, she didn't say anything about it.

I was packing up my backpack after school when Piper suddenly appeared at my side, leaning against the bank of lockers and frowning. I jumped a little when I saw her, and her frown deepened.

"I've been standing here for like five minutes," she said. "I was beginning to think I had to do a backflip to get your attention."

I forced a grin that felt awkward as I hoisted my backpack and closed my locker. "Sorry. I'm a little preoccupied."

"No kidding?"

I gave her a dirty look, thinking now she would surely ask

me what was wrong. I still hadn't decided what to tell her, though I was leaning toward the same cat story I'd told the police and my dad. She'd talked me through some pretty awful times as my parents' marriage had broken up. I started lots of those conversations in tears, and they mostly ended with me calm and smiling. Even laughing sometimes. I could have used a good dose of her sunny outlook right now, but I didn't have the guts to tell her the truth. She had always been very accepting of me, but I didn't know how any sane person could accept this particular story.

"I'm going to head over to Rare Vintage and do a little shopping before I go home," she said. "Wanna come with?"

Rare Vintage is a vintage clothing store Piper was in love with. It was within walking distance of our school—not that it mattered, since Piper's parents had given her a Volvo for her sixteenth birthday. My parents, on the other hand, had told me in no uncertain terms that if I wanted my own car I had to earn the money to buy it myself. They both grew up poor and made huge successes of themselves—my mom is a corporate lawyer and my dad the youngest police commissioner in Philly's history—and they thought giving me things they couldn't have afforded at my age would spoil me. Never mind that, without a car, my commute to school was pure hell, involving a couple of long walks to and from the train station as well as a thirty-minute train ride.

"I can't," I told her, making a regretful face even though Rare Vintage is not my favorite place. Maybe Piper has enough extra cash lying around to drop on fancy beaded flapper dresses she'll never wear, but I don't. "I'm grounded."

Except for my dad confiscating my phone and not letting me use the Internet, being grounded wasn't that big a deal for me. Most of my schoolmates lived out in the suburbs, and with me not having a car, it was really hard for me to hang out with them outside of school. On most days, I went straight home, and being grounded wasn't going to change that. Though if I weren't grounded, I'd have gone to Rare Vintage just as a chance to spend more time with Piper. She had about a bazillion friends, and getting a spot on her social calendar was something of a challenge.

Piper raised her eyebrows in surprise. "You've been getting into trouble without me?" she asked with mock incredulity. "How *could* you?" She lowered her head and put a hand to her sternum as if heartsick.

I laughed and let a little of the tension ease out of my shoulders. Even if I couldn't get myself to confide what had happened last night, maybe spending time with her—even if it was only a few stolen minutes—was the best thing for me.

Piper glanced at her watch. "What time is your train?" she asked.

"Three thirty," I told her, not looking forward to the long, cold wait on the platform. It was still in the twenties out, and the train platform was open and windy. The colder and more miserable the weather, the less likely the damn train would come on time.

"Hmm. I bet if I give you a ride home, I can get you there with time to spare."

I bit my lip, thinking about it. I knew my dad. He would still be at work when I got home, but since I was grounded, he would definitely call and make sure I was at home when I was supposed to be. And Piper was a little fuzzy on the meaning of punctuality. Chances were that, if I went with her, I'd be home late even with the ride.

"If we don't beat the train home," she wheedled, "you can always tell your dad it was late. It's not like it's never delayed or anything."

"True," I said. My dad would never have to know I'd defied him. And it would feel good to give this unfair punishment the respect it deserved.

Piper didn't wait for my answer, just slipped her arm through mine and gave me a tug toward the parking lot.

We weren't in the store more than about five minutes before Piper's phone rang, and I knew immediately by the goofy look on her face that the call was from her current boyfriend, Luke. I hadn't managed to have a single boyfriend yet, myself—going to an all-girls school and not having a car combined to make meeting boys really tough—but Piper went through them like popcorn, one moment head over heels in love, the next bored and looking for a new adventure.

Piper gave me an apologetic smile before retreating to one of the changing rooms so she could have a private conversation with Luke, leaving me browsing the racks aimlessly.

I was the one who introduced Piper to Luke, though I kind of regretted it. There's a gated courtyard behind my house, and Luke lives in the house across the courtyard from me. I'd had a crush on him for forever, but he never showed any sign of being interested in me in that way. For my seventeenth birthday, my dad had hosted a cookout in the courtyard. Piper was there, of course, but I'd also scraped up the courage to ask Luke. When he'd said yes, I thought maybe there was some glimmer of interest after all. But then he'd come to the party, and he'd met Piper, and that was that.

I'd never told Piper about my crush, so it wasn't like she intentionally stole the boy I was interested in. But I couldn't help a little twinge of jealousy every time I saw them together. I kept waiting for them to break up—they'd been together almost four months already, which was a record for Piper—but so far they were going strong. So strong that she was on that phone with him *forever.* I could hear her giggling from the back room as I kept glancing at my watch. Time was ticking away, and even if we left right that moment, I was going to have to lie to my dad and tell him my train was late.

I finally grew impatient and stomped back to the dressing room, pulling the curtain open and giving Piper a meaningful look before tapping my watch. She lowered the phone from her face for a second to glance at the time, and her eyes went wide.

"Oh, shit!" she said, raising the phone once more. "Sorry. I lost track of time. I've gotta go."

I couldn't hear whatever it was Luke said to her on the other end of the line, but it made her blush and smile. "I love you, too," she said.

I turned my back to her so she wouldn't see the sour face I made. There's nothing quite like hearing your best friend saying "I love you" to the boy you've had a secret crush on for years. Maybe I shouldn't have kept it secret. Piper had certainly made no secret about her attraction when she'd met him. She'd flirted with him from the moment I introduced them, and he'd lapped it up.

But then, Piper was beautiful, and witty, and brimming with self-confidence. How could Luke *not* have fallen for her? And why would he settle for an ordinary, socially awkward shy girl like me when he could have Piper? Even if I'd had the guts to tell him I liked him, and even if he liked me back, Piper would have dazzled him.

*Maybe if you'd told Piper you wanted him, she wouldn't have made a play for him,* I reminded myself. Hell, if I'd told her, she'd most likely have thrown herself into a quest to hook me up with him.

Maybe that's what I'd been afraid of. If she'd tried to play matchmaker and it didn't work, I'd have been utterly humiliated. And with Luke living so close, I'd have my nose rubbed in that humiliation practically every day.

No. Better for him to be with Piper, even if it did make me jealous. Jealous was better than humiliated.

Piper finally got off the phone, and we hurried to her car. "I'm so sorry," she said as we piled in. "You should have come and interrupted me sooner. You know how I am with time."

I snapped my seat belt closed while she started the car. She was right, of course. I *should* have interrupted her sooner. But I hadn't, and it was too late to change that.

"It's okay," I told her, insisting to myself that it was. I'd let her talk me into missing the train because I wanted to spend time with her. Instead, I'd spent my time browsing alone through a store I had no interest in while she talked on the phone. The cold, hard truth was that although Piper was my best friend, I wasn't hers. If she were to disappear from my life, I'd be devastated; if I were to disappear from hers, she'd be sad for a while, then get over it. When you make friends as easily as she does, you just don't get as attached.

"No, it's not okay," she said, surprising me. "I was being rude and inconsiderate, and I'm sorry."

I sighed. Sometimes Piper annoyed the hell out of me, but she was still a nice person and a good friend. I'd just have to learn to be more assertive with her. She'd gotten off the phone the minute I'd pointed out how late it was. If I'd done that fifteen minutes earlier, we wouldn't be having this conversation.

"Hey, I know you forget the rest of the world exists when you're talking to Luke," I told her with a smile. "It's my job to remind you."

Mentioning Luke brought the smile right back to her face, as I'd known it would. "Well, he is a little distracting," she admitted. "Somehow, we've got to find a boy for you. It would be so cool if we could go on a double date."

Yeah, right. Because I would so enjoy seeing Piper and Luke make out. "What do you mean, 'somehow'?" I asked, belatedly. "Is it that hard to imagine a boy liking me?"

Her eyebrows rose, and she turned to look at me. "No, dummy. It's just hard to find a way for you to meet them."

"*You* never seem to have any trouble," I muttered. "And watch the road, please. My dad would kill us both if you got in an accident."

She laughed, but thankfully turned her attention back to the road. "I don't have trouble because my parents let me have a social life. If your dad would loosen up a bit, meeting boys would be a whole lot easier."

Yes, it would. Thanks to being part of Piper's social circle, I was often invited to parties, but my dad would never let me go. I had to be able to prove to him that there would be no drugs or underage drinking at these parties, and I never could. Probably because there *would* be drugs and underage drinking. It was pretty frustrating to have a friend who was so popular and not be able to take advantage of the situation. I'd spent a lot of time in middle school longing to be part of the in crowd, and now, with Piper, I could have that—if only my dad would let me.

"Maybe," I said. "But I don't see that happening anytime soon, do you?"

She made a face. She wasn't any more fond of my dad than he was of her. "Doesn't he realize that by this time next year you'll be in college and making these decisions for yourself?"

I shrugged. "Yeah, but that's the excuse he uses for why it's perfectly fair for him to keep me under lock and key now. If he says 'A year isn't as long as you think' one more time, I'm going to scream."

We stopped at a red light, and Piper turned to me. "He does realize that just because there may be other people around doing drugs and drinking, that doesn't mean *you'll* be doing it, right?"

I winced, because it sure would be nice if my dad *did* realize that. I've never been the type to give in to peer pressure, even back when I was in middle school and those peers were making me miserable. I'm no angel, but I may be a teensy bit of a control freak, and the prospect of getting drunk or high when surrounded by strangers at a party held no appeal.

Piper rolled her eyes. "Jeez, does he even *know* you? I'd probably die of shock if you turned into a lampshade-wearing party animal just because people around you were drinking."

"He's a cop. They don't, as a general rule, have a lot of respect for teenagers."

She waved her hand in dismissal. "But we're not talking about some generic teenager. We're talking about *you*." The look she gave me held more than a hint of pity. "It kinda sucks if he doesn't get the difference."

She was right. It did. But I didn't see much chance of it changing.

The expression on Piper's face changed from one of pity to

31

one of calculation. "Maybe this is a case of what he doesn't know won't hurt him."

Uh-oh. I knew that look. "Whatever you're thinking, the answer is no. I'm in enough trouble with my dad already."

The light turned green, and Piper faced front, but I could still see the little smirk on her lips. *That girl's a bad influence,* my dad whispered in my head. He wasn't entirely wrong, but I couldn't swear that wasn't one of the reasons I liked her so much.

"You can't spend your whole life trying to make your dad happy," Piper said. "You have the right to have some fun. You're coming out with me Saturday night."

"Even *my* dad won't be working on a Saturday night. I don't see myself sneaking out with him in the house." But the thought of going out with Piper on Saturday night kicked my pulse up a notch. I didn't know what she had planned, but I was sure it would be exciting. An adventure.

"So we'll tell him you're coming to spend the night at my place," Piper said easily. "He can't object to a sleepover, can he?"

I snorted. If the sleepover was at Piper's, yes, he could. He didn't trust her as far as he could throw her. "I'm grounded," I reminded her.

She wrinkled her nose. "True. Hmm. Give me a couple of days, I'll come up with a better excuse."

"A better lie, you mean."

She grinned at me. "Your point being . . . ?"

I sank a little lower in my seat and crossed my arms. It wasn't like I had any problem with lying to my dad. If he had his way, my entire life would consist of doing chores, going to school, and studying. If I had a dollar for every time I'd told him I was studying when I was actually reading a romance novel or messing around online, I'd have enough to buy that car I wanted so badly. But this was a whole different level of lying—and there was more risk I'd get caught at it.

"Seriously, Becket, what's the worst that can happen? Your dad can yell at you and ground you for longer, but is that such a terrible risk to take?"

Once again, she had a point. One problem with my dad's No Privileges policy was that he didn't have much in the way of privileges to take away for punishment.

"What the hell," I decided. "You only live once, right? If you can come up with a cover my dad can swallow, then you're on."

Piper grinned and offered me an awkward high five, thankfully keeping her eyes on the road and one hand on the steering wheel. "I love a good challenge," she said. "Now, tell me how you managed to get yourself grounded."

Thinking about what had happened last night put a damper on my momentary defiance high. I wished I could just convince myself it was some kind of nightmare, but every time I tried to sell myself a logical explanation, I kept getting stuck on Bob. All well and good to come up with reasons why I might have been seeing things or misinterpreted what I saw, but there was no question that Bob had seen something freaky, too.

I told Piper the cat story. She laughed her ass off, and I knew she was going to give me a hard time about it for the foreseeable future. But at least she didn't think I was crazy.

# CHAPTER THREE

Jimmy shivered and pulled his flimsy jacket tighter around him as he hurried down the quiet street. He should have worn his heavy coat, but he hadn't wanted to deal with it during dinner, and it had never occurred to him that he wouldn't be going home until the ass end of morning. He'd never gotten lucky on a blind date before and certainly hadn't been expecting it tonight. Winter had eased up a bit and it was above freezing, but only by a degree or two. He turned up the collar of his shirt and buried his hands in his pants pockets, but that didn't help much.

He was shivering, and his feet felt like lumps of ice, but there was still a warm, contented glow in his belly. It had been the best damn blind date ever. The sex alone had been out of this world, but the connection he'd felt with Maria went so much deeper than that. He didn't generally think of himself as the romantic type, but he couldn't help thinking that tonight he may very well have met the One.

The fastest way to get back to his own apartment was to cut through Logan Circle, and he was all for the fastest way. In the daytime, there were always people around, taking in the view of the impressive fountain in the center of the circle, but at this hour sensible people were shut up tight in their heated homes, not taking in the sights, and Logan Circle was deserted.

For reasons he didn't understand, his footsteps slowed when he got within a few yards of the fountain, and the hair on the back of his neck prickled.

At the center of the large circular fountain, there was a raised area with three larger-than-life bronze statues reclining. The highest jet of the fountain rose up from between those figures, and jets all around the perimeter of the circle sent water streaming toward the center. From where Jimmy stood, the feathery jets veiled the figures in the center, revealing only shadows and glimpses.

Jimmy blinked. It had to be his imagination, or just his tired mind messing with his memories, but he could have sworn the bronze figures were reclining farther from the center than they used to be. He took another few steps, moving away from the jets on the edge so he had a better view of the center.

There were steps in the center of the fountain—people often cavorted in the water or sat on those steps on hot summer days—and there were raised sections in the steps for each of the statues. The statue closest to Jimmy was a hollow-eyed naked woman lying on her side with her head raised so she was staring out at anyone who stood near the edge. She was kind of unsettling on the best of days, her eyes shadowed, her stare holding a hint of malevolence, at least in Jimmy's opinion.

And the more he looked, the more Jimmy was convinced the statue wasn't where it was supposed to be. Its hand was usually propped on the top step, its body draped over the rest of the stairs. But now it was lying at the bottom of the stairs.

Jimmy swallowed hard and rubbed his eyes. It had to be an illusion of some kind, or just some kind of brain fart.

When he dropped his hands from his eyes, Jimmy's insides turned to pure ice. Because the statue wasn't reclining anymore. It was sitting up, one arm draped over its knee, the other hand resting casually on the bottom step.

Jimmy's breath came in soft little gasps, white puffs of frozen air emerging from his mouth like smoke. He was seeing things. He had to be. Either that or Maria had put something in his drink—but if she'd done that, surely he'd have felt the effects before now. He shook his head, as if that movement would make the sight before him change.

The statue's lips curled up into a smile, and Jimmy cried out, stumbling backward, in such a hurry to back away that he tripped over his own feet and landed on his butt. The statue's smile went broader, metallic muscles rippling as it slowly rose, those hollow eyes fixed on Jimmy.

Jimmy no longer cared if his mind was playing tricks with him or whether he was having a psychotic episode or what. The look in that statue's eyes was pure malevolence, and Jimmy wasn't hanging around to see what would happen next.

He sprang to his feet, the combination of cold-numbed feet and terror making him clumsy. It didn't help that he couldn't seem to tear his gaze away from the crouching statue.

Finally, Jimmy got his feet under him and forced himself to look away. He ran for all he was worth, looking frantically around for another person, preferably a cop with a gun. If they hauled him off to the loony bin, it would be worth it. But there was no one in sight.

Behind him, there was a metallic screech and a sound like a giant hammer beating down on concrete.

He couldn't help it, couldn't stop himself from looking over his shoulder, though if he'd been in his right mind he'd never have slowed himself down by looking back.

A terrified scream tore from his throat when he saw that the statue was giving chase, its arms reaching for him.

This can't be real, *his mind insisted*. I'm having a nightmare, and any moment I'll wake up in a cold sweat.

*But then a pair of giant metal arms grabbed him and lifted him from the ground. He struggled, kicking and flailing, but it was like being bound with steel bars, the grip so strong it squeezed the breath right out of him. He tried to scream again, but there wasn't enough air in his lungs. The arms squeezed more tightly, and he felt what he was sure was a rib breaking.*

*This was no dream, no matter how impossible it seemed.*

*Keeping a crushing grip on Jimmy, the statue loped back to the fountain. Though every motion hurt, Jimmy kept struggling, the will to live stronger than any pain. He let out a startled little bleat when the statue let go.*

*Jimmy landed in the ice-cold water, on his hands and knees. He came down so hard his teeth sliced into his cheek, and blood trickled from his lips, staining the water. He managed one full breath before the metal hand grabbed him by the back of the neck and shoved his face into the water. His nose made solid contact with the concrete floor of the fountain, and more blood stained the water.*

*The icy water sent shards of pain whipping through his body, and the chill stole what little air he'd managed to suck in. He tried to hold his breath, but the hand stayed clamped around his neck, holding him down as he thrashed and struggled and suffered. Until, eventually, he was perfectly still.*

. . .

When Piper comes up with a cover story, she doesn't mess around. Her parents have friends in high places—including, it turns out, an old college buddy of her dad, who works in the Princeton admissions office. Princeton was far from my first-choice college—it was too close to home, for one thing—but it was on my list, and it was a place my dad would dearly like to see me go. I have the grades to get me there, and the SAT scores to boot, but so do thousands of other people who don't get in. Which meant a chance to schmooze with someone who might help me get into Princeton was an opportunity my dad couldn't let me pass up, even if I was grounded.

"My mom invited Dr. Schiff and his wife for dinner on Saturday night," Piper told me on Thursday morning, when we passed in the hall at school. "I asked if I could invite you, and she said it was fine."

I looked at her skeptically. "Dinner with your parents and a couple of their friends doesn't sound like the kind of Saturday night outing you were talking about." Actually, it sounded a bit like my vision of hell. I find Piper's parents kind of snobby, and socializing with them and a guy who'd be studying my every word to see if I was Princeton worthy would be torture. He'd probably run back Monday morning and put me on some kind of Do Not Admit list.

"Oh, we won't be joining them for dinner," Piper assured me. "We can beg off at the last minute. My mom won't mind. My dad'll probably be irritated, but he'll get over it."

It sounded awfully rude to me—both to Piper's parents and to Dr. Schiff. But Piper and her folks didn't live by the same kind of rules I did, and if she didn't think her parents would mind, then who was I to question it?

Piper must have seen the acceptance in my eyes—either

that or she had just *assumed* I would accept. "Good. It's settled then. I'll have my mom call your dad so it sounds all legit."

"And what will I tell my dad when he gives me the third degree afterward?" He'd probably want a line-by-line report of what I'd talked about with Dr. Schiff, as well as a careful analysis of how I thought the evening went. Dad *really* wanted me to get into an Ivy League school.

"Make something up," Piper said easily. "I'll introduce you to Dr. Schiff before we leave, so at least you'll have *met* the guy. It's not like your dad is going to call up my folks and ask them to verify your story."

Piper talked about all this like it was no big deal, and for her, it probably wasn't. Obviously she did this kind of thing all the time, and if her folks knew about it, they apparently didn't care—or had given up on trying to stop her. For me, it was a different story. I'm not some kind of goody-goody, and I'd gotten in trouble with my dad—and my mom, when she was still living with us—more than once, but it was always for small things. You know, like failing to do my chores or talking back to them or lying to them about something trivial, like whether I'd done my homework.

Lying about where I was going was a much bigger deal. And sneaking out with Piper when I was supposed to be chatting up someone who could help me get into Princeton was off the charts.

But as Piper had pointed out, the worst my dad could do was ground me for longer, and that was only if he ever found out.

"We're going to have so much fun!" Piper promised, and she looked almost giddy with excitement.

. . .

Since I was supposed to be going to Piper's place to meet and have dinner with Dr. Schiff, I had to dress like I was going to an interview, not like I was going out for a night on the town. Piper refused to tell me what she had planned, but she did say I couldn't wear the black pants with the button-down silk shirt and low-heeled boots I would leave my house in. I couldn't very well sneak a change of clothes by my dad that night, so I stuck some jeans, sneakers, and a T-shirt in my backpack on Friday morning and put them in Piper's car.

She was supposed to pick me up at seven thirty for an eight o'clock dinner, but Piper is allergic to getting anywhere on time, so it was almost eight already when she knocked on my door. Bob greeted her arrival with a bark that rattled the windows, and my dad didn't immediately call him off. I think Bob was kind of talking for the both of them, because my dad had been looking at his watch every five seconds since seven thirty, and there was no hiding the irritation on his face.

If I'm being perfectly honest, I was a bit irritated myself, even though I'd been expecting her to be late. The last thirty minutes would have been tense even if I weren't nervous about what we were about to do, and fending off my dad's barbed comments had been no fun. I'd defended Piper loyally, but really, is it that hard to show up at least *close* to on time?

"It's a subtle power play," my dad had said. "Showing you that her time is more valuable than yours."

I just rolled my eyes at that one.

Dad finally called Bob off, but he answered the door himself instead of letting me do it. Internally, I groaned, knowing this couldn't be a good thing. I couldn't see the look on his face, but I could see Piper's and the way her eyes widened. There weren't many people who could intimidate her, but my dad was one of them.

"I suppose Becket misheard you," he said. "She thought you said you were picking her up at seven thirty."

Yes, my dad has all the subtlety and tact of a wrecking ball. "Cut it out, Dad," I said, trying to slip past him and out the door before he changed his mind about letting me go. "It's not that big a deal."

"Sorry, Mr. Walker," Piper said, blinking innocently at my dad. No one calls my dad Mr. Walker. It's either Pete, or Commissioner Walker. Piper knows that. And while I didn't think being late had been any kind of power play, I suspected calling my dad Mr. Walker was. Telling him that, just because he was the police commissioner, it didn't mean he was anyone special. "Traffic was terrible, and then it took forever to find a parking space."

Her claim of traffic delays on a Saturday night was questionable, but trouble finding a parking space was completely believable. I don't think my dad bought it, but at least he didn't completely humiliate me by calling my best friend a liar to her face.

"I expect her home by eleven," he told Piper sternly.

"Okay," she said, but we all knew she would treat that curfew as a guideline rather than a rule.

My dad finally let me get past him, and with only the briefest good-bye, Piper and I hurried off down the street. It was another cold night, the temperature somewhere in the twenties, and I decided I should strike all colleges north of the Mason–Dixon Line off my list. I wanted to go somewhere where it was warm all year long, even if that meant no Ivy League for me. I hoped Piper hadn't had to go too far to find that parking spot.

We turned the corner, and the wind whipped our faces. I saw Piper's red Volvo parked only half a block away and hurried my footsteps, eager to get inside where it was warm, but Piper grabbed my arm.

"One stop first," she said, grinning at me. "Tonight will be more fun if we have some male companionship."

And that was when I realized that this wasn't going to be a night on the town with just me and my best friend after all.

If she noticed the disappointment that stabbed through me, she gave no sign as she reached up and rapped on the door of Luke's house. She was filled to the brim with excitement and energy, practically vibrating with it, but my heart had taken up permanent residence in my toes. I had lied to my dad—and put myself at risk for the worst punishment he could think up—for some girl time with Piper and a side dish of the forbidden. Being the third wheel on a date was *not* what I'd had in mind.

"I dropped your change of clothes off with Luke before coming to get you," Piper said. "I decided it would have been too much of a pain to drive all the way back to my place so you could change. Besides, we don't want to eat into our fun time."

"But you said I would get to meet Dr. Schiff," I protested, in what I'm afraid might have sounded a bit like a whine.

Piper made a something-smells-bad face. "Believe me, you're not missing anything. He's a long-winded bore, and as far as I can tell, he has no sense of humor. Don't worry—we'll come up with something creative to tell your dad."

Luke's door opened and Piper darted in, pulling me in behind her. I seriously considered telling her I had a queasy stomach and would rather stay home after all. That lie had little to no chance of getting me in trouble—though my dad would be disappointed I didn't get a chance to impress Dr. Schiff—and lying in bed feigning stomach woes would be more fun than watching Piper hang all over the boy I'd been too shy to make a play for.

Piper didn't give me a chance to say anything before she flung herself into Luke's arms, leaving me to close the door behind us. Luke laughed and hugged her back, hazel eyes dancing.

"Long time no see," he said in that delicious baritone voice of his. He was wearing a faded T-shirt for some band I'd never heard of over comfortably lived-in blue jeans, and even though he was my neighbor and I saw him all the time, my voice froze in my throat when he met my eyes over Piper's head.

"Hey, Becket," he said. "Glad you can come with."

I had no reason to believe he really meant that, but I wanted to. And though it was totally lame of me, I realized I couldn't pass up the chance to spend time with him, even if it made me sad and jealous. So, no queasy stomach for me.

I hate my full-out smile because it shows too much gum, so I kept my lips a little tight as I smiled back at him. I probably looked like I was grimacing in pain. "Me too. But you know you'll be caught in the Circle of Doom if my dad finds out about this."

Luke shrugged casually. "It's a chance I'm willing to take. Why don't you go ahead and get changed so we can hit the road? Your clothes are in the bathroom." He pointed down the hall.

"Okay," I said, then hesitated a beat, feeling like I should say something else. Something sophisticated, or at least witty. But my mind went blank, as it had a tendency to do around Luke, and I hurried toward the bathroom before the silence could become awkward.

When I closed the bathroom door behind me, I let out a sigh of relief. How was I going to get through an entire night in Luke's presence without making him think I was a gibbering idiot? I was always a little shy, but not like I was in Luke's presence. I couldn't say two words to him without second-guessing myself, and tonight was far from the first time I'd had my mind go completely blank while talking to him.

"Cheer up," I muttered to my reflection in the mirror over the sink. "With Piper around, he won't be paying any attention to you anyway."

I changed into my jeans, folding my nice outfit carefully, worried that it would develop telltale wrinkles. Then I spent a couple of minutes in front of the mirror practicing my no-gums smile. It looked a little fake, but I'd rather look fake than flash half an inch of gums.

I took a steadying breath. It was already clear I was going to be way out of my comfort zone tonight, but maybe it would be good for me. My dad kept me too isolated, too sheltered, and I needed to get out into the world a little more or college was going to give me a bad case of culture shock.

Determined to have fun, I bravely rejoined Luke and Piper.

# CHAPTER FOUR

It turned out Piper's idea of a fun Saturday night was getting some friend of hers to sneak the three of us in through the back door of a nightclub on South Street. Which, I have to admit, seemed pretty exciting at first. No one under twenty-one was allowed into the club, and yet there we were, getting a sneak peek of what it would be like when we were legally old enough to drink. My dad would totally have a heart attack if he knew where I was, and there was no denying the glow of satisfaction that gave me.

The glow faded pretty fast once we got inside. The music was so loud it made my teeth vibrate, and it was some obnoxious techno crap with a relentless thumping beat and no melody. The club was packed to the gills, and although it might have been twenty degrees outside, it was probably around ninety inside.

Since we hadn't come in the front entrance, we didn't get to check our coats. Which meant someone would have to keep an eye on them all night or they might walk off. Why anyone would bother to steal a coat from inside a nightclub I don't know, but it was just a fact of city life that you couldn't put anything down anywhere and expect it to still be there when you got back.

There wasn't anywhere to sit down, but there was a cluster of standing-room-only tables off to one side of the dance floor, and we hovered until one of them opened up, then piled all our coats on it. Luke fought his way to the bar and got us each a beer, but before anyone had taken more than two sips, Piper was tugging him toward the dance floor. He looked over his shoulder at me, obviously uncomfortable with the idea of leaving me alone at the table. I wasn't exactly comfortable with it myself, but I gave him a smile and a thumbs-up anyway.

Left with no company save three empty coats, I felt the faint prickle of tears in my eyes. I blinked rapidly in an effort to stave them off. Piper was out on that dance floor, dancing with abandon, her body gyrating to the beat as she steadily sipped from her bottle of beer. She leaned toward Luke and said something that made them both laugh. With nothing to do but people-watch, I let my eyes drift around the room and saw that Luke wasn't the only guy in the place who appreciated Piper's dancing. If Luke got tired, there would be a stampede of volunteers eager to take his place.

I took a sip from my beer and tried not to make a face. Disgusting stuff, though I fully intended to try to develop a taste for it in preparation for college. I'd never be the wild party animal type, but I hoped to at least blend in.

There were plenty of people out there dancing without partners, mostly groups of girls who seemed to be having a good time without the help of any guys, but I would have been way too self-conscious to just go out there and dance by myself, even if I didn't have to keep an eye on the coats. I felt like the world's biggest loser.

I spent about five minutes throwing myself a pity party, but then Piper returned to the table and pushed me out toward Luke on the dance floor.

"Your turn!" she shouted in my ear.

Lucky for me it was kinda dark in there, so Piper couldn't see how red my face turned. Me, dance with Luke? I could barely remember how to breathe in his presence.

Piper gave me a bright smile and another push. "He doesn't bite unless invited to," she said with a laugh. "Now get out there."

Luke was beckoning to me, so I plastered on what I felt sure was a frozen smile and forced myself out onto the crowded floor.

*It's not like it's some romantic slow dance,* I told myself. Piper would never have sent me out if it were.

The good news was that the music was too loud for conversation, so I didn't have to make a fool of myself stumbling over words. The bad news was that, well, I had to dance. The floor was so jam-packed the only dance move I could do without bumping into someone was a vaguely rhythmic shuffle. Luke was about ten times as coordinated as me, but he didn't seem to mind my pathetic dancing, and I tried to have fun. Sweat trickled down my back and glued my hair to my neck. Eventually Piper cut in, and I was more relieved than disappointed.

Luke and Piper made every attempt to include me, and we all took turns sitting out and keeping watch over the coats. But despite their best efforts, every time it was my turn to sit out I felt a little lower, a little more like a third wheel who just didn't belong. Maybe it was because I couldn't get enough beer into me to make much of a dent in my inhibitions.

That was one problem Piper most definitely did not have. I didn't keep track of how many beers she drank, except it was a lot, and her dancing got progressively wilder and more sexual. Sweat plastered her already clingy shirt to her body and shone on her skin, and her movements became less co-ordinated. Already, I was dreading what would happen when it was time to go home. There was no way I was letting her get behind the wheel of a car in her condition, but I wouldn't be at all surprised if she put up a fight.

The alcohol seemed to give Piper a limitless supply of energy, and after a while she stopped taking her turn watching the coats. Once she was drunk enough, even Luke seemed to have become optional to her, and eventually he and I were left standing at the table together while Piper danced on in a little all-girl cluster toward the edge of the floor. I noticed with some relief that Luke was drinking a Coke rather than a beer.

"We're not letting her drive," I shouted at him, hoping like hell he would be on my side.

He shook his head, then reached into his pocket and pulled out a set of keys on a Hello Kitty key chain. They definitely weren't his, and I breathed a sigh of relief as he flashed me a wry grin.

"Not my first time around the block," he yelled back. I could barely hear him over the music, which was so monotonously repetitive I longed for my iPod and some earbuds. I hoped my top wasn't showing sweat stains and that my makeup hadn't melted off. How Piper could keep dancing with such energy in this heat was a mystery.

I glanced at my watch and saw it was almost midnight. So much for my eleven o'clock curfew. I fished my cell phone out of my pocket and saw I had three missed calls from my dad. Great. I hoped Dad hadn't called Piper's house looking for me when I didn't answer. Luke caught me checking and leaned in closer so he wouldn't have to shout quite as loud.

"What time did you tell your dad you'd be home?" he asked.

"Eleven," I replied glumly. Piper was obviously having a blast, drinking and dancing, even flirting a little, which I didn't think Luke much appreciated. Prying her away was going to take a major effort.

Luke winced in sympathy. He knew my dad. "We'd better get out of here, then," he said.

I wasn't exactly having fun, but I might have felt compelled to argue anyway—if Luke had waited for a response. Instead, he immediately waded out onto the crowded dance floor and shouted something into Piper's ear. Still dancing, she made a pouty face at him. I didn't need to hear them to know she was telling him she wasn't ready to leave yet.

I don't know what Luke said to her—he appeared to try several different tactics—but eventually she gave in. I noticed she had to cling to his arm to keep herself upright, and when she got back to the table, it took both Luke and me to get her into her coat.

We left the same way we came in, through the back door. Piper puked into the gutter before we were halfway back to her car. I hoped getting some of the alcohol out of her would sober her up just a little, but no such luck. She was so unsteady on her feet that I thought Luke was going to have to carry her, and when she spoke her words were so slurred I couldn't understand her. I had the feeling I wasn't missing much.

When we got to the car, Luke handed me the keys, and I opened the door. Luke then guided Piper in so she could lie down on the backseat, where she passed out immediately. Luke shook his head at her as he closed the door. I wondered how many times she'd ended up passed out when one of their dates was over.

"I thought maybe with you here she wouldn't get so drunk," he said, giving Piper a rueful look as he reclaimed the car keys.

I didn't say so, but that seemed a little idealistic of him. Piper was who she was, and you either accepted the whole package or you didn't. There were things about her I didn't like—and she'd added a few entries to the list tonight—but I knew I had to take the bad with the good. Tonight had been nothing like I'd planned or hoped for, but I'd still had plenty of good times with her in the past. It was worth putting up with moments like this. "Moderation just isn't her thing."

Luke laughed. "Yeah. Guess you could say that."

He got into the car, and I did too, though I was super conscious that I was sitting in the front seat next to him, where Piper ought to be. A hint of panic fluttered in my belly. When Piper was around, I never had to worry much about what to talk about, because she was never at a loss for words. If a moment of silence threatened, she jumped smoothly and easily into the breach. But Piper was passed out, and I was tongue-tied around Luke in the best of times. What was I supposed to say to him after a night like tonight? Would he think I was totally standoffish and rude if I just savored the silence after the cacophony of the club?

"Sorry tonight wasn't much fun for you," Luke said as he started the car and pulled out into traffic.

"What? Oh. No. It was great." I felt my face heating with a blush at my spastic response.

He gave me a knowing look. "What could be better than standing at a table watching the coats?"

My blush deepened, and I hoped it was dark enough that

he couldn't see. "I danced!" I said, but even I could hear how defensive I sounded.

"There's nothing wrong with not being into the nightclub scene."

My hackles rose, though I knew he was just trying to be nice. I'd tried to act like I was having a great time, tried to lose myself in the music—which was hard when I actually hated it. Why couldn't he just pretend he hadn't noticed I was miserable?

"It's not really my thing, either," Luke continued, surprising me. "But Piper loves to dance, so I go with her."

I glanced over my shoulder at Piper, who was still dead to the world. "That isn't all she loves to do," I mumbled. How did she get away with coming home drunk like this? Were her parents okay with her drinking? Or did they just not care?

"I tried to get her to slow down," Luke said, and this time he was the one who sounded a little defensive. "But once she gets started . . ." He shrugged instead of finishing the sentence. "I'm just glad she doesn't give me a hard time about taking the keys away."

Yeah, me too. If it had been just me and Piper tonight, the way I'd expected, would she have given me her keys?

I knew the answer to my own question. She would have fought me on it. There was no way I would have gotten into the car with her behind the wheel in the shape she was in, but would I have been assertive enough to stop *her* from getting in? I don't think of myself as being particularly weak willed, but sometimes Piper felt like a force of nature, and I'd let her have her way so many times.

I didn't like where my thoughts were taking me, so I yanked my mind away—and immediately saw the flaw with having Luke drive Piper's car.

"How are you going to get home?" I asked. Piper's house was out near the Main Line, so it wasn't like he could hop on a bus or subway to get home once he'd dropped her and her car off.

"Piper's folks will call a cab for me, or one of them will give me a ride. They're just thankful I don't let her drive."

Clearly this wasn't the first time he'd ended up in this situation. If so, it seemed like kind of a shitty way to treat your boyfriend. Piper was the only one of the three of us who'd really been free to have fun tonight, and it was only because she knew I'd stand there and guard the coats and Luke would stay sober so he could drive her home.

I can't say it was the first time I'd ever allowed myself to think that my dad's view of Piper was more accurate than mine, but I found his voice in my head harder than usual to dismiss.

"She's a handful," Luke said, though he looked at her in the rearview mirror with a smile that said it wasn't so much a complaint as an observation. "But she's worth the trouble."

Maybe he and I both needed to stop drinking the Kool-Aid.

# CHAPTER FIVE

Remember how I said there wasn't much my dad could do to me in punishment if he found out the truth? Well, I was wrong.

He was waiting up for me when I got home, and just as I'd feared, he'd called Piper's house to check on me when I didn't answer my cell. Piper's mom ratted me out, of course, and to say my dad was furious is an understatement. The fight we had was truly epic, and I ended up not just grounded but confined to my room. He made sure I had nothing to do other than homework and college applications, stripping all the books from my shelves and blocking the Internet on my computer.

I said some awful, hurtful things while we were yelling at each other, and it wasn't until afterward that I realized how much I'd sounded like my mom, in those final, miserable months before she moved out. I don't know how long she and Dad had been fighting in private, but they'd gone totally public with it in the year or so before their divorce, the fights getting louder, more frequent, and nastier as time wore on. Having been an unwilling witness—or at least listener—to many of those fights, I knew where Dad's weak spots were. Poking a wounded bear rarely turns out well, but after the disappointment and discomfort of my night on the town, I couldn't seem to help myself.

It wasn't until I woke up on Sunday morning that I started to feel really bad about it. After all, I *had* lied to him, and in a big way. I'd known exactly what I was getting into when I decided to go out with Piper, and I'd done it anyway. A parent who wouldn't get pissed off about what I'd done was probably a parent not worth having.

I was allowed out of my room for meals and bathroom breaks only, and I slept so late it was lunchtime by the time I made it downstairs. Dad was in the kitchen scrambling eggs when I dragged in, still in my pj's. There was a full pot of coffee waiting, and I helped myself. Dad's face was tight and unhappy, and he didn't say good morning. The silence between us felt like a physical force, daring us to break it.

He was still royally pissed at me, and I could hardly blame him. My own anger had faded into resignation and a heavy dose of shame, not so much for disobeying him but for the things I'd said. Once upon a time, we'd been really close, and I'd thought having this time with just him and me living together would make us even closer. So far, it had turned out just the opposite.

The silence was still too oppressive to break. Dad poured what had to be at least six scrambled eggs into the sizzling pan, and I noticed his coffee cup was empty. I couldn't seem to force myself to speak, so I just grabbed the cup and refilled it for him. As peace offerings went, it wasn't much, but I figured it was better than nothing.

"Thanks," he said with a gruff nod.

At least he was willing to speak to me—and make me eggs, because although he was a big eater, I knew all those eggs in the pan weren't only for him. I tried to think of a way to apologize for the things I'd said last night. Especially the accusations that he had neglected his family in favor of his career—a favorite refrain of my mom's, even though it was a case of the pot calling the kettle black.

In the end, I swallowed all the inadequate words I came up with. I believe that words have power—as I'd proven the night before, when I'd wounded him with them—but sometimes they just aren't enough.

"Do you want me to put on some toast?" I asked instead, vowing that when breakfast was over I would go into my solitary confinement with no complaints or delays.

Piper was waiting for me by my locker first thing Monday morning. It was a rare show of punctuality from her, but I was still too pissed off about our crappy excuse for a girls' night out to be very impressed.

It wasn't really Piper's fault that our Saturday had been so miserable. Since she had no idea how I felt about Luke, she couldn't have realized how unappealing being a third wheel on her date would be to me, and she really had gone out of her way to make sure I was included. She danced with me, and she made sure Luke danced with me, and I could hardly blame her for the fact that I'd hated the nightclub. How could she know I hated loud, overheated, overcrowded nightclubs when I hadn't even known that myself? I should just chalk it all up to a learning experience and get over it.

Sometimes, Piper comes off as being totally oblivious to other people, but she was still capable of surprising me. I thought I'd done a pretty good job of hiding my feelings on

Saturday night, but the first words out of her mouth when she saw me were, "I'm so sorry about how I acted at the club."

I wanted to laugh it off, maybe pretend I didn't know what she was talking about. In some ways, it felt almost ungrateful to complain. But after having spent all of Sunday shut up in my room with nothing to do but work on college applications— my dad hadn't even let me out to do chores or walk Bob or anything—I was in too brittle a mood to manage it.

"Let's just forget about it, okay?" I said, staring at the buttons on my coat as if I needed absolute concentration to get them open. Out of the corner of my eye I saw Piper lean against the bank of lockers, letting me know she planned on hanging around.

"I promised myself I'd stop at two beers," she said. "I should have remembered that once I get a couple of beers into me, I forget all about promises like that. It was selfish and stupid and words can't describe how sorry I am."

There was an unfamiliar hitch in her voice that made me look up and meet her eyes. She wasn't crying, but the remorse on her face was so genuine I couldn't help but believe it.

I won't say the anger went away, but its intensity lessened. There were so many other things I had hated about Saturday night, but at least Piper was apologizing for the one thing I could blame her for in good conscience. It was more than I'd expected to get from her.

"I'd suggest you try apologizing to my dad," I said, "only I'm not sure getting within a mile of him would be a good survival strategy."

She smiled tentatively. "Are you suggesting your dad doesn't like me?"

"Shocking, I know."

I took my coat off and shoved it in my locker. Piper frowned at me.

"You're out of uniform," she commented.

I groaned. Shit! "I was hoping no one would notice."

Thanks to my stint in solitary confinement yesterday, I'd completely forgotten the one Sunday chore that absolutely had to be done: laundry. I hadn't remembered until this morning, when I'd had to dig through my hamper in search of a uniform. I found a tunic that probably wouldn't wrinkle if an elephant slept on it all night, but all of my button-down white shirts were a mess. I'd had to settle for a long sleeve white polo, hoping the tunic over the top would disguise its nonregulation placket.

"Maybe no one else will," Piper said doubtfully.

But if *Piper* noticed, I would never get through the whole day without at least one of my teachers noticing. "Dad's probably going to send me to military school if I get a detention on top of everything else."

Piper eyed me appraisingly, cocking her head, then frowned and shrugged. "Don't know if it's going to work," she said, more to herself than to me, "but might as well try."

Without another word, she grabbed my arm and tugged me into the ladies' room across the hall. Then she reached up and started unbuttoning her own shirt, which she'd paired with a uniform kilt that was probably at least an inch shorter than regulation. "Give me your shirt," she ordered.

I should have had more coffee that morning. It took me a beat or two to realize she was planning to switch shirts with me.

"You don't have to do that!" I quickly argued, once I figured it out.

"Of course I don't have to," she said. "But it's the least I can do after getting you into trouble with your dad this weekend."

"But you'll get a detention for sure!" At least my tunic covered my placket and gave me an outside chance of getting away with it. There would be no hiding the fact that it was a polo shirt instead of a button-down if Piper wore it with her kilt.

Piper already had her shirt off and was handing it to me. "No one's going to be shocked, disappointed, or pissed off if I get a detention. Can you say the same? Now come on and give me your shirt."

I looked at her lean figure and then down at my own much more curvy one. "What are you, a size two or something?" I asked.

Piper waved the question off. "Just try it and see. If it doesn't fit, it doesn't fit."

The thought of letting Piper take a detention in my place didn't sit well with me, even though what she said made perfect sense. I'm not the kind of person who feels comfortable letting someone else take the blame for me. That didn't stop me from pulling my tunic and shirt off over my head and taking the shirt she offered me. My dad was going to go ballistic if I came home with a detention, and I didn't need any more drama at home.

Unfortunately, no amount of breath holding was going to make Piper's shirt button over my boobs. Another half an inch or so of play and I might have made it, but as it was, there was no way.

"It's the thought that counts," I said as I handed the shirt back to Piper.

"Sorry, Becks," she said. "I wish I could have helped make it right."

I gave her a quick, impulsive hug. "You don't have to make anything right. All is forgiven, okay?"

And it really was. My irritation had vanished as if it never existed. Piper wasn't always an easy friend to have, but she *was* a good one. My life was richer for having her in it, even if my dad was incapable of seeing that.

"Maybe you'll get lucky," Piper said. "Maybe I'll be the only one in the entire school who notices."

"Maybe," I agreed unconvincingly.

As it turned out, I was right not to be convinced. I didn't even get past homeroom without getting the little pink slip of doom.

My school is small enough that it wasn't worth having a detention period every day, so everyone got the joy of serving on Friday afternoons. Which sucked, because it meant I had the damn thing hanging over me for the whole week—and that didn't exactly help the atmosphere at home. I don't think my dad was capable of getting any *more* angry with me, but the detention helped prolong my stay in the doghouse. He didn't force me to stay in my room anymore, but I was still thoroughly grounded, with no phone, Internet, or TV privileges. And things always felt tense when we were in the room together.

It didn't help that the city was experiencing a sudden and unexplained crime spree. There were more murders in that one week than there had been in the previous two months, and they weren't confined to only the bad neighborhoods. Dad told me about some guy who was found floating in the fountain at Logan Circle, which felt uncomfortably close to where we lived.

The crime spree meant he had to work even later hours than usual and that everyone was putting pressure on him to somehow fix it. I couldn't really blame him for being grumpy, under the circumstances.

That didn't make detention any more fun. There were five of us—four juniors and me, because apparently the seniors had been behaving themselves this week—sitting silent in that classroom, working on our homework or daydreaming. The teacher didn't care what we did as long as it didn't involve cell phones, tablets, or talking. Thanks to being grounded, I was already well ahead in my homework, so I decided to work on one of the many college essays I would have to write, grumbling to myself and wishing each application didn't have a different essay question.

The weather had gotten warmer, the air just chilly now instead of freezing. As I worked on my essay and watched the sunlight fade as sunset approached, a bank of fog rolled in. For the millionth time, I wished my dad would get me a car, even if it was just some used clunker on its last legs. It was going to be almost completely dark by the time I got out of detention, and I knew from experience that the fog would be creepy as hell on this campus even in broad daylight. The streetlights were shaped to look like old-fashioned gas lanterns, and when there was fog, the damn things gave the place a Jack the Ripper vibe.

When detention was over, I hitched my backpack over one shoulder and set out into the fog, following the curve of the long driveway that led past the athletic fields to the school's front gate. Several cars zipped by me as my fellow detainees were whisked home by their parents, and then there was nothing.

The fog was blocking out what little light was left from the setting sun, and I might as well have been walking through the campus at midnight. Thick as paste, it cut visibility to next to nothing. I knew I wasn't alone on the campus—there were probably still teachers working, and the school's beautiful Victorian main building even had faculty apartments for those who wanted the convenience of living close to work. But I couldn't *see* anyone. I couldn't even see the lights from any of the buildings. All I could see were those faux gaslights looming in the impenetrable fog.

It was actually kind of pretty, as long as you could convince yourself there wasn't some serial killer lurking in the fog on the off chance a tempting victim wandered by. I laughed at the workings of my imagination, though I have to admit it was a little harder to shake off the silliness after my encounter in the alley.

I made it to the biggest of our athletic fields, which is situated at the bottom of a small hill and lined by weeping cherry trees that are breathtakingly beautiful in the spring. However, in the fog the bare branches added just that much more creepiness to the atmosphere. The heavy fog pooled at the base of the hill, making the athletic field invisible, so that it looked like the hill led into the abyss. I willed my imagination to take a break, but it had so much to work with it was having a blast.

Knowing I was being ridiculous, I nonetheless fished my keys out of my backpack. There was an air horn on the key ring, and I felt a little less vulnerable having it in my hand.

The field hockey team must have had a home game, because there was a full plastic trash barrel at the base of one of the cherry trees. Someone had knocked it over, and trash spewed onto the grass and sidewalk all around it. In other circumstances I might have set it upright again—though I'd have left it to someone else to put the trash back in—but to-night I was in too much of a hurry to get to the train station, where there would be other people in sight. I swerved to avoid the spill of empty Gatorade bottles and PowerBar wrappers on the sidewalk and kept right on moving.

I was only a few steps past when I heard a strange metallic crunching noise behind me. I hadn't realized how eerily silent it was until that noise startled me into an embarrassing squeal. I looked behind me, but all I could see was the trash barrel and its contents. Nothing that would explain the noise. Then again, thanks to the stupid fog, someone could be standing ten feet away, and I wouldn't have seen them.

I swallowed hard as my neck hair rose, and I was overcome with the same feeling of *wrongness* I'd felt when I'd started down that alley.

"It's your imagination," I reminded myself out loud.

A wisp of wind suddenly swirled through the fog, strong enough to roll one of the outlying plastic bottles back into the rest of the trash.

There shouldn't have been any wind. Wind and fog don't go together. And yet, another gust tugged on the edge of my coat as it blew past, swirling into the trash can and emptying the rest of its contents onto the sidewalk and the grassy hillside.

I blinked, knowing it was impossible for wind to act like that. And yet the visual evidence was right there in front of me. Three crushed aluminum cans. More food wrappers. A torn Ace bandage. A broken pencil. An apple core, brown and dis-gusting, along with desiccated orange peels and a half-eaten banana black with rot.

*Wrong, wrong, wrong,* my inner alarm screamed.

The wind kept gusting, first into my face, then from behind me, then swirling, and with each gust the trash moved—but didn't blow away.

A shape started to emerge from the trash. A head. A torso. Two arms, two legs.

*Not possible.*

I stood frozen and staring, trying to convince myself I wasn't seeing what I was seeing. It was just darkness and fog and the memory of what had happened in that alley working together to make my mind play tricks on me. I willed the shape to go away, to become just a random pile of trash. I wanted to be able to laugh at myself for making something out of nothing.

And then the man-shaped pile of trash sat up, and I no longer cared if I was imagining things or having a nightmare or just hallucinating. Clutching the straps of my backpack close to me to keep it from thumping my back, I turned tail and ran into the fog, away from . . . whatever that was.

My pulse was pounding in my ears, but it wasn't loud enough to drown out the strange rustling and clanking noises behind me. A quick glance over my shoulder revealed a shadowy, fog-blurred figure loping toward me in a ground-eating stride. I faced front and put on more speed, my breath coming in frantic gasps while my mind revolted at the impossibility of what was happening.

*This can't be real,* I told myself, but I kept running anyway, because it sure as hell *felt* real.

The school's iron gates loomed in the fog ahead of me, and I sprinted for them. I still heard the rustling and clacking, but it didn't seem to be as close as before. I wasn't about to pause and check it out.

I made it through the gates but felt no temptation to slow

down. Every instinct in my body screamed at me to run faster, even though my legs were burning and I couldn't seem to get a full breath into my lungs. I would be safe if I could make it to the train platform, where there were other people around.

A car drove by, and the fog was probably so thick the driver didn't even see me. Which meant crossing the street without a careful look both ways was probably dangerous, but nothing was going to slow my legs down. I was relieved to make it across the street without becoming roadkill, but that relief was short-lived.

A figure suddenly appeared in the fog right in front of me. I screamed and tried to dodge around, but I was going too fast. I crashed into someone, who made a startled-sounding grunt and fell backward onto the sidewalk with me on top.

# CHAPTER SIX

I was so panicked by what I'd seen—what I *thought* I'd seen—that my first assumption was that the trash creature had somehow gotten in front of me and cut me off. I lurched to my feet, expecting an attack, but my brain finally kicked in and saw that the figure lying on the pavement in front of me was not made of trash.

He looked to be around my age, maybe a little older. He propped himself up on his elbows on the pavement, blinking startlingly green eyes and shaking his head as if groggy. I'd crashed into him *really* hard. I was going to have bruises from the impact tomorrow, but he'd probably gotten the worst of it, since I'd ended up on top. He put his hand to the back of his head, running his fingers over his short black hair, most likely searching for blood.

I was now rational enough to recognize that I'd crashed into a normal human being, not a monster made of trash, but I still had plenty of adrenaline coursing through my veins. Under my coat I was drenched in fear sweat, and my heart was hammering.

I looked behind me, straining my ears for the distinctive rustling sound the trash man had made as it chased me, but there was no sign of movement in the fog. That gut-clenching sense of wrongness was gone too. I kept watch on the area in my peripheral vision as I turned back to the boy I'd knocked over, feeling like a complete idiot.

There was no monster made of trash chasing me. A short laugh—half hysteria, half relief—escaped me before I could cut it off. It had been my imagination after all.

*Oh yeah?* whispered an insidious voice in my mind. *Why don't you just stroll on back there and give that trash can another look then?*

No way in hell.

I didn't want to imagine what color my face was when I met the green gaze of the boy I'd knocked over. He'd stopped patting his head in search of injuries, and he didn't look groggy or woozy or anything. If his head had hit the pavement when we fell, it probably hadn't hit that hard. At least that's what I tried to tell myself.

"I am so, so sorry," I said, wondering if I'd rather face the trash man than this particularly awkward moment. Now that I'd gotten a real good look at him, I could see that the guy was drop-dead gorgeous. Like actor or boy band lead singer gorgeous. Those eyes of his were almost too green to be real, and although he was wearing a leather bomber jacket, it was open and revealed a faded T-shirt hiked up enough to give me a glimpse of washboard abs.

His lips turned up into a grin, and I knew I was compounding my impression of a drooling moron by standing there staring at him instead of helping him up. Wishing the pavement would swallow me, I reached out a hand. Still grinning, he took it, though he sprang to his feet with almost no help from me.

"No problem," he said, not letting go of my hand. "Most fun I've had in a week." He winked at me.

I couldn't seem to force my lips into an answering smile. "Are you all right?" I asked.

Maybe I was still suffering from an adrenaline overdose, but I didn't like the way he was keeping hold of my hand. I'd had it drummed into me since I was a little girl that strangers—especially strange men—were to be treated with caution and suspicion. This guy might be really nice to look at, but that didn't mean he was trustworthy. And the fog was still thick enough to make this stretch of pavement as isolated as a dark alley. Cars passed by once in a while, but even if the headlights hit us on the way by, I wasn't sure anyone inside could even see us.

"I'm fine," he said. "And you?"

"I'm okay." I tried to pull my hand away without seeming to pull away, but he didn't take the hint. The keys I'd been gripping when I ran had flown out of my hand when I'd fallen, and I saw them sitting on the pavement a couple of feet away. My pulse had finally started to calm, but now it was accelerating again.

I was nerving myself up to pull away a little more forcefully, afraid it was going to turn out badly no matter what. If he didn't let go, then I'd know I was in deep trouble, and if he *did* let go it would probably mean I'd be offending a perfectly nice guy whom I'd just bowled over and possibly injured.

To my immense relief he followed the direction of my gaze and saw my keys. He let go of my hand to retrieve them, holding them out to me with a flourish.

"I believe these are yours," he said, his eyes dancing with amusement, though I wasn't sure what he found so funny.

"Um, thanks," I said, taking my keys and not putting them away. If he noticed or understood the implications of that act, he didn't show it.

"Seriously," he said, the amusement changing into an expression of concern, "are you all right? You looked pretty panicked when you ran into me. Did something happen?"

*Yes, I was chased by an imaginary monster made of trash.*

"I'm fine, really. And I'm sorry I was so clumsy. I, uh, thought I was going to miss my train."

He raised an eyebrow, and I knew I was blushing again. It was a lame excuse that didn't come close to explaining the headlong run—especially when there was no telltale rattle of a train approaching the station—but it was the best I could come up with on short notice.

Thankfully, he didn't press. "Uh-huh." He nodded skeptically. "Would you like me to walk you to the station?" He looked all around at the lingering fog and the dark that lurked beyond the halo of each streetlamp. "It feels kind of like the set of a horror movie around here, doesn't it?"

I hesitated. The idea of walking alone through the fog and dark was not appealing, but the train station was so close, and I had no idea who this guy was. I would feel like the world's biggest idiot if I encouraged him and he turned out to be some psycho.

He smiled at me in an obvious effort to put me at ease. "I'm Aleric, by the way." He held out his hand for me to shake. "If you know my name, I'm not a stranger anymore, right?"

Yes, I was being completely transparent in my caution, but it didn't seem to offend him. And really, if he was some kind of bad guy and wanted to do me harm, he wouldn't need my permission to walk with me to the train station to do it.

"Becket," I said, shaking his hand, braced for him to hold on too long once more, but he didn't.

"Pleased to meet you. Now let's get you to your train."

We started walking toward the station, and I couldn't decide whether I felt better for having him at my side or not. My whole body was still in red alert mode. Aleric seemed perfectly harmless as he walked beside me, and in truth he was being quite the gentleman, after I'd knocked him over like that. But knowing that didn't lessen my paranoia.

"Do you go to Edith Goldman?" Aleric asked.

"What gave me away?" I responded with a forced smile. Normal, witty banter was just what I needed to get my head back on straight. Not that I'm usually good with witty banter, especially not with people I've just met.

Aleric laughed at my dumb joke, which made me feel a little better. "I don't know. Maybe the backpack, the location, and the uniform? I'm a regular Sherlock Holmes, you know."

"I can see that. Do you go to school around here?"

It seemed like a logical question, but I knew there weren't any boys' or coed schools within walking distance. And come to think about it, what *was* he doing walking around here by himself in the dark? There were sidewalks here, sure, but it wasn't exactly a pedestrian thoroughfare. The vast majority of the foot traffic was from students going to or from the train station.

"Nope," he said. "I'm not in school."

I couldn't tell if he meant he'd graduated already or if he was a dropout or what.

We reached the parking lot just outside the train station, and I could see a handful of people on the far side of the tracks, waiting for the train into the city. The train going deeper into the suburbs must have left recently, because the near side of the tracks was deserted.

Yet another knot of anxiety began to form in the pit of my stomach. You were supposed to walk through the tunnel under the tracks to get to the other side, but in my frazzled state of mind there was no way I was walking into a no doubt deserted tunnel, whether Aleric was by my side or not. In the bright light of day, I wouldn't hesitate to run right across the tracks, but the fog and the dark gave me pause. I checked my watch and saw that I still had more than five minutes before my train arrived, and the empty platform on this side said this track should be clear too. But just because no trains were scheduled to stop here in the next couple of minutes, it didn't mean there wouldn't be some express train blowing through. I'd *probably* hear it coming from a mile away, but crossing the tracks with so little visibility was technically not safe.

"Thanks for walking me to the station," I said to Aleric. "And sorry again for barreling into you like that."

He reached out to shake hands in parting, forcing me to shift my keys into my left hand if I didn't want to leave him hanging. But we were in full view of the people on the other side of the tracks, so my paranoia took a momentary breather and I stuck my keys in my pocket so I could shake. His gaze flicked first toward the stairs leading down to the tunnel, then to the empty tracks. One corner of his mouth tipped up in a knowing grin. I guess it was better he found my caution amusing, rather than insulting, but I would have preferred he just pretended not to notice.

"It was a pleasure running into you," he said, his inflection making clear that the pun was very much intended.

I rolled my eyes and hoped I didn't look as embarrassed as

I felt. I wished I could just erase the last ten minutes or so from my memory. I was kind of looking forward to a tense, strained evening at home with my dad. At least that would have some feeling of normalcy.

"Thanks again," I said, because I couldn't think of a clever comeback. Then I looked carefully both ways and, seeing no sign of the lights of an oncoming train, hurried across the tracks. A couple of adults waiting for the train gave me reproving looks, but I wasn't flattened by a train, so that was good.

When I looked over to the far side of the tracks, Aleric was gone.

I spent the entire train ride brooding about what might or might not have happened in that fog. Half of me was *sure* I'd seen exactly what I'd thought I'd seen, but the other half was equally sure it couldn't be true. The problem with that second half was that if it hadn't really happened, I was pretty low on plausible explanations. I mean, sure, I have an active imagination, but still . . . It was hard to accept that I had seen a totally innocuous pile of trash lying there and somehow translated that in my mind into a man-shaped nightmare that chased me.

Unless I was losing my mind, that is. Maybe I was experiencing psychotic episodes, or having hallucinations. Maybe I had a brain tumor. Maybe I should come clean with my dad about the baby incident and tonight's nightmare and he could make an appointment for me to see a doctor.

The thought made me shudder, and my mind instantly rejected it. I felt perfectly normal almost all the time. If I had a brain tumor or was going crazy, surely I'd have more symptoms than this. And the weirdness would happen more often. Right?

By the time the train reached 30th Street Station and I began the trudge home, I had decided I would wait and see. If I saw something else impossible or just weird, I'd suck it up and tell my dad the truth. I tried not to let myself imagine what kind of tests the doctors would do to find out if I had a brain tumor. I also tried not to let myself think about what would happen if they ruled out a physical cause for my hallucinations. I wasn't spectacularly successful at that, either.

Usually, I wouldn't be even mildly worried about walking the streets of Center City alone at night. I'd lived all my life in Philly, and I did it all the time. I kept a city girl's level of awareness at all times, but I'd never really felt threatened. There were always people around, and plenty of light. But tonight my threat radar was on a hair trigger.

The first stage of my journey home involved crossing over the Schuylkill River on the Market Street Bridge. There was plenty of traffic, both pedestrians and cars, and my rational mind said I was perfectly safe. Nonetheless, I found my gaze darting around suspiciously, taking in every detail of my surroundings in a way I never had before.

I doubt it would have caught my eye if I wasn't still suffering from the aftermath of my possible attack at school, but when I got near the end of the bridge my footsteps slowed and I stared. The railing on the side of the bridge ended in a stone pedestal, on top of which perched a stone eagle. I had passed this eagle I don't know how many times and had never really looked at it closely. But my mind was telling me it looked different tonight, even though I couldn't conjure an image of what it usually looked like.

I had a vague notion that the eagle was usually just sitting there on its pedestal, gazing majestically out at the city. But tonight its head was slightly lowered, its beak open as if in a shriek, its posture suggesting it was about to leap off and attack some unsuspecting prey. I quickly glanced at the matching figure on the other side of the street, and it, too, looked poised to attack.

It had to be my imagination running wild with me again. No one else walking by was giving the eagle even a brief glance. Then again, the changes were pretty subtle. If I hadn't already been in a vulnerable state of mind I probably wouldn't have noticed it myself.

I let out a heavy sigh and shook my head. That was the explanation right there—I was in a vulnerable state of mind, and so the stone eagle suddenly looked menacing to me.

"Get a grip, Becket," I muttered to myself, shaking my head. I fixed my gaze on the pavement in front of me, ordered myself not to go looking for weirdness, and continued on my way home.

# CHAPTER SEVEN

The following Monday morning, when I walked to the train station, I paused to take a close look at the eagles. They looked perfectly normal. Not at all threatening. Their heads were up, their beaks closed, their posture rigid and upright.

Obviously I'd let the power of suggestion get the best of me on Friday night. That was the only logical explanation for what I'd thought I saw.

I can't say I convinced myself, and I felt all cold and shivery for the rest of the trip into school. There comes a point when "logical" explanations stop being logical, and I was perilously close to that point.

I decided I *really* needed to talk to someone about what was happening to me. Someone who wouldn't force me to go see a doctor but who might have a little more perspective. The only logical candidate for such a conversation was Piper, but the trick was to get her to hold still for it. Her crammed social calendar made it so I had to plan any get-togethers well in advance, and that was hard to do when Dad still had my phone under lock and key. My best chance was to lurk near her locker and catch her before school started. I wasn't about to talk about the craziness in school, where just about anyone might hear, but maybe she'd have time to go for a cup of coffee or something after school. It would get me home late once again, but I'd just have to take responsibility for keeping an eye on the time and making sure I wasn't so late I couldn't blame the train for it.

Piper was already at her locker when I got there, still dressed in her coat, so she couldn't have beaten me in by more than a few seconds. I noticed she was wearing a pair of skinny jeans under the coat, and assumed she also had a kilt or tunic on and was just wearing the jeans to keep her legs warm. Or maybe she was planning to change before heading off to homeroom.

"Hey there, Becket," she said cheerfully as she opened her locker and then slipped her coat off.

I was momentarily at a loss for words, because when she took her coat off I could see that not only was she not wearing a tunic or kilt, she also wasn't wearing a white button-down shirt. Instead, she had on a faded black T-shirt with a huge marijuana leaf splashed across the chest. Even on the occasional days when we were allowed to come to school out of uniform, that T-shirt wouldn't have passed muster.

Piper grinned at my shocked expression. "What do you think? Will they send me home or just give me a couple of detentions?"

You get detention for wearing stuff that doesn't quite meet the uniform code. You don't get it for completely *ignoring* the code. Not only was she going to be sent home, she was probably going to be suspended.

"What are you doing?" I asked her, shaking my head.

"I'm sick of school," she said. "My grades wouldn't get me into Harvard or Yale or anything, even if I wanted to go there, and just going to Edith Goldman is enough to get me into someplace like Temple or Drexel. So why should I be wasting my time in boring classes?"

"Have you been drinking?" It was the only explanation I could come up with for what I was hearing. No, Piper had never been an exceptional student and had never done more than the bare minimum she needed to get acceptable grades, but she'd never treated her education this dismissively before. She and I had talked about our college plans less than a month ago, and though she wouldn't be applying to all the power schools I would, she definitely had some selective schools on her list and had shown every sign of caring where she went.

Piper laughed. "It's a little early, even for me, so no." She shrugged. "I just had an epiphany over the weekend. It really doesn't matter where I go to school, or even *if* I go to school. Shit like that only matters if you have career ambitions."

"And you don't?" She'd never told me specifically what she wanted to do with her life, had always said she'd figure it out when she was through with college, but I'd always had the sense she wanted a career of some sort, even if she didn't know what career it was.

"Don't look so surprised. You don't either, do you?"

She gave me a challenging look, and I found myself looking away. It frustrated my parents to no end that I couldn't blurt out, "I want to be a ___." Both of them had known from the moment they started high school what they wanted to do with their lives, and they'd aimed themselves at their goals like guided missiles. My older sister was like that, too—a chip off the old block. She was in her first year of med school and had never seemed to consider any possibility except becoming a doctor. No waffling, no doubts, no indecision.

Not me. I didn't know *what* I wanted to do for a living. My college counselor at school told me that was fine, that I had plenty of time to make a decision and that things would be clearer when I was away from home and had dabbled a bit at college. She said that very few people went into college knowing what they wanted to be, and that most of those who thought they did found out they were wrong before they graduated. My parents did not agree.

Piper touched my shoulder. "Sorry, Becks. Didn't mean to throw salt in the wound."

"Just because I don't know what I want to do, that doesn't mean I don't have ambitions," I said. My ambitions were vague ones—get a good job that paid decently in a field I enjoyed— but that wasn't the same as not having any.

"I know. You might not know what you want to do, but you know you want to do *something*. I guess I realized this weekend that I . . . don't."

"What does that even mean?"

"It means my parents will support me no matter what I do, so I might as well do what makes me happy. Hell, I might not even go to college at all, although maybe if I find a good party school I should go for a couple of years just to have that experience."

"So you're saying your big goal is to mooch off your parents for the rest of your life?" I asked incredulously. I'd thought I knew Piper pretty well, but it was beginning to look like I didn't. Or like something had happened over the weekend that had fundamentally changed her outlook.

"Basically, yeah." She shook her head. "How many times have I told you that you should live your own life and not the life your parents want for you? I can't believe you never pointed out what a hypocrite I was being."

I had no idea what to say to that. As far as I could tell, Piper had never cared what her parents wanted her to do, had always gone her own way with barely a second thought.

She glanced at the clock on the wall. "You'd better hurry if you want to get to homeroom on time. I'm cruising to get *myself* in trouble, not you." She winked at me.

I felt like I was standing in the presence of a stranger. Piper had always been wild, but nothing like this. I was also surprised that she'd bothered paying attention to the time. Maybe this was another bizarre "incident," another hallucination or manifestation of my brain tumor.

Obviously I wouldn't be talking over my situation with Piper after school, because even if she was somehow miraculously not sent home, I wasn't sure I could have a heartfelt conversation with *this* Piper. No, I was just going to have to keep all my worries buried deep inside and try to ignore them.

Hopefully all the weird Twilight Zone stuff was over now, and one day I would look back at this time and laugh.

Ha-ha.


Piper wasn't the only one in my life acting kind of strange. My dad seemed to be a little bit more tense and distracted every day. He'd always worked long hours, but his super-overtime was usually sporadic. For the past week or so it had been constant, and it seemed like even when he was at home his mind was still at work.

"Crime spree still going on?" I asked him on Tuesday night.

It was almost nine thirty and he'd just gotten home. I'd fixed myself some spaghetti for dinner and was reheating the leftovers while he slumped at the table and looked exhausted.

"What?" he said, rubbing his eyes and blinking, his mind still lost in whatever was troubling him. "Oh, the crime spree. Yeah. It's . . ." His voice faded out and he shook his head.

"It's what?" I asked with a chill of unease. I didn't like seeing the haunted expression on his face, the uncertainty in his eyes. His duty had been behind a desk for years now, but before that he'd been a homicide detective, constantly faced with the worst humanity had to offer. He'd seemed to me to be psychologically bulletproof. Maybe everything he'd seen had been damaging to his psyche, but if so, he'd hidden it from me and my sister, and maybe even my mom. Certainly he'd never looked then like he looked now.

Another shake of his head. "I don't know. It's like there's a full moon, only times ten. The moment the sun goes down, the weirdos come out of the woodwork."

I frowned as I retrieved his dinner from the microwave and set it down in front of him. He'd shown himself to be surprisingly self-sufficient since Mom moved out—I'd had no clue he was capable of cooking before then—but tonight he was obviously just too exhausted for the effort and accepted my offer to feed him.

"Isn't that normal, though?" I asked. "Isn't crime and stuff usually worse once it gets dark out."

"Sure. Just . . . not like this."

I pulled up a chair as Dad idly stirred his spaghetti around without eating it. He still had that distant look in his eye, like he wasn't quite in the room with me.

"Not like what?" I prodded.

He sighed and gave me an assessing look that I assumed meant he was trying to decide how much to tell me. Mom had never let him talk about his job in much detail—she said she didn't want my sister and me to be subjected to the ugly reality of police work, but I think she was protecting her own sensibilities more than ours—so he was really used to censoring himself.

I met his eyes and tried to look as mature and prepared as possible. Whatever was going on out there, whatever he was having to deal with, I wanted to know about it. I figured it couldn't be as weird or upsetting as the crap I was dealing with, after all.

I must have looked like I could handle it, because he nodded and started to talk, still choosing his words carefully.

"Usually when there's a crime spree, it's small stuff and it's kind of the usual suspects. Like during that heat wave we had a couple years back. People were crankier than usual, so there were a lot of fights and domestic disputes. Most of the people we arrested had records already. But this one . . ." He shook his head. "It's not small stuff, not bar fights and domestic violence. It's murder and assault and perfectly ordinary-seeming people helping themselves to stuff that isn't theirs. And a constant stream of people calling 9-1-1 with ridiculous shit we're required to respond to, no matter how obvious it isn't real."

I suppressed a shiver, thinking of my own fateful 9-1-1 call a couple of weeks ago. If I'd told the truth about what I'd seen, my call would certainly be counted with the rest of the "ridiculous shit" that had been reported lately. Dad must have thought about that call, too, because he suddenly averted his eyes and dug into his spaghetti.

Now was the perfect time for me to come clean about that night, to tell him that I'd seen something impossible and had been too embarrassed to tell the truth. I could tell him I was worried, and he would take me to the doctor and I would find out if there was something wrong with me. He'd opened a door, and I could choose to walk right on through.

But I just couldn't do it. I told myself I didn't want to burden him, that he was already too tired and dispirited, that maybe it was all over and I'd never have to think about it again. But I think the truth was that I didn't really want to know what was going on with me. The way I saw it, there were three possibilities: something was physically wrong with me (i.e., the brain tumor theory); I was going crazy; or it was some bizarre anomaly that was all over now. Option three was probably a pretty fragile possibility to hang my hopes on, but options one and two were both too terrible to contemplate. I would face them if and only if I had no other choice.

*Jill Jameson had forgotten to bring her umbrella when she'd left for work this afternoon. She'd specifically checked the weather report and had seen there was an eighty percent chance of rain, but it slipped her mind when it was time to leave, and the rain hadn't started yet. No rain had fallen for the entirety of her shift at the restaurant, but when it came time to walk home at just after midnight, a light drizzle started.*

*Jill turned up the collar of her coat and tucked her hands in her pockets, hunching her shoulders. Raindrops spattered on her glasses, creating artistic blurs and prisms out of the city lights around her. She tried wiping them off once, and then the rain started in harder, and she stuck the glasses in her pocket. Now everything was a consistent blur, but her eyesight wasn't so bad that she couldn't make her way home.*

Cold water seeped down the neck of her coat, making her shiver. Her breath fogged the air, and she cursed herself for being an airhead. She should have left the umbrella right in front of her door as soon as she'd seen the weather report, instead of trusting herself to remember it later.

The rain came harder and harder, chasing all but the hardiest of pedestrians indoors. Jill was getting thoroughly drenched, and water was collecting in the gutters, flowing like a whitewater river. A taxi raced by, sending a huge splash of dirty water her way, with no sign of apology. Jill cursed the driver and groaned as the water started to penetrate the thick padding of her sneakers.

Hurrying her footsteps, Jill reminded herself she'd be home and warm and dry in less than ten minutes.

Up ahead of her a section of sidewalk right near the curb was blocked off with sawhorses, traffic cones, and yellow caution tape. There was still room to get past, but it required walking over one of the city's ubiquitous basement entrances—a pair of metal doors set flush with the sidewalk. Usually those doors led to freight elevators or stairs that made it easier for businesses to get supplies, but these particular doors were situated in front of a vacant lot.

Doors like these opened outward, and people walked over them all the time without a second thought. Jill, however, always tried to avoid them when possible. It was a silly superstition, but she always felt as if the doors might give way beneath her.

She hesitated for a second, thinking about going around on the street side of the construction, but a blocked drain had created a virtual lake in the gutter and she decided the metal doors were the lesser of two evils. Her feet were wet, but short of squelching, and she hoped to keep it that way.

Jill plunged forward, figuring she'd be past the metal doors in two steps, but she tripped over something and came down hard on her hands and knees. The impact on those metal doors was startlingly loud, and though they held her weight, there was a hint of give to them.

Cursing again, Jill turned to see what she had tripped over and found her foot had somehow gotten tangled in a straggling end of caution tape that stretched between a pair of sawhorses. It was true she couldn't see all that well without her glasses, but the tape was bright yellow. She wasn't sure how she could possibly not have seen it when she'd hurried forward. She glanced briefly around for a Good Samaritan who would offer her a hand up, but the only people in sight were on the other side of the street, their heads invisible under hoods or umbrellas.

Jill tried to shake the tape off her foot, but it was wrapped all the way around her ankle. With a grunt of frustration, she sat on her butt and reached down with both hands to disentangle herself.

It wasn't until her hands were inches from the tape that she noticed it wasn't normal caution tape. She should have been able to pick out the word Caution from the black markings on the tape, but instead she saw what looked more like a pattern of streaks and spots. She pushed rain-soaked bangs out of her eyes and looked again, but the streaks and spots didn't resolve themselves into letters. Actually, they looked kind of the like the markings you might see on a snake's skin.

As soon as that thought entered Jill's head, the band of

yellow around her ankle tightened, and the loose end of the tape raised itself up from the sidewalk.

There was no wind. No explanation for the movement. None that made sense, anyway.

Jill wouldn't quite say she was afraid, not yet, because she was sure there was a logical explanation for what she was seeing. But she would admit to being unnerved, and she gave her foot a hard yank, hoping to break the tape.

It didn't work, and the metal doors on which she was sitting gave an ominous creak. Whatever she'd gotten tangled up with, she'd be more comfortable extricating herself if she were sitting on the actual sidewalk instead of the doors.

She tried to stand up and work her way over to the sidewalk, but before she'd even reached her feet, more tape wrapped itself around her other ankle, tugging her off balance.

Jill fell once more, her butt hitting the doors with an echoing clang. Now she was scared, because there was no logical explanation in the world for what had just happened.

The caution tape oozed free of the sawhorse, both ends now moving on their own, wrapping themselves around her legs. She'd handled a boa constrictor once, had felt the strange undulations of the muscles in its body as it moved, and the tape felt exactly like that.

Jill tried to scream, but her throat was tight with fear and very little sound came out. Certainly not enough to be heard over the roar of the bus that passed by in the street. She tried to wave to the passengers for help, but they probably couldn't even see her with the sawhorses and tape and orange cones in the way.

The tape was now twined around both her ankles, and its coils squeezed tighter and tighter until she couldn't feel her feet.

She tried again to stand, or at least to get to her hands and knees and crawl. She didn't care about the metal doors anymore, just wanted to get out from behind the construction so somebody could see her and help her.

She made it to her hands and knees as the tape continued to squeeze. She lurched forward, pulling with her hands because her legs didn't seem to be working at all. She was almost to the edge of the doors, almost onto the sidewalk on the other side of the construction. She was convinced she'd be safe if she could just get to where someone could see her.

The doors groaned again, as if straining under a great weight, and then—impossibly, because the hinges weren't angled that way—they started to open inward.

Jill screamed again, louder this time. Maybe loud enough for someone to hear, although she couldn't see anyone running to the rescue. The metal was slick from the rain, and even the slightest incline was enough to send her sliding back into the center, where a gap was forming.

She clawed at the edge of the doors, losing a couple of fingernails in a vain effort to pull herself away from the widening gap.

The doors continued to open, the motion smooth and effortless, as if the doors were designed to open that way. One end of the caution tape unwound itself from her ankle and plunged into the gap between the doors.

She tried to use her newly freed leg to propel herself off of the doors, but she couldn't even feel her foot.

The doors continued their inexorable opening. Gravity and rain-slick metal were working together to pull Jill toward that opening, through which she could see nothing but impenetrable darkness. But the tape decided to help the process along anyway.

Jill felt as if a two-ton anchor had just latched on to the bottom of the tape around her ankle. Even using both hands and her one free leg to resist, there was nothing she could do.

Screaming, she slid into the opening, wedging there for a moment because it wasn't large enough to admit her. Then the doors opened just a fraction more, and she was dragged down into the darkness below.

# CHAPTER EIGHT

The good news was that Dad decided to give my cell phone back before my official grounding was over—not because I'd been such a perfect angel (the detention was proof that wasn't the case), but because he didn't like the idea of me being out in the city without a way to call for help if I needed it. Apparently the crime spree and wacko 9-1-1 calls were still in full force.

The bad news was that the crime spree made it so Dad was literally never home even close to on time. And even when he *was* home he was on the phone practically all the time. Which meant that not only was it up to me to stock our groceries and make our meals, I was also stuck walking Bob every night, once after dinner and once right before going to bed, if Dad wasn't home yet.

I know walking the dog a couple of times a day doesn't sound like much of a hardship, especially with one as well-behaved as Bob, but reports said we were having the coldest November in more than a century, and I had no trouble believing it. It didn't matter how cold it got, or if it was pouring down rain, or even if there was a freaking blizzard. Bob still had to go out, and I still had to clean up after him. All of which made me jealous of people who lived out in the 'burbs and had fenced-in yards.

Although Bob's intimidating presence made me feel pretty safe, I still kept a careful eye on my surroundings when I walked him, feeling a heightened sense of awareness both because of the crime spree and because of my own recent . . . misadventures. I was using a different dog-walking route these days, avoiding the alley by the church, but there was nothing on my new route I hadn't passed a thousand times before over the years of living here. Apparently I'd never really bothered to *look* at my surroundings before. Not closely anyway.

It was when I was walking Bob right before bed on Thursday night that I realized how truly oblivious I usually was to what was around me. For instance, I'd never noticed before that the metal grille the proprietor of a nearby antiques store lowered over his windows at night had wickedly sharp little burrs at regular intervals. You could see what was in the window through the grille, but heaven help you if you tried to, say, stick your face in the window to get a better look at something.

I stopped and frowned when I noticed the burrs, and Bob took that opportunity to mark the shop as belonging to him. There used to be a homeless guy who frequently hung out on the stoop next to the shop, and I could have sworn I used to see him sitting with his back against that grille sometimes. Though now that I thought of it, I hadn't seen him in a while. Maybe the owner had added the burrs to discourage just that kind of thing, and that was why the homeless guy had moved on.

I continued on around the block, and I noticed several more little oddities. Like the knocker on one of the doors on a row of houses being in the shape of a tongue. It was a small thing, but I wondered how I'd never noticed and had a little laugh at it before. It was possible whoever lived there had just installed it, though, so maybe there was nothing strange about my not noticing.

Then there was the iron railing on the sides of the stoop of another house. I'd noticed its highly ornamental ironwork before and had somehow thought the design in the center was a fleur-de-lis. Maybe that's what it was *supposed* to be. But the bulb in the middle didn't come to a point like it usually would in a fleur-de-lis, and the two petals on each side of it curled so much they were almost circular. How could I not have noticed before how phallic that design was? Again, it seemed like something I would have had a laugh at in the past. I must have been blind not to have seen it.

On Friday morning I decided to take advantage of having my cell phone back and take snapshots of a couple of the oddities I'd noticed the night before. I wanted to ask my dad if *he'd* ever noticed them. I figured he must have, because his cop instincts made him super observant.

And that was when I took yet another step into the Twilight Zone. I left my house a little early so I'd have time to walk around the block before heading to the train station for school, but when I came to the antiques shop, its grille was up and there was shadowy movement inside, so no chance there. I hurried forward until I reached the row of houses with the tongue door knocker. There were five houses, and I could have sworn it was the one in the middle with the red door that had had it, but this morning there was no sign of the tongue. All the door knockers looked perfectly normal.

Perhaps the owner had decided the tongue was too weird,

I told myself, but I couldn't hold back a shiver of apprehension. It reminded me a little too much of the eagle incident.

I kept rationalizing and headed on to the house with the phallic design in its railing. There was no way the owner could have switched *that* out overnight.

But when I got there I saw that the design in the center was clearly a fleur-de-lis. I supposed if I squinted at it and looked at it sideways it might look a little phallic. But I was dead certain it didn't look the way it had when I'd walked Bob last night.

*That damn brain tumor is acting up again,* I told myself, trying to laugh it off.

Maybe, thanks to my dad's stories about all the whacked-out stuff that was happening at night, I'd somehow made myself sort of paranoid. Maybe last night I'd been actively looking for something to be strange and had convinced myself I'd seen it. Damn it, I was going to stick to logical explanations as long as I possibly could.

I snapped a quick picture of the railing on my phone before I left to catch my train. Surely I'd shattered the illusion now that I'd seen the railing in the bright light of day, but I wanted that photographic evidence in case my eyes or memory started playing tricks on me when I walked Bob later that night.

I spent the day trying not to obsess. Not only did I do a piss-poor job of it, but I was so lost in my own head that I couldn't seem to concentrate on the inconvenient pop quiz my teacher sprang on us during calculus class. I'm really good at math—obviously, or I wouldn't have been taking calculus—but my skills failed me that afternoon, and I knew I'd be lucky if I got a C.

I consoled myself with the thought that, unlike my mom, my dad didn't pore over my every grade and share his opinion of my performance. But that thought evoked a strange twist of yearning in my chest. I'd gotten over the worst of missing my mom within a month or so of her moving to Boston, but every once in a while her absence would rise up out of nowhere and smack me in the face. I talked to her on the phone every week, and I'd be going up to Boston soon to spend Thanksgiving with her and my sister, but that wasn't the same.

If my mom were still living with me, would I have confided in her about all the strange things that had been happening? I wasn't sure I would have had the nerve, because talking about it would somehow make it all more real, but I *might* have. She was warmer and more approachable than my dad. At least more so than my post-divorce dad. But then she wasn't warm and nurturing enough to hang around in Philadelphia for my last year of living at home, and her taking that job in Boston had forced me to decide between her and my dad. Maybe she used to be someone I could have confided in, but she wasn't anymore.

I was not a bit surprised when, shortly after I got home from school, my dad called to let me know he'd be home late. Again.

"Maybe you should call when you're *not* going to be late," I quipped. I meant it as a joke, but I could tell from the tone of his voice that Dad didn't take it that way.

"I'm really sorry, honey," he said. "If there was any way I could—"

"Relax, Dad. I was just kidding."

But was I? I honestly didn't know if there was something passive-aggressive about that little joke. I had to admit, I was pretty sick of being home alone all the time.

"I'm sorry anyway," Dad said, and I wanted to kick myself for putting the guilt trip on him, whether it had been semi-intentional or not. He was doing the best he could, and I knew that.

I fixed myself some tomato soup and a grilled cheese for dinner, too lazy to put together something that required any actual effort, then fed Bob and prepared for what I feared would be the ordeal of walking him. I didn't know what I was going to see on our little stroll around the block, but at this point I knew I would be unnerved by the time I got home, either way.

I bundled up against the cold and clipped on Bob's leash. "Let's do this," I muttered under my breath.

But when I reached the front door I found myself hesitating, not sure I had the courage to face what was out there. Or what *wasn't* out there.

Bob whined and scratched at the door, giving me an impatient look.

I took a deep breath and finally found my courage. My cell phone was tucked away in my pocket, and within a few minutes I would know whether I should be fearing for my sanity or fearing that something genuinely goose bump–inducing was happening.

Out into the cold I went, Bob leading the way. I had the brief, cowardly thought that I should choose a different route, but Bob knew the way, and I didn't argue.

We passed the antiques store with its barbed grille, but since I hadn't seen it during the day, I didn't know whether those barbs were unusual or not. When we got to the house that may or may not have had a tongue-shaped door knocker the night before, I saw that the door was open and some guy was going at the knocker with a screwdriver. So apparently the home-owner *was* messing around with the knocker.

Hope surged through me, and my knees felt weak with relief. I wasn't crazy, and nothing spooky was going on. There had been a logical explanation all along.

The relief and hope both retreated when I remembered the phallic railing and my inability to come up with any logical explanation for it. Certainly that homeowner wasn't changing the railing back and forth within the span of a single day.

Bracing myself, I continued on my route. As soon as I turned the corner up ahead, the railing would come into sight, though it would be too far away to make out details yet. Bob slowed us down by taking care of business, but then we were rounding the corner, heading toward the railing in question. My eyes homed in on it immediately, and I stared at it with single-minded purpose as we approached.

My stomach did a nausea-inducing backflip when I got close enough for a good look and saw the unmistakable phallic symbol in a circle of iron at the center of the railing.

I swallowed hard and came to a complete stop, shaking my head. Bob gave me a curious look, no doubt wondering why we'd stopped, but he was perfectly content to spend a little time sniffing around.

Reaching into my pocket, I pulled out my cell phone and brought up the photo I had taken just this morning. In that photo, the emblem in the center of the railing was clearly a fleur-de-lis. I closed my eyes, squeezing them tight, then ventured another peek at the railing in front of me. Everything about the house looked exactly the same now as it did in the photo—up to and including the house number on the weathered gray door—except for that railing.

This was no trick of the light or of my imagination. The railing did not look the same now as it had this morning. Period.

The realization made my head spin and my pulse race.

With shaking hands I raised my phone and took another picture of the railing. I was thinking that maybe I could show the two pictures to Dad tonight when he came home, though I wasn't sure I could wait that long to get confirmation of what my eyes were telling me. Maybe I'd just send the two pictures to Piper and ask her what she saw.

But apparently seeing a phallic symbol with my own two eyes after confirming earlier that it was a fleur-de-lis wasn't enough weirdness for one night, because when I pulled up the photo I had just taken . . .

There was the fleur-de-lis, right smack in the middle of the railing where it was supposed to be.

*It has to be the wrong photo,* I told myself, but I knew it wasn't, even as I flipped to the previous photo on my phone and saw the daytime shot. One was clearly taken during the day, and one was clearly taken at night. I rubbed my eyes and looked at the railing again, but that phallic symbol remained firmly in place. Mocking me.

I tried taking a photo again. When I looked at the camera view, I saw the phallic symbol, but when I actually snapped the picture, the fleur-de-lis was back.

I felt near hyperventilating and was probably white as a ghost. A kind-faced lady walking by looked like she was thinking of asking me if I was all right, but then she saw Bob and kept moving. Bob doesn't even have to bare his teeth to make people think twice about getting close to him. I considered asking the lady to look at the railing and tell me what she saw, but if I was going crazy, the last person I'd want to confirm it for me was some stranger who just happened to be passing by.

The cold was starting to get to me, and I was hovering on the edge of panic. There was nothing more I could do while standing out here staring at the railing, so I somehow managed to gather myself enough to make my way home.

# CHAPTER NINE

Once home, I made myself a big mug of hot cocoa in the vain hope that it would somehow soothe me. I was spooked enough that I seriously considered adding a splash or three of something from Dad's liquor stash, but my head was feeling swimmy enough already.

I kept looking back and forth at all the photos I'd taken. All the photos that looked pretty much exactly the same, and with about as boring a subject as you could ever hope to see. If I was going crazy, or if it was all some hallucination caused by a brain tumor, wouldn't the nighttime photo look identical to the real thing?

Somewhere in the midst of my brooding and staring, I realized I had moved past the stage of wanting to keep the weirdness in my life a secret. Whatever was happening, whether it was something going terribly wrong with me or terribly wrong with the city, I wanted to know. And until I had outside confirmation one way or another, I would keep bouncing back and forth between being convinced I was crazy and being convinced Philadelphia had entered the Twilight Zone.

I found myself constantly looking at my watch, willing Dad to get home at a semi-reasonable hour just once, but that was wishful thinking. If only the photo had turned out . . . At least then I'd have been able to share it with Piper and talk this whole thing over with her on the phone while I waited for Dad. My stomach was churning, and my head felt all thick and achy with anxiety. I couldn't sit still, and I couldn't come close to concentrating well enough to do my homework.

I wanted to know the truth about that stupid railing so badly that I briefly revisited the idea of stopping some stranger on the street to ask them what they saw. Then I wondered why it had to be a stranger.

I knew most of my neighbors by name, and I went through them one by one, considering who was most likely to be home, who was most likely to help me, and who was most likely not to haul me straight to the hospital if it turned out the phallic symbol was all a figment of my imagination.

Which all sounds very logical and methodical, but I knew before I even started the process that there was one person and one person only I could even *consider* approaching. Even if the thought of picking up the phone and calling him out of the blue—or worse, knocking on his door—made me want to dive under my bed and hide.

I had found the nerve to call Luke exactly once, when I'd invited him to my birthday party. I'd come really close to chickening out, sure he was going to laugh at me (behind my back, not to my face, because he was too nice to do that), because I knew I was going to be my usual inarticulate self the moment I heard his voice. Also, I was sure he was going to say thanks but no thanks.

My invitation had been as clumsy and awkward and generally embarrassing as I'd expected, but he had shocked the hell out of me by saying yes.

Of course, asking him to come to my birthday party, especially when it was being held about thirty feet from his back door, was different from asking him to come with me and confirm whether I was a lunatic or not. I didn't think I could face the latter conversation, so I came up with a cover story.

I called Luke's number before I gave myself time to think about it any longer. The phone rang three times, and I suppressed a groan as I remembered it was Friday night. Luke and Piper were probably out on a date somewhere. It was silly of me to expect him to be home.

I lowered the phone and was millimeters from hitting the Off button when suddenly Luke's voice said, "Hello?"

I jerked the phone back up to my face so fast I dropped it, my hands suddenly sweaty. I winced as it clattered on the floor; then I snatched it up and prayed I hadn't just broken it.

"Hello? Luke? Are you still there?"

"I'm here," he answered with a little chuckle. "Everything all right over there?"

I was glad he couldn't see me, because I was sure my face was bright red. He must have thought I was totally spaztastic. "Um, yeah. Fine. I just dropped the phone."

*Because I'm a total klutz and lose all hand–eye and brain–mouth coordination whenever I talk to you.*

There was a momentary pause. "Seriously, are you all right? You sound kind of . . . I don't know, freaked out?"

I let out a slow, silent breath. I reminded myself that I'd spent an entire car ride sitting in the front seat with Luke while Piper was passed out in the back, and I had managed it without making a total fool of myself. I'd felt almost at ease with Luke by the end of the ride, and I tried to call up that feeling now.

"Well, I guess I kind of am," I said, truthfully enough, before I launched into my mostly untrue explanation. "Nothing's wrong. It's just, I have to pick up some stuff at the store, and my dad says there's been a serious crime spree going on lately. I'm sure I'm overreacting, but I really don't want to go out alone at night after some of the stuff he's been telling me. I'd take Bob, but he can't go into the store with me, so I was wondering..."

My voice trailed off because I felt like such an idiot. I may be a cautious city girl, and I may pay extra attention when I walk around alone at night, but I wasn't even remotely scared to walk two blocks to the grocery store. Luke probably thought I was a pathetic wimp, and I wondered how I'd ever managed to convince myself this was a good cover story.

But if Luke thought my request was weird, he did a great job of hiding it. He didn't hesitate even a little bit before he said, "Sure, I'll go with you. I'm sure there's something we're low on around here. There always is. I'll be right over. If you're ready to go now, that is."

There was a strange, fluttery feeling in my chest. I couldn't tell if it was panic or excitement or a little of both. I instantly scolded myself for the excitement, if that's what it was, because Luke was just being nice and walking me to the store. It wasn't like I'd just asked him out on a date or anything. So my palms were sweating and my pulse was thumping *entirely* because I was worried about what he would see when we passed the railing in question. Absolutely, definitely the only reason.

"Thanks so much," I said in a rush of breath. "I feel like such a chicken asking, but—"

He made a short, dismissive sound. "You're not a chicken. You're just being practical. I saw on the news tonight that a woman was jumped in a parking lot not three blocks from here. I wouldn't let my *mom* walk to the store alone at night right now."

I suppressed a shiver. Dad had talked about the crime spree in very basic terms, and I hadn't asked for details. I certainly hadn't realized anything had happened that close to our home, though Dad had said it was happening all over the city. Maybe asking Luke to walk with me to the grocery store wasn't such a bad idea after all. If I'd actually needed to go to the grocery store, that is.

"Thanks again," I said. "I really appreciate it."

"No problem. See you in a few."

I bundled up and took one more look at the photos on my phone as I waited for Luke to arrive. Those photos remained stubbornly the same, the railing appearing identical both day and night. I might be going nuts, but it seemed I was at least *consistently* nuts.

I shoved the phone into my pocket when Luke knocked at the door. Bob barked loudly enough to rattle the windows, running to the door and preparing to rip the potential intruder's throat out.

"Bob!" I shouted over the racket he was making. "At ease!"

When my dad gave that command, Bob would shut up practically midbark and politely move aside so that Dad could get the door. With me, the response time was considerably slower, and he stayed parked in front of the door, so I had to shove him out of the way.

"Sit," I ordered him sternly.

He parked his butt down obediently, looking up at me with wide, innocent eyes. His tail thumped against the floor, and he wasn't snarling, but his neck hair was still suspiciously fluffy looking.

"It's just Luke," I explained, as if I thought Bob would understand me. "You know Luke. The guy who gives you Milk-Bones?"

For whatever reason, Bob had never warmed to Luke, always watching him suspiciously whenever they were out in the courtyard together. Dad had Luke give Bob treats in an effort to foster good will, a tactic that met with mild success. Bob still didn't seem to *like* Luke, but he tolerated him.

I checked through the peephole to make sure it really was Luke before I opened the door. He gave me a lopsided grin and held out his hand, showing me the Milk-Bone in his palm. "I came prepared with a peace offering for the man of the house," he said.

I gave a little snort of laughter and opened the door wider. Luke might not be Bob's favorite person, but a little bribery went a long way.

Bob's tail thumped louder on the floor, his ears perking forward, his eyes fixed on the treat in Luke's outstretched hand. A thin whine rose from his throat, and he leaned forward eagerly, but he waited for me to give him permission before he stood up and swept the Milk-Bone off of Luke's palm.

"Good boy," Luke said, giving Bob a quick scratch behind the ear. "We're best friends now, right?"

Bob licked his chops, and I could almost hear him saying, *Sure, we're friends, as long as you give me another treat in the next five seconds.*

Belatedly, I noticed that Luke was carrying an empty grocery bag. Because, duh, he thought we were going to the grocery store.

"I'll be right back," I told him, then darted to the kitchen to grab a bag. If Luke saw the railing and saw nothing but a fleur-de-lis, I would just have to go through with the grocery shopping charade and try to act natural.

I gave Bob a pat on the head on my way out, then locked up and tried to keep myself relatively calm. Which was a pretty tough challenge when Luke was around, even when I wasn't fearing for my own sanity.

"Sorry about Bob," I said, because I felt the need to say something and it was the only thing that came to mind.

"Don't be," Luke said as we started off toward the grocery store. "You don't want a wuss for a watchdog. He's just doing his job."

There was a reason I had such a crush on Luke, and it wasn't just because he was hot.

"You have your own supply of Milk-Bones now?" I asked.

Luke smiled. "Your dad gave me a box so I could always be prepared."

I tried to think of something else to say, some way to make conversation, but I sucked at small talk, and the knots in my stomach were making it hard to think.

What if Luke didn't see what I saw? That would have to mean I was going crazy, right? I knew without a doubt that I was totally going to freak out if he didn't see it, but even if I was bound for the loony bin tomorrow I didn't want to have a meltdown in front of Luke. I could just imagine trying to explain that I'd asked him to come with me to the store to show him the penis-shaped thing on the railing but that, oops, I seemed to be the only one who could see it. I would never be able to look him in the face again. Assuming they ever let me out of the padded cell.

*Remember, it could be a brain tumor,* I reminded myself. Because that prospect was so much more appealing than being insane.

My palms were sweating inside my gloves, and I was gnawing on my lip. I risked a quick glance at Luke, wondering what he was thinking. Did he think my lack of conversation was rude, or just awkward? And could he tell just by looking at me that I was a bundle of raw nerves?

Of course he caught me looking, which sent a flush of embarrassment to my face. I wished I had Piper's self-confidence, her gift for making easy conversation. Not to mention her looks. If I were anything like Piper, I would laugh it off if a guy caught me staring at him, instead of blushing beet red and wishing the sidewalk would open up and swallow me.

"Why aren't you out with Piper tonight?" I found myself blurting. Because I had all the subtlety and tact of a charging rhino.

His jaw clenched, and he looked straight ahead. "She's been acting weird lately. Really pushy, even for her."

I hadn't talked to her much since she'd been suspended, but I had to admit something had felt a bit off each time I had. Like I only had about a third of her attention. And she'd more than once suggested I skip school to spend the day with her, something she had to know I would never do. She kept trying to convince me it wouldn't be that big a deal. This from the girl who'd tried to switch shirts with me not that long ago because she understood that getting a detention was a big deal to me. I just didn't get it.

"Should I ask what she was pushing you to do, or do I not want to know?" I asked. *Or is it none of my business,* I added silently.

"She's at a rave tonight. I'm okay with sneaking into bars once in a while, but I'm not into the rave scene."

I wouldn't have thought Piper was, either. I mean, sure, she was a little wild, and she obviously loved to drink. I wouldn't have been surprised to learn she'd tried pot, or maybe even X, in a controlled environment. Still, she'd always seemed to have a spirit of self-preservation—for instance, making sure she had a conscientious guy like Luke around to do the driving when she was totally shitfaced.

We walked in silence for a few moments. We were nearing the corner, and soon we would be turning it and the railing would come into view. My pulse rose a notch.

"Should I have gone with her?" Luke asked softly. "Just to watch over her, I mean?"

I had to pull my head out of my own butt to make sense of what Luke was asking me. I blinked at him in surprise, seeing that he really wanted to know my opinion. I guess he felt bad about putting his foot down.

I had to admit to being a little worried about Piper, worried about what might happen to her if she was out at some drug-riddled party with no one to rein her in. But Luke was supposed to be her boyfriend, not her bodyguard.

I shook my head. "She wouldn't have let you watch over her," I said, and knew immediately that I was right. "I saw what she was like once she got a couple of drinks in her."

Luke acknowledged the point with a nod and a resigned sigh, but I could tell he still felt bad about it. Sometimes being Piper's friend was downright exhausting. I imagined being her boyfriend was about ten times worse.

We fell silent as we turned the corner and the railing came into view. We weren't close enough to make out any details yet, but I found myself holding my breath and staring at the thing intently as we approached, wondering which version I would see now. Maybe it would be back to the fleur-de-lis. I didn't know what conclusion I would draw if that was the case.

But as we got closer and closer and I kept staring, the details of the phallic symbol became steadily clearer, and I knew the moment of truth was almost upon us. My heart was hammering, and my ribs felt unnaturally tight in my chest. I sensed Luke looking at me quizzically, but I couldn't take my eyes off the railing.

"What are you looking . . . ?"

Luke's voice trailed off. I finally tore my gaze away from the railing and saw that Luke was now staring at it too, his eyebrows raised, his jaw open.

"What the hell?" he said with an almost choked-sounding laugh. "How long has *that* been there? I never noticed it before."

I felt suddenly dizzy and breathless. "So you see it, too."

Luke's brow furrowed and he cocked his head at me. "Of course I see it. What do you mean?"

I swallowed hard and pulled my phone out of my pocket. I meant to show him the photos I'd already taken, but realized at the last moment that he would probably think I'd doctored them somehow, so instead I handed it to him and said, "Do me a favor and take a photo of it."

He looked even more puzzled. "What? Why?"

I crossed my arms over my chest as if I could hold myself together that way. "Just do it. Please."

He was still looking at me funny, and I couldn't blame him. And just because he saw the phallic symbol, it didn't mean the photo would work the same way for him as it had for me. My mouth was completely devoid of spit, and I was so tense I felt I might shatter at the slightest touch.

Luke shrugged and took the photo, looking at me afterward as if awaiting further instructions.

"Now bring the photo up," I whispered, my throat almost too tight to let any sound out.

I knew Luke saw exactly what I saw when he brought the picture up, because he let out a little cry of surprise and dropped the phone.

# CHAPTER TEN

I'd accuse you of playing a prank, if I could only figure out how you could've pulled it off," Luke said.

We'd skipped the grocery store and gone back to my place to try to sort through what we'd both seen. So far, Luke was still trying to fight it all off, come up with a logical explanation. Me, I was finally beginning to accept that something totally impossible was happening. But then, I'd been fighting the weirdness for almost two weeks already, so I had a head start toward acceptance.

I'd made us a pot of coffee, just to have something to do with my hands, and now we carried our mugs out into the living room and sat on the couch. Bob was being unusually clingy, sticking to my side like glue. I was lucky I didn't spill my coffee, considering the number of times I found him in my way.

When Luke and I sat on the couch, Bob jumped up on the seat between us, circling the spot and whacking us both in the face with his tail before he plopped down and made himself comfortable.

"You're not allowed on the sofa," I reminded him, and he gave me a look as if to say, *Your point being . . . ?*

"He senses we're freaked out," Luke said. "Dogs are good at that kind of thing."

"That doesn't mean he's suddenly allowed on the sofa," I said. But instead of grabbing his collar and demanding he get down, I found myself laying my hand on his head and scratching behind his ears. He gave a happy sigh and laid his chin on my thigh. "I'm such a pushover," I muttered under my breath, but there's nothing like petting a dog to soothe frayed nerves, and my nerves very much needed soothing.

Bob wagged his tail once in response, dipping some of his feathery tail hair into Luke's coffee in the process. Instead of looking annoyed that he was stuck with the wrong end of a dog practically in his face, Luke just set the coffee aside and shook his head.

"I still can't quite believe what I saw," he admitted. "Why hasn't anybody else noticed?"

"How often do you actually *look* at a railing when you walk past it?"

He shrugged, unconvinced. "Yeah, but still . . ."

"And how do you know no one else has noticed it?"

"I think if someone had noticed, we'd have seen it on the six o'clock news by now, don't you?"

"Seen *what* exactly? When we tried to take a picture of it, it didn't show up."

"Well . . . they'd *talk* about it at least, wouldn't they?"

I thought about my dad, about all the late hours he'd been working, about how he was always on the phone even when he was home. And I thought about him telling me that they were getting lots of weird 9-1-1 calls at night.

"I think maybe people *have* noticed," I said. "And I think maybe the powers that be are trying to keep it quiet." I told him about what was going on with my dad. "It's not just that one railing that's changing," I said.

Bob had filled up every spare inch of space on the couch between us, his butt tucked up against Luke's leg. Luke laid his hand on Bob's back and started stroking idly. Bob twitched a bit, as if unsure whether he wanted to grant Luke that privilege, but then he relaxed and accepted the extra attention as his due.

Luke's phone bleeped with a text message, and he frowned briefly when he saw it, typing out a quick reply.

"I should go," he said. "My mom's wondering why a trip to the grocery store is taking so long."

We both stared at the empty grocery bags draped over the arm of the couch.

"What should I tell her?" Luke asked.

"I don't know. I guess it depends on whether you think ignorance is bliss." I chewed on my lip for a moment. "Are you mad at me for getting you involved, for showing you what was going on?"

"Of course not!" he responded with gratifying haste. His gaze dropped to his hand, which was almost invisible as he stroked Bob's thick coat. Bob raised one of his front legs to let his servant know where he wanted to be scratched, and Luke obliged.

"You're definitely winning Bob over," I told him with a little smile. "I've never seen him ask for a belly rub from anyone except me and my mom. Not even my dad." Dad and Bob had more of a professional relationship than an emotional one, though I knew Dad loved Bob in his own way.

"It'll have to be a quickie this time, Bob," Luke said, giving Bob's belly a pat. "But let's do it again sometime, okay?"

His words caused a not-unpleasant quivery feeling in my stomach. It sounded like maybe Luke wanted to see more of me. I mean, sure, it was Bob he'd actually suggested he wanted to see more of, but Bob and I were a package deal.

*He's still Piper's boyfriend,* I reminded myself. So if we ended up hanging out now and then, it would have to remain platonic. Even if he and Piper were to break up, I wasn't the kind of girl who would date her best friend's ex.

I wrenched my mind away from the direction it was going, knowing I was getting way ahead of myself and making too much out of a few casual words.

"Thanks for coming with me tonight," I said. "I seriously thought I was going crazy."

He gave me a dubious look. "And you actually feel *better* knowing it's real?"

"Misery loves company?" I said with an apologetic shrug. "Are you going to tell your mom?"

He frowned. "Haven't decided yet. I'll have to explain why I'm not bringing home any groceries, but I don't know . . . Are you going to talk to your dad?"

"Yes," I said, with no hint of uncertainty. My dad and I had been butting heads an awful lot in the last year or so, and we were never going to go back to being as close as we were before the marriage went south, but I was convinced he knew way more than he was telling me, and I planned to get him talking.


It was nearly midnight by the time Dad got home. I was waiting up for him on the living room sofa, trying but failing to work on a history term paper that was due on Monday. Mostly,

I just stared at the screen of my laptop and zoned out, but other times I managed a sentence or two that I invariably deleted five minutes later. Bob was stretched out beside me on the couch, his head against my hip, but he'd long ago fallen asleep and wasn't much company. I was pretty tired myself, but not overly eager to face whatever dreams my mind planned to throw at me tonight.

Bob woke up the second he heard the key in the lock, and he was off the couch and doing a welcome home dance before the door even began to open. I quickly brushed the dog hair off the middle seat and fluffed up the cushions. The leather might still hold a hint of *eau de chien,* but based on the look on my dad's face, a dog on a forbidden couch was the least of his worries.

I swear he was looking older every day. The bags under his eyes were growing more pronounced and darker, and the brackets around his mouth had gone from shallow trenches to veritable canyons.

"What are you doing still up?" he asked, rubbing at his eyes and stifling a yawn.

*Maybe now isn't the best time for this conversation,* I thought to myself. It didn't look to me like Dad needed one more thing on his plate right now, so maybe I should just leave it until morning.

The problem was, if things stayed true to form, he wasn't going to look much perkier in the morning—he might even look worse, if the phone ended up ringing at some unholy hour—so there was no point in putting it off.

"I need to talk to you about something," I said, and though he tried to hide it, I could see the hint of worry that sparked in his eyes.

"Any chance it can wait until morning?" he asked. "I'm dead tired."

I was tempted to take the out he'd just given me, to spend a few more hours trying to pretend that everything in my world was normal. But denial no longer seemed like such a hot idea, and I wanted to know how much of what I'd seen might be real. After all, just because the fleur-de-lis had turned into a phallic symbol didn't mean I'd really been chased by a trash monster or that I'd really seen a baby turn into a pile of dust and blow away.

"No, I don't think it can," I said, searching his eyes to see his reaction. He's usually pretty good at hiding what he's thinking—one of the many "flaws" my mom harped on during their epic fights as the marriage ended—but he didn't do such a great job this time.

I'd suspected from the moment Luke and I had talked about it that some of the weird things that were happening in the city and keeping my dad at work so much were the same brand of weird I'd been experiencing, and the look in my dad's eyes was all the confirmation I needed.

Walking gingerly, as if his bones were aching, he made his way to his favorite chair and dropped down into it with a groan. "What have you seen?" he asked.

At least he wasn't bothering with a useless denial. "Enough to make *The Twilight Zone* seem like a documentary."

He winced and rubbed his eyes again.

"What's going on, Dad?"

He shook his head and sighed. "I wish I knew, Becks. I wish I knew." He leaned forward and rested his elbows on his thighs, hands clasped between his knees. "What really happened on the night you called nine-one-one?"

I was surprised to find I was still harboring a fair amount of anger about that night. My response made it out of my mouth before I had a chance to think better of it. "You already made it clear that you know the One True Answer to that question, and nothing I have to say about it is worth listening to."

"I made a mistake," he admitted. "But it's not like you were telling me the truth, so don't mount your high horse just yet." The words came out mildly reproachful rather than angry, and that helped defuse my own fit of pique.

"If you didn't believe the plausible explanation, then you would never in a million years have believed the real one," I said, with no heat.

"Maybe not then," he agreed with a nod. "But I'm listening now. I doubt it's any stranger than a lot of the nine-one-one calls I've been hearing about lately."

That was far from a comforting thought. However, it seemed he was ready to hear me out and that he wasn't going to haul me off to have my head examined inside and out.

Bracing myself to relive the terrible experiences of that night in the alley, I told my dad the truth.

D ad sat in stunned silence for an uncomfortably long time after I stopped talking. I couldn't tell what he was thinking, except that they weren't good thoughts. His eyes looked so distant I almost felt like he was no longer in the room with me.

"Do you believe me?" I asked when his silence became unbearable.

Dad shook his head slightly, but he was just bringing himself back to reality, not saying no. He blinked and his eyes refocused.

"I think I liked it better when I thought it was a prank," he admitted. "But yes, I believe you. There have been so many impossible things happening lately. . . ." He made a frustrated-sounding grunt. "Eventually you realize they can't *all* be made up."

"Do some of these impossible things have to do with stuff physically changing at night?" I asked.

Dad's little start of surprise was the only answer I needed, and I told him about the railing—and about taking Luke with me to see it and confirm that my mind wasn't playing tricks on me.

Dad leaned back in his chair as if he didn't have the strength to hold himself upright anymore. "We've been hearing stories like that since a couple of nights after you made that call. Not very many at first, and we just assumed people were making it up or were on bad trips or not right in the head. But every night we get more calls, and I've seen reports from officers with impeccable records confirming some of them."

"Then why isn't it all over the news?" I asked, wondering if he'd have a more convincing answer to that question than Luke had.

He gave me a significant look. "In what way would splashing sensationalist headlines all over the place improve the situation?"

I wasn't exactly a newsie, but being the daughter of the police commissioner, I was probably more conscious of current events and news than most people my age. I raised an eyebrow at my dad and said, "Since when do reporters care whether their reports improve the situation?"

He conceded my point with a nod—it was a rare police

commissioner who thought very highly of the press. "They might not, but I do, and, more importantly, the mayor does."

"So what you're saying is you're suppressing the story."

"To the best of our ability. But unless the madness stops, we're not going to be able to hold it back much longer. A day, maybe two, tops. The only thing that's helped keep it under wraps so long is that no one can capture anything on camera. Can you imagine a mainstream news channel going on air with the photo of a perfectly ordinary parking deck and claiming there are gargoyles on it even though you can't see them?"

I could see where he was coming from, and it made sense that the traditional news outlets would listen to the mayor and police commissioner when they suggested they not report anything until they had something with which to back up the story. "What about the tabloids? They don't mind being thought of as crackpots."

My dad made a sour face. He didn't much like the mainstream press, but he loathed the tabloids. "Take a look at some of the headlines next time you're in the grocery store. They're reporting it—it's just that no one really believes what they read in tabloids."

Not ordinarily, maybe, but I had a feeling that the people who were seeing the changes were much more receptive to what the tabloids had to say right now.

"It's a mess out there, Becks," my dad said. "The crime spree and the craziness seem to be related, and they're both getting worse every night. I don't see myself getting home at a normal hour in the near future, but I think it's best you stay inside as soon as the sun goes down. If you need anything at the grocery store or whatever, get it when it's still light out. Take Bob out right before sundown, and then I'll walk him again whenever I get home. He can hold it that long if he has to."

Bob had gone to sleep at my dad's feet, but he woke up at the sound of his name, raising his head to look at Dad and wag his tail. He probably wouldn't have been so cheerful if he understood English.

"Isn't that going a little overboard?" I asked. "I feel pretty safe with Bob, and if he ever starts acting like he did in that alley, I know better than to ignore it now."

"I know. But *I'd* feel a whole lot safer if I knew you were indoors." He scrubbed a hand through his hair. "It's killing me that you're home alone so much. If something happened to you . . ." His voice choked off, but I got the message.

I wanted to argue, because what Dad was describing sounded almost like being grounded again. Under house arrest. But it wasn't as if I went out a whole lot at night, at least not during the school year. And it was obvious the stress was already getting to my dad. The last thing he needed was to have me adding to it by tempting fate just to prove something. Staying inside once the sun went down seemed like a damn good idea, at least until things got back to normal—assuming they ever did.

# CHAPTER ELEVEN

The news broke the very next day. It started slow, just one local news station having the guts to mention that something genuinely bizarre might be happening. The talking heads worded everything very carefully—lots of "claims" and "alleges" and other words to help cast doubt on the story—but predictably, that first news story brought all the wackos out of the woodwork. The trouble was, it was hard to tell the difference between the wackos and the people who had legitimately seen bizarre changes.

My dad, of course, was called into work first thing in the morning, even though it was a Saturday, and once the news started getting out, I knew it was going to be another marathon day for him. I made sure our pantry was well stocked so I wouldn't have to go out after dark, then tried once again to work on my term paper.

Unfortunately, I didn't have the willpower to disable my Internet connection while I worked, and I kept getting sidetracked by "breaking news" as more and more legitimate news outlets picked up the story. Most people were calling it all a case of mass hysteria, and the groundless, often ridiculous speculations would have been laughable if I weren't dealing with my own case of "hysteria." The reporters seemed to think that starting every theory with "We don't want to speculate, but . . ." meant they could say whatever they liked, without a shred of evidence. Some evil mastermind had put hallucinogens in the Philadelphia water supply. Some new virus had sprung up out of nowhere and was spreading. Philadelphia was experiencing the first effects of a terrorist attack using previously undocumented biological or chemical weapons. And those were just the ideas the *legitimate* news sources were throwing out there. Never mind the tabloids, with their aliens and government conspiracies.

I wasn't the only one keeping an eye on the stories as the news went national. My sister called to see if I was okay. I lied and told her everything was fine, because that was the path of least resistance. I love Beth, but she's five years older and we've never been super close. She was the poster child for everything my parents valued—drive, determination, decisiveness—so of course we had almost nothing in common.

My mom's phone call came about thirty seconds after I hung up with Beth. We were barely past hello before she was telling me to pack a bag and catch a train to Boston until whatever was going on in Philly was smoothed over.

"I have school," I reminded her. "I can't just abandon ship."

"Of course you can," she said. "You can keep up with your classwork from home, and you'll be off on Thanksgiving break in a couple of weeks anyway. I'm sure your father is camped out at his office, and I don't like the idea of you being home alone all the time."

Her voice fairly oozed with righteous indignation. Just because she and my dad were now divorced, it didn't mean they'd stopped fighting, and it didn't take a rocket scientist to see my mom was spoiling for one of those fights. I'd tried playing peacemaker when my folks were still married, and it hadn't gone well. But when I thought about how hard my dad had been working lately, how haggard he looked, I knew I had to head my mother off at the pass. Dad didn't need her haranguing him on top of everything else.

"I've got Bob," I reminded her, keeping my voice conspicuously light. "And the press is exaggerating like you wouldn't believe. It's really not that big a deal."

The prospect of heading off to Boston for an indefinite stay held no appeal. Maybe I'd be safer there, but my mom was as much of a workaholic as my dad, which meant I'd be spending most of my time alone in her condo in a strange city where I knew no one. No thanks.

The fact was, as screwed up as everything was around here, this was my home. I'd used school as an explanation/excuse for why I chose to stay with Dad instead of moving with Mom, but that had only been one of my many reasons. At least when Dad left me home alone for hours on end it was for a good and important reason. Mom did it because she was at the beck and call of her corporate clients, who thought the bottom line was the only thing that mattered in the world. I would never admit it to her, but that was an excuse I couldn't muster much respect for. Especially when she complained so bitterly about Dad's hours.

"But with everything that's going on—" she started, but I cut her off.

"I'm fine, Mom. And I don't want to miss school. I'd never be able to keep up, and you know I can't let my grades tank my senior year if I want to get into a good college." Our teachers reminded us of how important our senior year grades were all the time, though I suspected their motives were somewhat self-serving. "It's not like there's rioting in the streets or anything." Yet.

I could tell my mom wasn't quite buying it, but she reluctantly backed off. I made a mental note to call my dad and let him know I hadn't told Mom what I'd seen. I had a feeling she'd be calling him herself sooner rather than later, and I didn't want him letting the cat out of the bag. If she knew I'd experienced some of the weirdness up close and personal, she would probably come to Philly herself and physically drag me off to Boston.

After getting off the phone, I made yet another valiant effort to work on my term paper. My brain still wasn't exactly laser focused, but I managed to get a couple of paragraphs written before someone knocked on the front door. I was up in my bedroom with my laptop sitting on my lap, and I frowned in annoyance at the interruption.

Bob was downstairs, barking like a hellhound. I wasn't expecting anybody, so I sat on my bed and waited for whoever it was to go away. As a general rule, no one who comes to your door unexpectedly in the city is anyone you want to talk to, especially during a crime spree.

Bob kept barking, and whoever was at the door knocked a second time. That was unusually persistent, and I wondered if there was any chance it could be Luke.

*Probably not,* I told myself. Luke would have known to call first. My dad was a walking PSA and was always preaching about how to maintain personal safety while living in the city. Not answering the door when you weren't expecting someone was one of his oft-repeated safety tips for women.

Even with this realization, I found myself putting the laptop aside and hopping off the bed. There was a third knock on the door as I was making my way down the stairs—Bob was barking so hard and loud I feared for the structural integrity of our house—and then my cell phone chirped. I pulled it from my back pocket and saw a text from Piper: *Come to the door before Bob barks himself to death.*

I stopped halfway down the stairs and stared at the message. It was *Piper* at the door? She had certainly heard my dad's safety lectures before, and the thought that she had shown up unannounced was slightly shocking.

*Coming,* I texted back, wondering what she was doing here. Getting a spot on Piper's social calendar was usually nearly impossible without extensive advance planning, and it was totally unlike her to just show up out of the blue like this.

Bob was majorly worked up by the time I got to the door, and it took some effort to get him to back off. He was still bristling, his lips twitching with barely suppressed snarls, when he finally obeyed my command to move aside and sit. Maybe I'd let him bark for too long and now he was having trouble reining it all in. He'd never bitten anyone before—except in training, when he was supposed to—but something about the way he looked now made me uneasy. I decided I'd rather be safe than sorry, so I grabbed his collar and led him into my dad's office at the top of the stairs and closed the door before finally letting Piper in.

The girl I let in my front door barely looked like the Piper I remembered. She'd cut her beautiful golden-red hair until it was so short on the sides you could see her scalp, and she'd dyed it white-blond. The longer section on the top was styled into a severe, punky-looking ridge that was kind of like a sideways-leaning Mohawk.

Piper grinned at my look of slack-jawed amazement, turning to give me a 360-degree view. "What do you think?" she asked when she faced front again.

"Um . . ." I struggled to find something suitably noncommittal to say, because there was no point in telling her the truth, which was that I thought it looked awful. "It's different," I finally said.

Piper laughed. "In other words, you hate it."

"I didn't say that!"

She snorted. "You didn't have to. You have the worst poker face I've ever seen."

Polite instinct told me to lie a little more convincingly, but I wasn't sure I was up to the challenge. The stark white color and the severe angles of her new haircut somehow leeched all the warmth and friendliness from her face, made her look unapproachable, even cold, despite her usual winning smile. The look set me completely off balance. There was no way I could convince her I actually liked it.

"What do your parents think?" I asked instead, but I already knew the answer.

Piper's smile turned into a self-satisfied smirk. "They loathe it, of course. My mom said I should wear a wig until it grows back. But hey, one of my cousins is getting married next weekend, and I bet my mom will let me out of going. She wouldn't want her snobby friends to see me with my hair looking like this. So it's a total win."

I wondered what Luke thought of all this, but I refrained from asking. "Did you just stop by to show me your hair?"

"Nope. Get your coat. I want to do some shopping. I need to get some clothes that go with my new look, and shopping is no fun alone."

I glanced at my watch and saw that it was three thirty. It would be getting dark in a little more than an hour, and that would leave precious little time for shopping. "Maybe some other time," I told her. "It's kinda late, and I don't want to be out after dark."

Piper made a dismissive noise. "You're not buying into all that bullshit on the news, are you?"

I shrugged, feeling not a bit tempted to tell her about my own encounters with the weird. "I believe we're in the middle of a crime spree and that the wackos are coming out in force at night. Maybe we can go tomorrow."

"We're going now," Piper said firmly. "I have my car, and I'll make sure you're back home safe and sound by dark."

"That's only an hour from now," I pointed out, not sure she had any idea what time it was.

"So it'll be a short shopping trip."

"You don't do short, remember?"

Her grin was still impish, even with the new crazy hair. "So don't count on me to keep track of time. You set an alarm on your phone, and when you have to go, you just say so."

I hesitated. It would certainly be more fun to go out with Piper than to sit around the house by myself for the rest of the day. But when had Piper *ever* managed to get me home by whatever deadline I or my father had set?

"Come on, Becks," Piper wheedled. "I know I have a bad track record, but you have to admit, it's not all my fault. You never speak up until it's already too late. As long as *you're* paying attention to the time, everything will be fine. Please?"

The fact was that getting out of the house for a while was a temptation too great to resist, and Piper's argument made perfect sense. It was true that when she'd made me late in the past, it was because I'd been unwilling to put on the brakes myself. As long as I trusted her to listen to me when I said it was time to go, there was no reason I couldn't spend the next hour or so doing a little shopping. It would get my mind off some of my troubles, and, as she said, I could set an alarm on my phone to make absolutely sure I got home before dark.

I'm not sure I was completely convinced by my own rationalization. But I went anyway.

Piper has money coming out her ears, so she tends to be a high-end shopper. Myself, I'm more of a bargain hunter. Not because my parents didn't have money but because they'd instilled their own innate frugality in both me and my sister. Since we were shopping specifically for Piper, I thought we'd go to a fashionable stretch of Walnut Street, where there was a mix of trendy chain stores and exclusive boutiques. But I could tell right away that wasn't where we were headed.

"Where are we going?" I asked her, already feeling a niggle of unease. Everything about this little scenario was strange, from Piper's surprising appearance on my doorstep to her ugly new hairdo, and I remembered Luke telling me she'd been acting strange lately, even pushier than normal.

Piper smirked at me. "You'll see when we get there."

I glanced at my watch. We'd eaten up a bunch of time already walking to Piper's car, since she'd parked three blocks away. "The further we get from my house, the less time we'll have to spend shopping." The stores on Walnut Street would have been a short drive, assuming we didn't have too much trouble finding somewhere to park, but we were already well past them and now had less than a half hour before sunset.

"Relax, Becks," she said, as she ran a red light. Someone honked indignantly, and Piper responded almost absently, flipping them the bird. "We'll have fun, I promise."

I frowned at my best friend and rechecked the security of my seat belt. "Are we really going shopping?" I asked. I was already sure there was something else up, but I had no idea what it might be.

Piper turned her head and winked at me, and I flinched at how close she came to smacking into some pedestrian who was trying to cross the street.

"Watch the road!" I snapped at her. Whatever she was up to, I knew I didn't like it. "What has gotten into you?"

"Remember how I said the other day that I had to find some way to set you up with a guy? Well, I found a way."

I suspect my eyes nearly bugged out of my head. "What? What are you talking about?"

"I met a guy last night at a party."

At the rave she went to without Luke, she meant. But I didn't want to explain how I knew about that, so I didn't say anything.

"He is seriously hot," Piper continued, "and he's also seriously unattached. He was hitting on me last night. I told him I was unavailable but I had a friend I thought he would like. So we're meeting him at the Bourse for coffee, then going to a movie."

For a moment I was stunned speechless. Piper had never pulled anything remotely like this before, and I felt like I was being ambushed. I was certainly willing to entertain the idea of letting her set me up with someone, seeing as it was nearly impossible for me to meet guys on my own. But at a time and place of my own choosing. The Bourse was about as far away from my house as you could get and still be in the heart of

Center City. And if I was going to risk being out after dark, it sure as hell wouldn't be for some movie at the Bourse Ritz, which showed art films and documentaries. I'd let Piper drag me to one once and had been so bored I practically fell asleep.

"You lied to me," I said, when I was finally capable of speech.

She shrugged, no hint of apology on her face. "I've known you a while, Becks. You wouldn't have come if I'd told the truth."

"You're right, I wouldn't have!" I answered with some heat. "And for your information, that's my prerogative."

Piper turned a corner and the Bourse came into view. It's a gorgeous old building near Independence Square, a historic Philadelphia landmark. It's a far cry from a teen hangout, containing offices, tourist shops, and an anemic food court. I had the sneaking suspicion that Piper had chosen it solely because it was so far away from my house. She thought the distance would make me into a captive audience. I seriously contemplated murder as Piper began circling the block in search of a parking space. The light was fading, sunset only minutes away.

"Turn the car around," I said, putting as much authority as I could muster into my voice. When Luke had told me Piper was getting pushier than ever, he clearly hadn't been exaggerating. "Take me home. Now."

Piper laughed and took aim at an open space by the curb. The space was open because of the fire hydrant on the sidewalk, but she didn't seem to care. "We're already here," she said as she maneuvered into her illegal parking spot. "What's the harm in just coming in for a few minutes and saying hello? If you don't want to do the movie after—"

"I said no, and I meant it." Sometimes I let Piper push me

out of my comfort zone because I figured it was for my own good. This was not one of those times. "Take me home, Piper."

She stopped the car and put it in park, then looked at me in triumph. "I'll take you home just as soon as we've had our cup of coffee, and not a moment sooner. Now come on."

"But it's dark already. You said—"

"It's four thirty in the afternoon, not one in the morning. Will you chill already?"

She got out of the car before I could protest more. I sat there fuming for a minute or two, so mad I could barely see straight. What did Piper think she was accomplishing? Did she honestly think there was any chance I would *like* the guy she was trying to force me into meeting? Even if he turned out to be Prince Charming, there was no way I could warm to him under the circumstances. Piper *had* to know that.

But she wasn't getting back in the car, and unless I knew how to hot-wire the damn thing, there wasn't much point in me sitting there.

I wondered if there was actual smoke coming out of my ears as I reluctantly climbed out of the car, glaring at Piper the whole way. The glare had no effect on her, and she merely stood there on the curb smiling at me, her eyes twinkling with amusement.

Wow. She actually thought this was *funny*. Who *was* this girl? Certainly not the Piper I'd thought I'd known. *That* Piper was often careless, but not actively malicious. If you had the guts to tell her she was being a bitch, she'd instantly recognize the truth of it and apologize. But I saw no hint today that she even knew an apology was necessary.

I averted my gaze, then checked my wallet to see if I had bus fare. This was one battle of wills I had no intention of letting

Piper win. I didn't have much in the way of cash, but it was just enough to get me home. If I didn't have to wait too long for a bus, I shouldn't have to spend more than about half an hour out in the city after dark. Surely the worst of the night madness didn't happen until later.

I glared at Piper one more time, hoping she'd see how serious I was and then relent and take me home. "I'm going to catch a bus," I told her.

That didn't seem to bother her a bit. "Suit yourself. You don't know what you'll be missing." Then her smile grew even broader, her eyes lighting up as she looked at something just over my left shoulder. "Or maybe you won't miss it after all."

The hairs on the back of my neck rose for reasons I couldn't explain, and I turned to see what she was looking at.

There was a boy walking briskly down the sidewalk toward us, waving and grinning. The boy Piper had hijacked me to come and meet, obviously. Although his face was instantly familiar, it took me a couple of seconds to place it. When I did, my jaw dropped open, and a chill shivered down my spine, because I don't believe in coincidence.

"Becket," Piper said, sounding so self-satisfied I longed to shake her, "I'd like you to meet my new friend, Aleric. Aleric, this is Becket."

The boy I'd literally run into when fleeing through the fog near school smiled at me, showing no sign of being surprised to see me.

# CHAPTER TWELVE

I was stunned speechless. What were the chances that I would run into Aleric when being chased by a trash monster at school, and then he would run into Piper at a party and arrange to meet up with me here in Center City? It's not like we lived in a small town.

"It's a pleasure to see you again," Aleric said. His words and his tone were perfectly pleasant, but there was something sharp and predatory in his expression, something that made me unwilling to shake the hand he offered me.

Piper jabbed me with an elbow, but that didn't make me feel any more inclined to shake Aleric's hand. His too-green eyes glittered with amusement. Far from being offended by my refusal to shake, he seemed to enjoy it.

"You sure do get around, don't you?" I asked him, and I was shocked to hear a faint quaver in my voice. Yes, there was something spooky and unnerving about Aleric—and about his showing up in my life for a second time—but surely there was nothing to be *scared* of. After all, we were in public, with plenty of people around. And he hadn't said or done anything that should make me afraid of him in anything but a shy-girl–meets–hot-guy way.

Aleric raised an eyebrow. "As do you."

"Wait," Piper said, sounding confused. "You two *know* each other?"

"I wouldn't go that far," Aleric said, his eyes locked on mine. "We bumped into each other once before."

"Wow," said Piper. "What a coincidence!"

"Either that or he's stalking me," I said, earning another elbow and a sharp sound of protest from Piper. I tried to make it sound like I was kidding, but I don't think either Piper or Aleric was fooled, even though Aleric laughed like I'd just told a great joke.

"I think the universe is trying to tell us something," he said when he finished laughing. "Let's get that cup of coffee. I'd like to hear more about your stalking theory. Personally, I think it would be kind of a neat trick to arrange to randomly run into your friend at a party. I'm sure you have a theory about how I pulled it off."

"Thanks," I said insincerely, "but no thanks. I was just on my way home."

Piper grabbed my arm to keep me from walking away. "What is *wrong* with you?" she muttered under her breath. If she thought Aleric couldn't hear her, she was delusional.

I jerked my arm out of her grip. If he was really some perfectly ordinary nice guy rather than some creepy stalker dude, then I was not only making a fool of myself but was also being unforgivably rude to him. But everything about him made me want to shrink away, despite his undeniably handsome face and his friendly smile.

"Next time you want to set me up on a blind date, ask my permission first," I snapped at Piper.

Because I thought there was a slim chance I might be overreacting, I smiled at Aleric as best I could. "Piper and I are having a disagreement," I told him. "Don't take it personally. I just refuse to let her get away with lying to me."

Piper groaned. "Oh come on, Becks. Get over it already. Where's the harm in getting a cup of coffee?"

"Everyone hates a liar," Aleric said, still smiling. His eyes seemed to bore into me, telling me he knew my every secret, my every lie.

My pulse was kicking as if I'd just run a mile, and my stomach kept wanting to turn over on itself. The sensation reminded me very much of how I'd felt when I'd approached the "baby" in the alley. My primal instincts had been right to warn me away then, and I was inclined to give them the benefit of the doubt now. Even though Piper didn't seem to sense anything at all wrong.

"Hey!" she said indignantly, though I seriously doubt he'd been talking to her. "It was just a little white lie. Let's not make it into some grand betrayal."

I didn't think now was the time and place to have it out with Piper, so I mostly ignored her as I took a couple of steps backward. "Nice to see you again, Aleric," I said, and no one could miss the sarcasm in my voice. "Just in case I end up 'accidentally' running into you again, you should probably know that my father is the police commissioner."

"For God's sake, Becket!" Piper said. Her face was turning red. I think she was actually embarrassed for me.

Aleric inclined his head. "I will consider myself warned."

His lips were still shaped into a half smile, and he showed no sign of taking offense at anything I'd said or done. Which I thought was a clear indicator that I wasn't overreacting. If he were just some normal boy who was letting himself be fixed up on a blind date, surely he'd be hurt, insulted, or royally pissed off about the way I was acting. Instead, he looked amused and unsurprised. This was not only how he *expected* me to act, it was how he *wanted* me to act.

I wished suddenly that I could have handled the situation with more grace and subtlety. I didn't like the idea that I was showing him my fear, that I was giving him what he wanted. But it was too late to change that now.

"Enjoy the movie," I said, sweeping my gaze over both Piper and Aleric. I would have liked to get Piper away from him, too, but she was obviously never going to listen to me. Besides, Aleric didn't seem even remotely interested in her. He was just using her to get to me, for reasons I didn't want to know.

It took an effort of will to turn my back and start walking briskly back toward Walnut Street, where I could catch a bus home.


I had the really uncomfortable sensation that I was being watched the whole time I walked to the bus stop. I looked over my shoulder only once, when I reached the end of that first block, but neither Aleric nor Piper was in view. I supposed they went into the Bourse to get that cup of coffee and have a good laugh at my expense.

There was a small crowd clustered at the bus stop, which I thought was a good sign. An empty bus stop usually means you just missed the bus. However, I stood there for over ten minutes before a bus finally roared its way toward us—and then roared right on past because it was already standing room only inside. Everyone at the bus stop gave a little groan and settled in to wait some more. Except me. I looked at the sky, which was now almost completely dark, and thought about how little I wanted to stand here for who knew how much longer waiting for the damn bus. And hoping the next bus that came by would have room.

On a sunny spring day, I would have happily walked home. It would take a while, and my feet would end up hurting by the end, but it would have been doable. Tonight, in the cold and gathering dark, the walk seemed impossibly long, and fraught with danger. Then again, at least if I was walking I'd be able to keep a little warmer. The temperature was steadily dropping, and I wasn't super bundled up because I'd thought we'd be inside, shopping, most of the time Piper and I were out.

I decided to compromise and walk part of the way, stopping at each bus stop and taking a look behind me to see if there was a bus on the horizon.

For fifteen blocks, I kept to that same pattern: walk a block, stop, look behind. And for fifteen blocks, I saw no sign of another bus coming. Each stop was crowded with irritated people, and maybe it was my imagination, but I could have sworn I sensed a strange feeling of tension in the air. Everyone I passed seemed furtive, and my threat radar was going off constantly. I also couldn't help noticing that the sound of sirens split the night way more often than usual. I tried to be aware of my surroundings for safety purposes, but not so aware that I'd notice any uncomfortable details, like railings displaying phallic symbols.

I was in the home stretch, beginning to feel like I would actually make it back to the house safely and without any undue weirdness, when a familiar car passed by me and pulled into the driveway of a parking lot in front of me, blocking my way. The window hummed down.

"Get in," Piper said, leaning across the seat so she could make eye contact.

I stopped in my tracks and shook my head at her. "You're kidding, right?" It was going to take some serious effort on my part—and a lot of sincere apologizing on hers—before I would even consider forgiving her. I realized with a pang that I was very likely in the process of losing my best friend.

Piper heaved an exaggerated sigh. "No, I'm not kidding. I just realized I was being a total bitch about this. I went about everything the wrong way, and I don't blame you for being pissed at me."

I folded my arms across my chest. I'd started home about forty minutes ago, and if she was just now catching up with me, that meant it had taken her a damn long time to come to that realization. Enough time for her to have a leisurely cup of coffee while chatting up Aleric, the two of them maybe commiserating about how badly I'd treated them.

"You're at least a half an hour too late with your apology," I told her. "I don't think you're a bit sorry, and I don't believe you even understand you did something wrong."

It was hard to see Piper's face in the darkened interior of her car, but I thought I caught a hint of an eye-roll.

"Of course I do," she said in a tone that was supposed to be placating but somehow grated on my nerves even more. "It doesn't take a rocket scientist to know that lying was a stupid move. I was just so proud of myself for talking Aleric into meeting you that I got tunnel vision."

My jaw clenched and I stared daggers at her. "Congratulations on achieving your impossible quest to get a guy to condescend to meet little old me. I'm sure it took a lot of lying and cleverness to make that happen." To my shame, my eyes were burning as if I were on the verge of tears.

Piper groaned. "You know I didn't mean it that way, Becks. I honestly thought you would like him. I admit, I'm an idiot, and my execution sucked ass. But my intentions were good."

Maybe so, but she had still lied to me. Still treated me as if what she wanted was way more important than what I wanted.

"Come on, Becks," she wheedled. "Let me drive you the rest of the way home, at least. You don't have to say you forgive me. Hell, you don't even have to talk at all, if that's what you want."

My feet were killing me. The temperature was still dropping. And the usual city dangers were magnified tenfold by my knowledge of the changes that were taking place. Walking the rest of the way home just to prove how angry I was seemed pointless.

Wordlessly, I climbed into the car and closed the door. I stared straight ahead as I fastened my seat belt, and I was determined that our short car ride would pass in silence. I expected Piper to start chirping at me with either more apologies or pointless small talk—she was never any good with silence—but she seemed to sense it would only make things worse.

We made it a little more than a block before Piper suddenly slammed on the brakes so hard I might have flown through the windshield if it weren't for my seat belt, which I had a feeling would be imprinted on my chest, come morning.

"What the hell?" I cried, bracing myself against the dash. I'd been staring out the side window, pointedly ignoring Piper, so I hadn't seen what made her stop. I turned to her and saw her staring forward, jaw dropped, eyes wide.

I followed her gaze, and couldn't contain a shriek.

Driving around Center City was a challenge to any car's shocks. Manholes, construction sites, potholes—you couldn't go a block without hitting one or even all three. So seeing a big pothole in the middle of Walnut Street wasn't exactly unusual. But the one that yawned across the street right in front of us was practically a canyon.

And that canyon possessed something that looked an awful lot like teeth.

As I watched in mute horror, the canyon opened wider, the asphalt moving as fluidly as flesh, until there was no way to move forward without driving into it. Behind us, someone was leaning on their horn. There are two lanes on Walnut Street, so when Piper didn't move forward, the guy behind us tried to veer around. He was yelling something through his side window and holding up his middle finger at Piper when his front tires hit the pothole.

There was a sound like nothing I'd ever heard before—a snap and a crunch and the bang of tires exploding, as the pothole . . . Well, I don't know any other way to describe it but that it bit down on the car that dared to try to drive over it.

The toothlike protrusions on each side of the pothole sank into the tires and then started crushing the wheels themselves. On the sidewalks, people had started to notice something was wrong—they couldn't have missed that noise—but I didn't think they had a clue what was actually happening. Not at first.

"Back up!" I ordered Piper breathlessly as the pothole widened to take in more of the car and then crunched closed again. The teeth had sunk in right at hubcap level, and the car lurched forward, its grille banging down on the road. The driver was screaming and fumbling with his seat belt, even as his back wheels spun and his engine revved futilely.

"Back up!" I said again, more loudly, as Piper just sat there and stared.

Pedestrians were starting to scream and panic, while behind us more cars were honking in annoyance. Piper finally broke out of her paralysis and put the car in reverse. Without bothering to look behind her, she floored it.

It was a good thing the car right behind us had stopped practically on our bumper. We didn't have time to build up any speed before we crashed into him. I glanced over my shoulder and saw that people in the cars behind us were starting to get out, trying to get a look at what had brought traffic to such a complete halt. When they were passed by screaming pedestrians, some of those drivers caught the panic and abandoned their cars, running blindly away from an unknown danger.

We were trapped, fenced in by the cars parked on the sides of the street and the ones that had come to a stop behind us.

"Maybe if I gunned it fast enough . . ." Piper suggested in a shaking voice.

The pothole seemed to rise up out of the street, sinking its teeth into the fender of the car it had caught, and tearing it off. The frantic driver finally tumbled out and joined the sea of fleeing, screaming people, until it felt almost as if Piper and I were alone in the street.

I didn't know how much mobility that pothole had, but I very much wanted to get out of there while it was still chewing up that other car. Piper sat frozen and staring in the driver's seat. I unhooked my seat belt, then reached over and put the car in Park, pulling Piper's keys from the ignition. Her hands were glued to the steering wheel, the knuckles stark white.

"Piper," I said in as calm a voice as I could muster, "we have to get out of the car."

She shook her head frantically, gripping the steering wheel even tighter. I wanted to open my own door and start running, but it was obvious that Piper was too panicked to function. I couldn't just leave her.

"It's not safe in here," I said. "Let's get out of the road." The pothole didn't seem to have any interest in the cars parked along the curb on both sides, nor did it show any signs of wanting to pursue the fleeing pedestrians—assuming it was capable of moving from its current spot. I figured that meant getting out of the car and running away was a damn good plan.

I opened my door, hoping the movement would inspire Piper to do the same, but she was still frozen. I closed my door and ran around to the driver's side, keeping a careful eye on the pothole while I did. It still seemed to be happily munching its kill, biting off hunks of metal from the car's exterior and then sinking its teeth into the engine. I opened Piper's door, grabbed her arm, and bodily yanked her out of the car. She fell to the asphalt with a little cry of distress, but at least that seemed to break her out of her paralysis. When I tugged her toward the sidewalk, she lurched to her feet and followed.

Feeling eerily removed from the situation, I dug out my phone and snapped a quick picture as the pothole reared up and snapped the car's front axle in two. Then Piper and I turned and ran.

# CHAPTER THIRTEEN

No other impossible creatures attacked us on the way to my house, though there was a marked increase in the number of sirens. From the sound of them, they were converging on Walnut Street. I also thought I spotted Aleric once, out of the corner of my eye, lurking in an alley on the other side of the street, but when I turned my head to look, he was gone. Assuming he'd ever been there.

I can't tell you how relieved I was when I closed and locked the front door behind me. I had no particular reason to assume I was safe indoors, except that every bizarre thing that had happened had happened outdoors.

Piper was shaking and glassy eyed, her face made even more ghostly white by her stark new dye job.

"Should I, uh, get you a drink or something?" I asked. I couldn't blame her for being freaked out, but she was beginning to worry me.

Piper blinked and shook her head. A hint of intelligence returned to her eyes. "What *was* that thing?" she whispered.

"Have you seen anything else strange at night lately?" I asked, because I couldn't answer her question. Maybe I was having an easier time accepting what I'd seen because of my previous experiences. My pulse had calmed, and though thinking about the pothole and its teeth made it pick up again, I wasn't anywhere near panic. Hadn't been even when we'd been in the car. I wondered if I was storing it all up for a nervous breakdown somewhere down the line.

"What do you mean?"

"You know. *Strange.* Things you can't explain. Things that seem to be impossible. Like a moving pothole with teeth. That kind of strange."

She opened and closed her mouth a few times as if struggling for words. You know Piper's in bad shape when she can't find words.

"Never mind," I said as gently as I could. "Why don't you just sit down for a bit. You're safe here."

Piper nodded and plopped down on the sofa. Bob, who seemed to have mellowed out while we were gone, walked over to her and nosed her hand, begging for a pet. Or maybe he just had that uncanny dog sense that told him she was upset and needed a little furry companionship. She stroked his head idly, and a hint of color finally came back to her face.

I suppose technically I was still mad at her, but I had no trouble putting that anger on the back burner. She looked so frightened and vulnerable right now. I wanted to comfort her, to tell her everything was going to be all right, but it was hard to say when I had such doubts of my own. I didn't know what was happening out there in the city, but it sure seemed to me it was getting worse instead of better.

I checked the photo I'd taken on my cell phone, wondering if I'd captured the toothy pothole any better than I'd captured the phallic symbol. I wasn't surprised when my photo showed a picture of a car with its front end smashed and broken sitting in a perfectly ordinary pothole. One with no teeth, and that was clearly not big enough to have caused the kind of damage the car had sustained.

I showed Piper the photo, then told her about my other adventures in photography. Which of course meant mentioning that I'd spent some time with Luke the night before. I thought the idea might spark a hint of jealousy or resentment in her, but instead she just looked guilty.

"I've been treating him like shit lately," she admitted. Her shoulders slumped, and she seemed to have lost the self-assurance that I had always figured was part of her basic nature. "And I've been a sucky friend to you, too. I don't know what's gotten into me. I've just been feeling so . . . frustrated. Like I can't make a single move without it being governed by rules. Go to school every day. Wear a uniform. Don't drink alcohol until you're twenty-one. Don't try drugs ever." She sighed hugely. "I know we need rules and all, but do we really need so many *stupid* ones?"

If she expected me to feel sorry for her, she was in for a disappointment. As far as I could tell, her parents let her get away with just about anything she wanted to, and hello, everyone has to live with things like going to school and drug laws. Did she think she deserved some special exemption?

I didn't put any of these thoughts into words. A rant wasn't going to help anything.

"Do you want to call Luke and ask him to come over?" I asked instead. I hoped maybe his would be a more sympathetic ear for her to pour her heart out to, but she shook her head.

"He hasn't seen the hair yet," she said with a wry smile. "I have a feeling he's not going to like it, and I'm not sure I can deal with that right now. I've had my fill of being disapproved of for a while."

I couldn't tell if that was a barbed comment aimed at me or if she was referring to her parents' disapproval of her hair or Luke's disapproval of the rave. Since fighting with her would be counterproductive, I chose to believe it wasn't aimed at me.

Piper heaved another sigh and dabbed at her eyes, though if she'd cried she'd managed to hide the tears completely. "How am I going to get home?" she wondered. "I mean, there's no way I'm going back there to get my car even if that thing turns back into a normal pothole."

I shook my head. "I bet the police have that whole area cordoned off by now anyway. Can your parents come pick you up?"

"They're at some charity auction tonight and they'll have their phones turned off. I probably won't be able to reach them until after eleven."

"We could call a taxi," I said doubtfully, but I wasn't sure how many taxis would even be on the road tonight. And hey, for all I knew, there were potholes with teeth popping up all over the city. "Or you could just wait until my dad gets home and he can maybe take you."

He'd know which streets were safe to drive on, if any.

Thinking about the chaos more potholes like the one we'd encountered would cause, I grabbed the remote and turned on the TV. The Special Report banner at the top of the screen told me things were bad even before the sound came on.

". . . are urging everyone in the Philadelphia area to stay indoors unless absolutely necessary," the reporter said. She was standing in front of the Art Museum, bundled up in a fashionable coat and scarf and doing her best not to look nervous.

Her best wasn't good enough, and she was obviously having trouble keeping her eyes on the camera.

The image on the screen changed to a couple of news anchors sitting at a desk, who looked a hell of a lot more poised and comfortable. I felt sorry for the woman whose job it was to stand outside, where all the chaos was happening, and tell everyone else to stay inside where it was safe. Cross TV news reporter off my list of potential future careers.

"In case you're just joining us," the male anchor said, "the rash of reports of unexplained phenomena at night has escalated in the city of Philadelphia. Authorities confirm that there have been multiple fatalities across the city but refuse to speculate as to the cause or scope of the issue. What follows are some graphic images captured on cell phone cameras by anonymous sources. Please be warned, these images are not suitable for all audiences."

The first image that came across the screen was dark and blurry, but you could make it out all right if you squinted. It was the body of a man, his face obscured in a half-hearted show of good taste. He was standing at the mouth of a vacant lot— one that had clearly been blocked off by a chain-link fence topped with barbed wire. Half of that fence was still attached to one of the neighboring buildings, but the other half was not only loose, it was wrapped around the man, from his ankles to his neck, in layers so thick you could barely make out his form within them. The man was quite obviously dead, and there was an amazing amount of what I assumed was blood splashed all around.

"Multiple witnesses at the scene of this murder," the anchorman's voice said, "report seeing this chain-link fence turn into barbed wire and wrap itself around the victim."

Beside me, Piper let out a long whistle. "Wow. Your dad and the rest of the police department must be *really* underwater if they're letting the press interview murder witnesses."

The image on the screen started to change, but I had no interest in seeing more pictures of dead people, so I switched the TV off. Piper didn't protest.

She was right, of course. The police would never allow the press to badger a murder witness until that witness had been thoroughly interviewed and had made statements. There had to be so much crazy shit going on that the police couldn't stop all the holes, and that thought was positively terrifying.

As of this morning, the story of Philadelphia and its "mass hysteria" had been starting to go public—hence the calls from my mom and sister—and I figured the current situation was going to add tons of fuel to the fire. I glanced over at our answering machine, surprised it wasn't blinking itself silly with messages from my mom and my sister both. They had to be worried, and my mom would want to get me on that train to Boston ASAP. Or maybe at this point a train was too slow. Maybe she wanted me on an airplane, this very night.

Feeling yet another chill of unease, I picked up the phone and wasn't entirely surprised to find the line was dead. I then tried my cell phone, but though I could see that I had a connection, I couldn't get a call through. Again, not entirely surprising. Practically everyone in Philly was probably trying to call someone or being called by someone. There's only so much traffic the airwaves can handle. Piper gave it a shot with her phone, just in case, but she had no more luck than I had.

"Do you think this is the start of the zombie apocalypse?" Piper asked, but she sounded too scared to make the joke funny.

I laughed anyway, a nervous giggle that momentarily threatened to run away with me. "No sign of zombies yet," I said, "but I'm going to double-check all our doors and windows, just in case."

There was no way any of our doors and windows were unlocked—Dad would never stand for that—but at least it gave Piper and me something to do other than brood and speculate. We checked each one together, wiggling each lock to make sure it was fully in place. Bob followed us every step of the way, practically glued to my leg, so that I almost tripped over him a couple of times. He wasn't usually this clingy—actually, he wasn't usually clingy at all—and I figured he was once again picking up on our anxiety.

"Maybe we should be watching the news," Piper said when we were finished. "I'm not sure I want to know what's happening out there, but not knowing is driving me crazy."

I agreed with her on both counts. I wasn't worried about my dad, because the police commissioner had no reason to go out in the field, but I of course knew a lot of his friends and co-workers. People who would be responding to any emergency calls that happened to come in and would therefore be out on the streets with the madness. I hoped all of them were all right, but without keeping an eye on the news, I wouldn't know the scale of whatever was going on. No, I probably wasn't going to see anything even remotely comforting, but I preferred to know.

Piper, Bob, and I were all on the stairs between the first and second floors, heading back down to the living room to park in front of the TV, when the lights went out.

"Oh crap," I whispered under my breath, while Piper said something far more colorful.

We both brought out our cell phones and used their feeble

blue light to guide us down the rest of the stairs, and then I went searching for candles. We didn't have a lot of power outages here in Center City, and when we did, they didn't last very long, but Dad was always prepared.

I found candles and matches in one of the kitchen drawers, and Piper and I lit enough of them so it wasn't pitch dark in the living room when we resumed our places on the sofa.

"What are the chances the power company will send someone out tonight to fix whatever's wrong?" Piper asked.

We both knew the answer. We were just going to have to hunker down in the darkness and wait for morning. I wasn't sure when or even if Dad was going to come home, but I knew he wasn't going to turn right around and drive Piper back to her own home. Not tonight.

"Guess you're staying the night," I said to her. "Maybe we can pretend this is a slumber party."

"Oh yeah, let's change into our nighties and talk about boys," Piper responded, showing that her sense of humor was still alive and kicking.

I hoped the outage was localized, because a blackout at a time like this could be catastrophic. The police were obviously already overwhelmed, and people get weird in the dark in the best of times.

"I'd suggest ghost stories, but, uh, no," I said, trying to match Piper's tone.

"No," she agreed with a dramatic shudder.

Bob, still being uncommonly clingy, had curled up at my feet and laid his head on his paws. I was edgy enough that I almost jumped out of my skin when his head suddenly snapped up and his ears pricked forward.

I didn't know what he was responding to—I hadn't heard

anything—but I breathed a little prayer under my breath that it was my dad coming home. I was badly in need of his strength and self-assurance. He would know exactly what to do, how we could stay as safe as possible in the face of whatever was happening outside.

My hopes that Piper and I were about to be under the protection of the police commissioner himself were quickly shattered when I saw the fur on the back of Bob's neck start to rise.

# CHAPTER FOURTEEN

I really hoped Bob was only bristling because Piper's and my anxiety was contagious. Silently, I begged for him to put his head back down and go to sleep, but instead he got to his feet and stared intently at the front door, hackles continuing to rise as his ears slowly flattened.

"This can't be good," Piper said, her eyes wide and frightened in the candlelight.

"The door's locked," I reminded her. "And we checked all the windows. And we have Bob."

"Uh-huh. A pothole grew teeth and attacked a car earlier tonight, and we're sitting here in the dark during a blackout."

Her case was more convincing than mine. I reached over and took her hand, which was cold and clammy. "We're safe here," I said with as much conviction as I could muster, as Bob stalked toward the door, his lips pulling back from his teeth and a low growl rising in his throat.

There was a sudden, loud bang on the door, one short, sharp sound that in no way resembled a knock and that made both Piper and me jump to our feet and cry out in surprise. Bob did not appreciate it, and his growl turned into a full-throated bark that made my bones rattle. He threw himself at the door, his claws ripping into the paint as he tried to batter his way through to whoever—or *what*ever—was out there.

"Becket . . ." Piper moaned, her hand tightening on mine as we both backed away from the door and Bob's fury.

If there were any other noises at the door, we couldn't hear them over Bob. My heart was pounding in my throat, and I had the now-familiar queasy feeling in my stomach. The flickering candles made the shadows dance all around us, but we'd only bothered to light the living room, where we were sitting. Beyond their feeble glow, everything was pitch dark.

There was another sharp crack, this time not from the door but from the front window. Piper screamed, and practically broke my fingers with her spastic grip. We couldn't see out the window because the shutters were closed, so there was no way to know what that noise had been. Bob abandoned his post by the door and roared over to the window, ears flattened, neck hair bristling, barking and snarling so viciously that even in the dark I could see the drool flying from his mouth. He rose up on his hind legs and scrabbled at the shutters with his claws.

The noise came again, this time from one of the side windows. Bob pursued it with single-minded fury. The side windows were set high in the wall, so Bob couldn't get at them directly. Instead, he propped his front paws on the wall and kept making fruitless little jumps.

"It's playing with us," Piper whispered, so softly I could barely hear her over Bob.

"Either that, or searching for a weakness," I whispered back. "It won't find one," I hastened to assure Piper when I heard the frightened whimper that rose from her throat. I might have been more convincing if I believed that myself.

I had no idea who or what was out there, and I had zero

interest in going to a window and trying to get a look. Then again, I didn't much like the idea of standing there cowering helplessly in the dark, either.

"I'm going to get my gun," I announced, pulling Piper with me as I sidled toward the coffee table to grab one of the candles.

I always called it "my" gun, but technically it belonged to my dad. He'd taught me to shoot, and he'd made sure I memorized the combination to the gun safe in case there was an emergency and he and his service weapon weren't around. I wasn't an expert marksman, but I wasn't a public menace, either.

I hauled Piper up the stairs while Bob continued to bark and snarl. Dad's gun safe was in his study. "Hold this," I ordered Piper, thrusting the candle at her as I knelt before the safe.

She held the candle low so that I could see the numbers on the combination lock. My hands were shaking a bit with nerves as I turned the dials. Bob's barking had moved to the kitchen now, which I supposed meant whatever was out there was continuing its survey of our defenses.

As the safe clicked open, I noticed that I had subconsciously started thinking of our stalker as "whatever" instead of "whoever or whatever." Maybe it really was a person out there, messing with us just for fun. But after encountering a fanged baby, a trash monster, and a living pothole, I found my assumptions shifting.

Dad's SIG Sauer was loaded and ready to go, because he didn't have it there for sport. It was meant for emergencies, and in an emergency you don't want to have to stop to load your gun before facing the enemy. I checked it over briefly and made sure there was one in the chamber.

"You look like you know how to use that thing," Piper said, sounding surprised for some reason.

I looked over my shoulder at her. "I'm the police commissioner's daughter. It would be pretty lame if I didn't know how to shoot a gun."

From the sound of it, Bob was back at the front door. Pressing myself against the wall, I tried to peek out the study window, which looked out over the front door of the house, but all I could see was a sea of black. It was so inky black out there that I figured the whole city must be out, because lights anywhere nearby should have provided at least a tiny hint of ambient glow.

Bob's frenzy was slightly muffled by distance, which allowed Piper and me both to hear a strange *click-click-click* sound. It was coming from outside, and to my ears it resembled the sound of claws on metal. It was coming from below, climbing higher.

"Shit!" I yelped, pointing my gun toward the window—which was the only possible way anything could get in this room—while moving backward away from it. "It's climbing the drainpipe!"

Thanks to the candle Piper still held, I could see nothing in the glass except a faint orange glow being reflected back at us, but my ears followed the sound as it rose, and I was tempted to fire blindly in that direction.

Not so tempted that I would actually *do* it, though. A gunshot would shatter the window, and if it didn't hit our stalker, then I'd be giving it free access to the study.

Bob had finally realized his prey had moved, and I heard the thump of his paws as he bounded up the stairs. He blew past Piper, then threw himself at the window. I half expected the thing to shatter on impact, but it didn't. His claws scrabbled at the glass—our house was going to be a wreck by the time this was all over—and he continued his furious barking.

I was torn between wanting to get as far away from that window as possible and wanting to be there and ready if whatever was out there broke through. I stood hesitating near the door, gun still held in a classic two-handed grip and pointed at the window. My finger wasn't on the trigger, though, because Bob kept leaping into my line of fire.

"We should go to a room with no windows," Piper suggested, tugging on my arm.

PSA: never tug on the arm of someone who has both hands on a gun. I was lucky my finger wasn't on the trigger, or I might have fired by accident.

"Careful!" I snapped at Piper, glancing at her in my peripheral vision and nodding toward the gun.

"Oops, sorry."

Whatever was climbing the drainpipe should have made it to the window by now, but if it was making any attempt to get in, I couldn't hear it over Bob. His desperate barking was getting on my nerves, making me even more tense, and I wished he'd give it a rest. I knew better than to try to silence him, however.

Abruptly, Bob turned away from the front window and leaped to the side window.

"Please, let's go somewhere safer," Piper begged.

I licked my lips, doing a quick mental inventory of the house. There were no rooms without windows, but the windows in the basement were only a few inches high, barely peeking above sidewalk level. However, we used our basement like many people use attics, meaning the place was crammed with boxes of junk, broken furniture, and stuff we plain didn't know what to do with. There wasn't much room to move around, and it was about the creepiest place I could imagine hiding from some unknown creature that was toying with us in the dark.

"The windows are all locked," I reminded Piper yet again. "And if it could break through one, I think it would have done it already."

"Right. So you should put the gun away and we should go downstairs and play cards."

I gave her a dirty look but didn't reply.

Apparently our stalker moved again, because Bob almost knocked Piper and me down as he charged past us, this time heading for what used to be my sister's bedroom. I lowered the gun and took a deep breath.

"It's not going to get in," I said, trying to reassure myself as much as I was trying to reassure Piper. "If it does, it'll have to go through Bob to get to us. And if it goes through Bob, there's always this." I held up the gun. "I'm not saying we should go play games, but I think we should both try to chill a bit." Ha-ha. Like that was going to happen. "Let's go downstairs, where we'll have more than one candle."

The light from the single candle Piper still carried was barely enough to penetrate the darkness, and the flickering shadows it cast made me want to jump out of my skin.

I don't think Piper was convinced of our safety—I know I wasn't—but she allowed me to coax her back downstairs, where we hastily lit even more candles. No amount of candlelight could equal the power of electricity, but it was better than nothing.

It wasn't long before Bob came flying down the stairs, once

more in pursuit of something we couldn't see. I would have thought he'd be getting tired by now, but he showed no signs of slowing down as once again he took up his post at the front window. The shutters were broken, crooked, and scratched all to hell from his last frenzy, but not enough to allow us to see outside.

I stood at the ready. I didn't point my gun, because I didn't want my arms to get tired, but I made sure that both Piper and I were far away from the window Bob was attacking so that, if it came to it, I'd have enough time to point and shoot before whatever was out there got to us.

I won't say I was relaxed—my heart was still pounding in my throat, and I still felt the occasional tremor in my knees, but I was beginning to feel vaguely secure. The thing outside continued to move from window to window, driving Bob out of his mind, but I had seen no sign that it could break in and get to us.

Our neighbor, a nice little old lady who always doted on Bob when she saw him, started pounding on the wall between our houses, complaining about the noise. If I hadn't been so scared, maybe I would have laughed about it. Short of shooting him, there would be no way on earth to silence Bob—even if I had wanted to. If nothing else, he kept us apprised of the creature's position, and he was a wall of fur and muscles and teeth between us and it.

The would-be intruder continued its leisurely course around the perimeter of our house, apparently interested only in us, not in any of the other houses in our row. It led Bob to the kitchen, where he threw himself against the door that led out into the courtyard. Mrs. Pinter, next door, banged on the wall once more, this time harder and louder.

Piper and I stood within the circle of candlelight in the middle of the dining room, neither of us speaking as we continued to track Bob's progress. Only the barest flicker of light reached into the kitchen, and the only visual evidence I had that he was in there was the occasional hint of movement as light glimmered on the lighter portions of his coat.

There was another exasperated bang on the wall, which I rolled my eyes at, but shortly afterward there was another sound that filled me with dread: Mrs. Pinter's back door slamming shut.

Our house was on the corner of the block, which meant that Mrs. Pinter couldn't see whatever was still keeping Bob busy at our back door, which opened on the side of the house rather than the back. I knew that Mrs. Pinter was stepping outside, either to investigate the source of Bob's distress or to come bang on our door and insist we make him stop barking.

I started running toward the back door, knowing there was no way I could get there in time to do anything useful. Sure enough, before I even made it to the kitchen, there was a shrill scream outside. Piper screamed, too, but I couldn't worry about her, not now.

Mrs. Pinter screamed again, and this time there was the unmistakable sound of pain in that scream. Bob was going even more nuts, and he was between me and the door.

Mrs. Pinter was still screaming, but her voice was noticeably weaker.

"Bob, at ease!" I shouted as loud as I could. I wanted to reach out and grab his collar, which is what Dad and I would usually do to get him out of attack mode, but he was in such a mindless frenzy I was afraid I might get my arm chewed off for my troubles. Not to mention that it was so damn dark in the kitchen—Piper had not followed me with her candle—that I was as likely to put my hand straight into his mouth as grab his collar if I reached for him.

Not surprisingly, Bob completely ignored my command. Mrs. Pinter let out a ululating wail that was abruptly choked off and followed by something thumping hard against the window. Bob dropped down to all fours, no longer scrabbling at the door with his claws, although he was still barking, snarling, and bristling.

"Bob, at ease!" I tried again. He glanced at me as if to say, *Are you crazy?* before returning his attention to the door. But he seemed more normal now, less frenzied.

I remembered that there was a flashlight in one of the kitchen drawers, and I dug around for it with my left hand while I kept my gun at the ready. Piper was still standing in the dining room, where we had been when Mrs. Pinter's door had first slammed. Her hand was clamped over her mouth, and her shoulders were shaking with sobs. The hand holding the candle wasn't too steady, and hot wax dripped onto the floor. It looked like it was all over her fingers, too.

I wanted to take the candle from her, sit her down on the sofa, maybe give her a hug. But there wasn't time for that. I had to see if Mrs. Pinter was okay. (I kept mentally telling myself that, but really what I wanted to know was if Mrs. Pinter was *alive*. Those screams . . . )

My probing fingers found the flashlight, and I was relieved to discover the battery wasn't dead. I shined the beam on the door, wincing when I saw streaks of blood on the white paint. Apparently Bob had broken a nail or two with his frantic efforts to claw his way through to whatever was outside. He was definitely beginning to calm down now, no longer jumping up or looking quite so intense. I had to hope that meant whatever had been stalking us was now gone.

"Come on, Bob," I said, "back off." I reached for his collar, and he put up only halfhearted resistance as I pulled him away from the door. I put the flashlight on the kitchen counter, pointing it at the door so I could undo the locks while holding the gun.

"What are you doing?" Piper screamed at me when I unlocked the first lock on the back door. She hurried toward me, her candle still dripping all over the place.

"I have to check on Mrs. Pinter," I explained. "She might need help." Which, frighteningly, was a best-case scenario.

"Who cares?" Piper responded, her voice high and shrill. "You can't open that door!"

I told myself her callous indifference to the fate of a nice little old lady was merely a side effect of her state of near panic. I shouldn't expect her to pick her words carefully under the circumstances.

But really, who would say "Who cares?" about something like this?

"I think it's gone," I said.

"You *think* it's gone? That's not good enough." She was in the kitchen with me now, and though she was obviously still frightened, there was a spark of anger in her eyes, too. "After all the effort that thing made to get in here, you are *not* just going to open the door for it."

I was reaching for the dead bolt, and Piper grabbed my hand to stop me. Bob didn't appreciate her tone or the gesture, and he turned his snarl her way.

"Let go of me," I said in as calm a voice as I could manage. "Bob's temper is on a hair trigger right now. This is *my* house, and I'm going to check on Mrs. Pinter. I have to open the door to do that."

Reluctantly, Piper let go, and when she saw I was not going to listen to her she retreated to the living room, leaving me to face whatever was out there, alone. Bob was still tense and agitated, but nothing like he had been before.

My hands were shaking as I twisted the doorknob and cracked the door open. It was still pitch black outside, and I didn't dare open the door any wider without the flashlight, so I held it in my left hand, the gun in my right, as I used my foot to nudge the door open. Bob gave a soft whimper but didn't seem inclined to dash off into the night. I ordered him to stay, just for good measure.

And then I stepped through the door and saw what had happened while Piper and I had cowered in the house.

# CHAPTER FIFTEEN

Mrs. Pinter was definitely *not* okay.

The first thing I saw when I shined my flashlight onto our patio was a spatter of red droplets on the flagstones. I gulped in trepidation as I let the light play over the entire area. I'm not a blood spatter expert, but it wasn't hard to tell that the blood on our patio floor had come from a source around the back corner of the house. And my flashlight couldn't reach that far unless I actually stepped outside.

I hesitated on the threshold. I did not want to see where that blood had come from. I did not want to step out from the relative safety of my house. But just because there was blood didn't mean Mrs. Pinter was dead, and I had to make sure she wasn't lying there desperately in need of help.

With a deep, shaking breath, I let the back door close behind me, training my flashlight beam on the surrounding walls and above, making sure our stalker wasn't just waiting for fresh meat to present itself. I saw nothing that didn't belong, nor did I see any sign of movement. Also, Bob was still quiet.

"It's gone, Becket," I told myself under my breath, but that didn't make me feel much better. Not with the blood on the patio or the sea of darkness that lay beyond.

I would have liked to hold the gun in both hands. It was heavy, and the grip was uncomfortably big for my hands. But I needed the flashlight, and I kept assuring myself that there was nothing to shoot.

I picked my way over the flagstones, avoiding the droplets of blood. A part of me couldn't help worrying that I was disturbing a crime scene, hearing my dad's voice yelling at the TV when some dumb cop show got it all wrong. I think that part of me was just trying to talk me into going back inside without investigating.

The darkness pressing in all around me was oppressive, and there was no traffic noise to help ground me in reality. Nothing but the occasional distant wail of a siren, nowhere near close enough to help.

Moving at the speed of about an inch per minute, I made my way to the corner at the end of our patio. The spray of blood droplets was denser here, and I could now smell its faintly metallic stink. My stomach turned over. I was pretty sure it took *a lot* of blood to make it smell that strongly.

Finally I forced myself around the corner, my breath coming short and steaming in front of my face, my light darting around the courtyard, trying to see everywhere at once.

Mrs. Pinter lay in a heap just a few feet from her back door. There was a pool of blood at the base of our house, just around the corner of the patio, and streaks of that blood led to where Mrs. Pinter lay. Like she had tried to crawl away from her attacker, although there was so much blood it was hard to imagine she had survived long enough to crawl.

A little mewling whimper rose from my throat, and if I'd had a free hand I'd have clapped it over my mouth to try to contain my own horror. I couldn't see all of Mrs. Pinter's body because she was all hunched in on herself, but there was no mistaking those sensible shoes, the flowery dress, or the drab cardigan.

I was shaking so hard I could hear my teeth chattering, and I knew for certain that Mrs. Pinter was dead. No one could survive losing as much blood as I saw spattered and pooled around the courtyard.

I remembered the thumping sound on the kitchen window right after Mrs. Pinter's screams had shut off, and I raised my flashlight to examine the window. Sure enough, there was a big splatter of blood there, though the thump had been too loud to be just the splashing blood.

Looking back, I think a part of my mind had registered the reality of what I was seeing well before I allowed myself to actually take it in. I'd already played the flashlight beam all around the courtyard, so there was nothing there I hadn't seen yet. I just really, really didn't *want* to see it. But there was only so long my subconscious could protect me.

There was a trail of blood droplets leading from the splatter on our window to the darkness across the courtyard, and with great reluctance I allowed my flashlight beam to follow that trail to its conclusion.

I couldn't stop the scream that tore out of me like a demon trying to escape.

Propped up against the far wall, where it had come to a stop after bouncing off the window of our house, was Mrs. Pinter's head.

I forgot all about my crime scene protocol worries, forgot about moving cautiously in the dark, forgot about making rational decisions. Forgot everything, basically. My mind filled with white noise as I turned and ran for the kitchen door, desperate to get inside. My feet skidded through blood, and I fell down hard on my hands and knees. I managed to keep hold of the gun, but the flashlight was jarred from my grip, and I was too panicked to reach for it.

Maybe it was just as well I ran the rest of the short distance in the pitch dark. I'd seen enough horror to haunt my nightmares for years already. I skidded and slipped and half-crawled, but I made it to the kitchen door and flung myself through, slamming it shut behind me and throwing all the locks. Then I collapsed in a shivering, hyperventilating heap on the floor, with my back propped against the door.

Bob whimpered softly at me in the darkness, coming over to nose my hand and then licking the skinned area on my palm from when I'd fallen.

"Stop that," I told him, then buried that hand in his thick, warm coat, clinging to him like I used to cling to my stuffed lamb when I was five.

I don't know how long it took—maybe five minutes—before I realized that unlike Bob, Piper hadn't come in to check on me. Surely she had heard me scream, and though she obviously wasn't the white knight type, once she heard the door close behind me she had to have known she wouldn't be running straight into danger if she came into the kitchen.

"Piper?" I called out, but there was no answer.

I had a brief, horrible thought that the creature had somehow gotten into the house while I'd been outside, that I would find Piper torn apart just like I had found Mrs. Pinter, but I quickly rejected the thought. I would have heard something, and Bob would have sounded the alarm and thrown himself into the fray.

I forced myself to my feet, keeping hold of Bob's ruff for

comfort as I called out to Piper once more. And once more received no answer. Figuring she must have run off to hide somewhere, I searched the house, room by room, calling for her repeatedly, but I couldn't find her anywhere.

It wasn't until I'd gone through the whole house a second time with no success that I thought to check the front door—and found it unlocked. While I'd been out finding the horror in the back courtyard, Piper had up and walked out the front door.

She had been adamant that I not open the courtyard door, but then she'd just strolled out the front door herself? With no warning? With no *car*? Where could she possibly have thought she was going? You couldn't *pay* me to leave the house in anything but a dire emergency at a time like this.

I tried her cell phone, of course, but it would take luck and hours of trying before I had a hope of getting a real live connection. I gathered up every last scrap of courage I could find and stepped out the front door to call her name, but I wasn't surprised she didn't answer. It had taken me too long to realize she was gone, and I'd spent so much time searching the house for her that she could easily be a mile away by now. Assuming she was all right. I couldn't for the life of me imagine what she'd been thinking. The part of me that was terrified for her battled with the part of me that was furious with her, leaving my emotions tangled and confused.

Struggling to keep all of the pieces of myself together, I sat down once more on the kitchen floor—I feared I would leave blood stains if I sat anywhere else—and started repeatedly calling my dad's cell, hoping that somehow, miraculously, I would get through.

. . .

The cops showed up before I managed to get through to my dad on the phone. Apparently, most of the people who lived around the courtyard had seen what happened to Mrs. Pinter—or at least the aftermath of it—and had been frantically trying to get through to the police. One of them got lucky at phone line roulette before I did, and soon there were red and blue flashing lights everywhere.

Even though I hadn't reached my dad on the phone, he showed up about five minutes after the first police car arrived, having been notified about a grisly murder happening right behind his house. When he came through the door, I practically threw myself into his arms, hugging him with all my strength and unable to suppress my sobs. He held me and murmured assurances that everything was going to be okay, and for a brief moment I felt like daddy's little girl again.

Eventually I got hold of myself and managed to stop crying, though it was much harder to stop shaking. I had blood on my clothes from having slipped and fallen in the courtyard, but I assured my dad I was unhurt except for my skinned palms. He was on the verge of insisting I let an EMT look at me anyway, but he relented.

His entire focus since he'd walked in the house had been on me, and when his officers tried to talk to him he was abrupt and dismissive with them in a way I knew wasn't like him. But despite his focus on my safety, he wasn't blind. He had to have seen all the damage Bob had done during his protective frenzy.

"What happened here?" he asked gently, like he was talking to a wounded animal.

"It's a long story," I told him between sniffles.

"Then let's sit down." He guided me toward the couch, but I balked.

"I don't want to get blood on it," I explained.

"I don't care about the damn couch," he said, his tight voice betraying his fear and protective anger. "We can get a new one or get it cleaned. Now sit down."

I knew the anger in his voice wasn't directed at me, so his tone for once didn't get my back up. I collapsed onto the couch and wondered if I could face the ordeal of recounting tonight's nightmare to my dad. Not that I had much of a choice.

"Promise you'll believe me," I begged him before I started, and he promised without hesitation.

And so I told him. Everything. Including Piper's attempt to set me up with Aleric, the attack of the living pothole, and the unknown, unseen creature that had tormented us so badly before it had finally killed Mrs. Pinter. I ended with Piper's baffling decision to leave the house while I was finding Mrs. Pinter.

Dad asked me a dizzying number of questions, and I belatedly realized I was making my formal statement. I suspected having my father do the interview broke about a million rules of protocol, but none of the officers at the scene was inclined to argue with him. Each and every one of them had a haunted, exhausted look that said the night had already stretched them to the breaking point. Big city police officers see amazing amounts of terrible stuff, but nothing like what had been happening tonight.

If Mrs. Pinter's death had been a normal murder, we would have had cops and detectives and crime scene technicians crawling all over the place for hours, meticulously documenting every detail, taking a zillion photographs without disturbing the evidence. But tonight the city was so overwhelmed with mayhem—and the mayhem was of such an impossible nature—that the authorities just didn't have the time to spend hours on the scene. They took plenty of photos and interviewed everyone whose house had a view of the courtyard, and then they packed the body into a medical examiner's van and were done.

The cops left, but my dad stayed. Feeling safe with him in the house, I finally changed clothes, dumping the bloodstained outfit in the trash, and took a shower. It was late enough that I could have fallen into bed directly afterward, but I was far from ready to face the specter of my dreams yet, so I went downstairs, where my dad was doing his best to tend to the wounds on Bob's paws. Our heroic dog had not only nearly torn the house apart, he'd also broken two nails and shredded the pads of his feet.

I was pleasantly surprised when the lights came back on just as Dad was finishing up with Bob and telling him what a good, brave boy he'd been.

"Keep the candles in easy reach," Dad warned as we went to work blowing them out. "I'll get us some extra flashlights and a couple of Coleman lanterns tomorrow."

I shuddered. "So you don't think we've seen the last of this."

He glanced at me and raised his eyebrows. "Do you?"

No, of course not. I had no good explanation for what was going on out there, but it seemed overly optimistic to hope it would just stop of its own accord and everything would go back to normal.

The next words were out of my mouth before I even realized I was going to say them. "Mom wants me to come live with her in Boston until all of this blows over."

When I'd talked to my mom on the phone in the afternoon, I had instantly rejected her suggestion. Funny how a few hours, an attack by a fang-filled pothole, and the decapitation of the nice little old lady next door had changed my perspective.

"Maybe that's not such a bad idea," I concluded, though I still hated to say it.

Dad's face looked grim, his eyes unhappy, as he turned to face me fully. "I would love nothing better than to have you out of danger," he said. "But I'm afraid that isn't possible."

I frowned. "Why not?"

"Because the city is now officially under quarantine."

# CHAPTER SIXTEEN

hat?" It came out as a high-pitched bleat, loud enough to alarm Bob, who rose gingerly to his wounded feet and started looking around for the threat.

Dad blew out a loud breath and rubbed his face. "No one knows why this is all happening, but the federal government is worried the city may be having some kind of outbreak. We can't capture any of the bizarre happenings on camera, so people who haven't personally witnessed something think we must be hallucinating. Until someone is able to prove that we don't all have some contagious disease, no one's going to be allowed in or out of Philadelphia."

"But . . . but they can't do that."

My dad nodded. "It's ridiculous to think they can effectively quarantine an entire city," he agreed. "The National Guard has been called in, and they're setting up roadblocks, but there's no way they can keep everyone in. And even if it *is* some kind of mutant virus—which I personally think is a theory with absolutely no merit—it obviously didn't just start tonight. The reports have been coming in for weeks, and the only thing different about tonight is the scale. People have been traveling in and out of the city every day, and if they're carriers of some sort, it's far too late to close the damn barn door."

I had been objecting on a moral/legal level, but the practical objections were just as compelling. I shook my head in disbelief. "So their theory is that every single person who's seen one of these strange phenomena is sick? And that this mutant virus is capable of making multiple people have the exact same hallucination?"

Dad shrugged helplessly. "I have a hard time thinking anyone actually believes that," he conceded. "But they don't know *what* to believe, and they'll grasp at any explanation they can find."

"Any explanation except that something supernatural is happening you mean."

It was the first time I'd fully allowed myself to think of what was happening that way. I'd clung to words like *weird* and *strange* and *bizarre,* but they didn't fully encompass everything that I'd seen and experienced.

"Can you blame them?" he asked. "If you weren't in the middle of it, do you think you'd believe it? Because I'm pretty sure I'd be grasping at some of those same straws if I were in their shoes."

He was probably right. Hadn't I spent a significant amount of time thinking that I might be going crazy, or that I might have a brain tumor? Had I ever once thought to myself that something supernatural might really be happening? And this even after I'd seen the evidence with my own two eyes. If I were some government official being told that the city itself seemed to be coming alive at night and trying to kill its citizens—but oh, yeah, we can't actually capture anything we say is happening on camera—I probably wouldn't buy it.

That realization did nothing to make the prospect of the quarantine any easier to contemplate.

The city of Philadelphia was a different world when Sunday morning rolled around. The supernatural crap stopped and the city physically returned to normal as soon as the sun came up, but life itself was about as far from normal as it was possible to imagine.

Dad wasn't comfortable leaving me home alone, even in the daytime—possibly because I was still in a state of shock over what had happened to Mrs. Pinter—so he took me to work with him. I sat in his office with my laptop, but he was in there for no more than fifteen minutes at a time because he was in nearly constant meetings and conference calls. Supposedly I was working on the history term paper, but who was I kidding?

I was worried sick about Piper, and I hated the fact that beneath that worry was an undercurrent of anger and hurt. She had, for all intents and purposes, abandoned me last night. As strange as she'd been acting lately, I couldn't believe she'd just walked out of the house like that, with no warning or even explanation. Dad and I had spent a while driving around the neighborhood looking for her, but we'd had no luck.

Phone service, both cellular and landline, was still sporadic, the lines constantly jammed, but with a little patience it was actually possible to get through. I called Piper's house and prayed she had gotten home safely last night. Unfortunately, her frantic parents hadn't seen or heard from her. Sharing any details about what had happened last night would only frighten them more, so I got off the phone as fast as possible. I thought about calling my mom—she had to be pretty frantic herself—

but I didn't want to tell her about what had happened last night. I knew fear for me would make her lash out, and I didn't want to listen to some rant about how my father should have dropped everything and rushed me to safety before all hell broke loose.

Mostly what I did was sit quietly and observe and listen to everything that was going on around me—which, considering I was sitting in the police commissioner's office, was a lot. And I learned a lot of stuff that the general population didn't know, because it wasn't being publicly reported. Like that there were hundreds of fatalities from last night's chaos, and that there were many, many more unexplained disappearances. People like Piper, who seem to have wandered away into the night, against all logic. Many of the friends and families of the missing people reported they'd been acting "strange" lately. Just like Piper, who'd barely been recognizable as herself yesterday. There was an underlying assumption—which people seemed reluctant to state out loud—that all or most of those people were dead, although their bodies had not yet been found.

The homeless population had been hit especially hard, and from listening to people talk, I got the impression that those who hadn't been safely inside a shelter had been wiped out almost completely, many dead, many missing. About the only good news was that there hadn't been the kind of rioting and looting one would ordinarily associate with a city in chaos. Most likely because the would-be rioters and looters had either been smart enough not to venture out or had paid the ultimate price if they had.

Not surprisingly, the city's residents—and those unfortunate visitors who were now stuck here—weren't too happy about the quarantine. There was no rest for our weary police officers, who had to take to the streets in record numbers to keep the peace. The Centers for Disease Control had been called in to examine volunteers who appeared to be "infected" with whatever fictitious disease the powers that be thought we all had. I suspected the quarantine would stay in effect even if the CDC doctors gave everyone a clean bill of health. I think the federal government had no idea what to make of the situation or what to do about it, so they were waving their hands like magicians, trying to make it look like they were taking action when they were in fact just as lost as the rest of us.

All day long, everyone watched the slow progress of the sun across the sky, trying to prepare for whatever the night would bring. Once the sun set, there would be no such thing as an off-duty police officer, and even those who were retired or still in training would be pressed into action. There was to be a four o'clock curfew, by which time everyone except law enforcement or emergency personnel was required to remain indoors. Every ambulance and fire truck would have a police escort, and teams of utility workers were assigned armed guards who would protect them should they have to roll out to keep the power on.

At around three o'clock, my dad finally had a brief chance to take a breather. He looked like he needed to sleep for about a week, and the stress was deeply etched into the lines of his face. I wished I'd taken my mom up on the offer to stay with her in Boston, because the one thing my dad didn't need was the extra stress of worrying about me.

"I don't know when I'm going to be able to make it home tonight," he told me. "I don't want you home alone, but I know it can't be comfortable for you sitting around the office all day."

To tell you the truth, it *was* getting pretty old. There was nowhere super comfortable to sit, and I couldn't just rifle through our pantry and fridge when I wanted a snack. Not to mention that I couldn't stretch out on my bed or walk around barefoot or sing along with the music on my iPod. Not without embarrassing myself, that is.

I'd thought Dad's words were a preamble to an apology, but I discovered he had actually made a plan—without consulting me first, of course.

"I've invited Luke to come over and spend the night in the guest room," he said, and my jaw dropped open in shock.

"You *what?*"

"I talked to his mother earlier today, and it turns out his dad was on a business trip in Chicago and now can't get home. And the hospital is going to need all hands on deck tonight, so she has to go in, and she doesn't want to leave him alone any more than I want to leave you."

I was too busy gaping at him to respond. I mean, seriously, could I be hearing him right? Had he really asked my best friend's boyfriend to spend the night at our house? Talk about awkward. Though admittedly, Dad didn't know about my secret crush on Luke, so he probably didn't realize just how epic the level of awkwardness was.

"Let me get this straight," I said. "You're inviting a teenage boy to spend the night alone with me at our house."

Dad waved his hand dismissively. "This is Luke we're talking about. I know he's trustworthy. And I know you are, too. Dr. Gilliam will feel a thousand times better knowing he's not alone in their house while she's at work."

"And you think I'll be safer with Luke there. No disrespect to Luke or anything, but we have Bob. And we have a gun." I could see from the look on his face that Dad was surprised by my resistance. I knew I was being unfair, making things more difficult, when that was the last thing he needed. I was being a selfish brat. But the idea of being trapped in the house all night with Luke had me near panic. "Isn't it a bit patronizing to think I'll only be safe if there's a male in the house?"

He blinked at me, totally taken aback. Which was fair enough. I wasn't sure what had driven me to say such a thing. My objection to being alone in the house with Luke had nothing to do with feminism.

"Honey, I suspect you'd be perfectly safe in the house all by yourself," he said. "For all the crazy stuff that happened last night, we don't seem to have a single credible report of a supernatural attack inside anyone's house. I don't think that's a coincidence. I think whatever is happening is outside only. But do you think you'd feel just as safe in that house alone as you would with someone else there? Imagine how you would have felt last night if Piper hadn't been there with you."

Piper had pretty much been no help at all, but if I was perfectly honest with myself, I had to admit that her presence had made me feel better. Her very helplessness had helped calm and steady me, if for no other reason than that I felt like I held her safety in my hands. If I'd been by myself, the terror might very well have overwhelmed me.

"And I'm not just doing it for you," Dad continued. "Luke doesn't have a dog or a gun. I don't think asking the two of you to buddy up for defense is remotely unreasonable. It'll make both his mom and me feel a lot better about not being able to be there."

He was right, of course. I was channeling Piper, thinking only of myself, of my own comfort. Just because Luke had a Y chromosome didn't mean he wouldn't be freaked out by being alone at night if some supernatural beastie tried to get into his house. And of course his mom would be worried out of her mind. She'd no doubt be seeing all kinds of horrible injuries in the emergency room. How could she not be terrified that something like that might happen to her only child while she wasn't there to watch over him? Never mind that her "child" was almost eighteen and outweighed her by like eighty pounds, all of it muscle.

"All right," I agreed, though in reality I didn't think my agreement was required. My dad and Luke's mom had already agreed to the arrangement, and I doubted either one of us had a say in it.

I'd suffered through more than my fair share of awkward, uncomfortable moments in my life, but the moment my dad closed the door behind him, leaving me and Luke alone in our house, was the new number one on my list.

It wasn't that I'd never been alone with Luke before, but somehow knowing he was spending the night raised the stakes to a whole new level. At least in *my* eyes—I saw no sign that Luke was even aware of the awkwardness, much less bothered by it. But, of course, he didn't have a crush on me and didn't know how I felt about him, so why would he?

"Have you heard from Piper?" I asked him, but I would probably have fainted from shock if he'd said yes. I would never have admitted it out loud, but there was a part of me that was convinced she was dead. I was doing my best to shore up my emotional defenses, to prepare myself for how I would feel if my suspicions were confirmed, but honestly, how prepared can you be for something like that? The only real loss I'd ever been exposed to was the death of Sadie, a retired K-9 dog my dad had taken in because her handler died in a car accident. Sadie had lived with us for two years, and most of her second year had been a slow decline from cancer. I'd had months and months to prepare myself for the eventuality of her death, but it had done nothing to lessen the pain when it happened.

If it had hurt that much to lose a dog, especially one who wasn't with us all that long, how much worse would it be to lose a person? My best friend?

"I haven't heard from her since she left for the rave," Luke said. "She was pretty mad at me for refusing to go with her."

I didn't know exactly how much Luke knew about the events of last night, but I knew my dad had told him that Piper had been with me and that she'd wandered off. I wondered if he blamed me for it, if he thought I somehow *let* her leave, but I didn't know how to ask him.

I shook my head. My crush on him notwithstanding, I had no right to feel awkward around him. Not now, when his girlfriend was missing, presumed dead. He was more unavailable than he'd ever been, and I should treat him like I'd treat any fellow human being, instead of like a boy I'd been crushing on forever.

It was almost four when Dad left, and though we still had about forty-five minutes until sundown, I went ahead and double-checked the locks on all the doors and windows. I also made sure our supply of flashlights, Coleman lanterns, and batteries would be in easy reach even if I was fumbling around in the dark.

"I should probably go ahead and cook some dinner now, in case we lose power later," I said, half under my breath. I had a habit of talking to myself when I was alone in the house, and I hadn't fully grasped that I *wasn't* alone until Luke answered me.

"You don't have to cook for me," he said. "I can just eat a sandwich or a TV dinner or something like that." He shook his head. "I should have brought food. I just didn't think of it."

I waved off his concerns. "I'd be cooking something for myself if you weren't here, so it's no big deal." Though if it were just myself, I might have gone for another grilled cheese and tomato soup dinner, which is one of my favorite comfort meals. "I haven't been shopping for a while, so I'm going to have to improvise, but I'll put something together."

Luke offered to help me, but our kitchen was tiny, and it was hard enough to move when Bob was constantly underfoot. It seemed the lower the sun sank, the clingier he got. Although, to be fair, I had defrosted some ground beef and was making a hamburger casserole that would have kept him riveted night or day.

At about four forty, with sunset only minutes away, I stuck the casserole in the oven and went upstairs to get the SIG. Dad had suggested I keep it with me at all times once the sun went down, and he'd even loaded up some extra mags for me, just to make sure I had plenty of firepower.

Luke's eyes widened in surprise when I came back downstairs with the gun in one hand and the extra mags in the other. I guess Dad had never mentioned to him that I'd be packing. I hoped he wouldn't turn out to be the kind of macho dipshit who thought it was his duty as the male to take the gun and guard the helpless girl. But then, if he were that kind of guy, I probably never would have had my little crush problem. There's nothing that turns me off more than a sexist asshole.

Luke got over his surprise quickly and grinned at me. "That is totally hot," he said, then blushed crimson and shook his head, gaze dropping to the floor. Which meant he couldn't see *me* blushing, which was a good thing. "Sorry," he said, rubbing the back of his neck. "That was totally inappropriate."

I guess he felt guilty for saying something flattering to a girl when his girlfriend was missing. Or maybe I was so firmly entrenched as his honorary kid sister that it felt kinda gross to describe me as hot.

Not that it was *me* he'd said was hot, at least not per se. I would never register on a guy's hot-o-meter all by myself. It was the chick-with-a-gun image he was reacting to, and I had no cause to feel that little stirring of warmth in my belly.

"No problem," I assured him. "I really hope we don't need this, but better safe than sorry."

I sailed past him into the kitchen, trying to act as if his words had had no effect on me whatsoever. I'd only put the casserole in the oven about five minutes ago, but I cracked the door to check on it anyway, just to have something to do and to give the moment of tension time to fade away.

"Smells good," Luke said. I think that, like me, he was trying to hurry us both past his uncomfortable declaration and steer us into safer waters.

I closed the oven door and shrugged. "It's not exactly a gourmet meal," I warned him. I was reasonably certain it would be edible, but all I'd done was throw some odds and ends together in a casserole dish.

"Hey, I saw beef and pasta and cheese. You hit all of the major food groups, so I'm happy."

I knew we were both casting anxious glances at the windows as the light inexorably began to fade. Wondering what the night would bring. And maybe also wondering if, when the sun rose in the morning, we'd be around to see it.

I know, morbid thoughts. But it was true that for a while now, each night had been worse than the one before, and last night had been terrible. That didn't bode well for tonight, and it was hard to put the reins on the dread.

I was pleased that the power stayed on long enough for my casserole to bake, and doubly pleased to discover that my Frankenstein's monster of a meal was actually pretty tasty. Luke certainly seemed to appreciate it, gobbling down seconds and then thirds.

He had almost finished that third serving when Bob, who'd been lying at our feet, staring longingly at each forkful of food that went into our mouths, leaped to his feet, bristling. I grabbed for the gun.

Bob rocketed toward the front door and started barking, seconds before a series of loud raps of the door knocker sounded through the house.

# CHAPTER SEVENTEEN

**B**ob was at his snarling, most ferocious best, and I was sure I looked as pale and frightened as Luke did. However, I'd already registered that the sound I'd heard was nothing like the feral battering of last night. This was the sound of the door knocker being used as it was intended, if with a little more force than necessary.

The knock came again, three sound raps, cutting through Bob's barking. Holding the gun with both hands, its barrel pointed toward the floor, I crept toward the door, wondering if it was possible there was just an ordinary person out there. Though I supposed any ordinary person knocking on a stranger's door after dark during this particular crisis was not to be trusted. And although Bob always barked when someone knocked on the door, there was an uncommon level of fury in him right now, just like there had been last night.

Luke was out of his chair, food forgotten as he stepped toward me. He kept behind me and a little to the left, making absolutely sure not to get in the way of my gun.

"You're not going to let whoever that is in, are you?" he asked, and I gave him a look that silently conveyed *Do you think I'm stupid?* "Just checking," he said, holding his hands up.

I crept a little closer to the door, though I supposed if I wasn't planning to let anyone in, there was no reason to get closer. I debated trying to get a peek through the peephole but decided I was more comfortable keeping some distance between myself and whoever or whatever was outside.

The knock sounded for a third time, the three raps louder and closer together this time and conveying a sense of impatience.

And then a voice shouted above the barking, a voice so startling it almost made me drop my gun.

"Call Cujo off and let me in already, Becks!"

It was Piper.

At least, it *sounded* like Piper. I'd seen more than enough not to take anything for granted. Luke and I shared one long, shocked look before we both started forward.

"Wait!" I said, blocking him with my arm. "Let's make sure it's really her before we open the door."

"Who else could it be?" he asked, but thankfully he listened to me and didn't rush to throw the door open.

I realized that although Luke had seen some strange things and had heard a bunch of strange stories, he hadn't seen things like the dissolving baby or the trash monster or the biting pothole with his own eyes, and there was a part of him still clinging to the illusion that the world was a normal, rational place. A notion I'd pretty much given up on over the course of the last twenty-four hours.

"Bob isn't acting like it's Piper," I said, and it was true. He always barked when she—or anyone else, for that matter—knocked on the door, but though he was loud and intimidating by nature, he didn't usually sound like this, like he wanted to rip the throat out of whoever was daring to request entrance into his territory.

I had to practically shove Bob aside so I could get to the peephole, and he continued to bark and carry on uninterrupted.

I don't know exactly what I was expecting to see when I looked out that peephole, but I'd obviously already convinced myself that it wasn't Piper, because when I saw her standing there, arms crossed over her chest, hip jutting to one side as she tapped her foot with impatience, my knees felt almost wobbly.

"Will you hurry up already," Piper whined. "It's freaking cold out here."

Feeling almost light-headed with relief, I shoved the gun into the back of my pants. My hands were shaking as I rushed to undo all the locks, my vision blurred with tears. She was okay. Against all odds, she was okay.

I wanted to fling the door open and throw my arms around her. I wanted to tell her how relieved I was to see her—and then spend the rest of the night yelling at her for torturing me and her parents and Luke by disappearing like that.

The problem was Bob. He was still pitching a fit, still very obviously in kill-the-intruder mode. If I opened the door, I feared he would go for Piper's jugular.

Luke obviously shared my concern. He pulled a Milk-Bone from his pocket. "Hey Bob," he beckoned, then whistled. "Come here, buddy. Look what I've got for you."

Bob paid no attention.

"What is the *matter* with you?" Piper shouted. "You can't seriously plan to leave me out here in the dark. Not after what happened last night."

"Hold on a minute!" I shouted, then grabbed Bob's leash and

clipped it on. I didn't know why he was freaking out so much. It made me think about how he'd barked at that baby-shaped bundle, how he'd tried to warn me that it was bad news, and I'd ignored him.

But I could see with my own two eyes that it was Piper out there. Surely my own eyes trumped canine instinct.

"Back up," I told Luke, then dragged Bob away from the door. Luke was happy to make way for us, and I directed him back into his seat at the dining room table. "Hold this," I ordered him, handing him Bob's leash. Luckily, I kept my own hand on it, because Luke wasn't prepared for Bob's strength and might have gone sprawling. He adjusted his grip more securely, and I let go.

"Hold tight," I told him unnecessarily. "And be ready to let go if I tell you to."

"What?" he asked, and almost lost his grip a second time.

I wiped my sweaty palms on my pants legs, then pulled the gun back out. "I'm worried there might be something *other* than Piper out there," I explained. "I'm probably being paranoid, but after last night I'd rather be safe than sorry."

I thought he might argue with me, but instead he frowned at Bob and nodded.

I opened the door cautiously, and although I didn't point the gun, I held it clearly visible in my hand. Piper glanced at that hand and her lips twisted in something vaguely resembling a smile.

"Someone's feeling kinda edgy tonight," she said as she slipped into the house.

"Aren't *you*?" I asked, keeping an eye on her as I closed and locked the door. If she'd been out on the streets alone at night, she should be a raw bundle of nerves right now. Luke and I had decided not to watch the news, but the frequent wailing of sirens announced that the city had not suddenly gone back to normal.

Piper stepped clear of the entryway and finally saw Luke sitting at the dining room table, holding on to Bob's leash with both hands. Bob tried to lunge forward when he saw her, but instead of looking intimidated, she laughed.

"I've gotta hand it to you, Becks," she said. "You move quick. I haven't been gone twenty-four hours, and already you're playing house with my boyfriend."

"I . . . What?" I shook my head, completely confused. This was not the tearful reunion I'd imagined.

"Don't be ridiculous," Luke shouted over Bob's barks. "Her dad and my mom didn't want us hanging around our houses alone. Where the hell have you been?"

My brain finally caught up with the conversation, and I understood that Piper was accusing me of stealing her boyfriend. Although she didn't seem even remotely upset about it, which I supposed meant she was kidding. But how could anyone make a joke at a time like this?

Piper laughed, for no reason I could discern. "Here and there. Out and about. You know."

Luke stared at her with his mouth open, as if he was trying and failing to come up with something to say. I couldn't blame him.

I thought Piper had acted weird yesterday, but that was nothing next to today.

"Are you on drugs?" I asked. Not that I believed any drug known to mankind could explain what was going on with her right now.

"Nope," she said cheerfully. "It's just that I've had a major . . ." She thought about it a moment. ". . . attitude adjustment." She laughed again, the sound strangely grating.

Bob's constant barking was giving me a headache, and I bet Luke's arms and hands weren't feeling so great either, as he struggled to hold the dog back. I really wished Bob would shut up—I'd gotten the hint already—but I knew from a combination of experience and common sense that yelling at him wouldn't help the situation.

"If it's not drugs, then you must be some kind of body snatcher–like thing," I said. I didn't actually believe that, but I was racking my brain to find some explanation for how much she had changed. "Like a pod person. Or you've got some parasite inside you. Or maybe it's a glamour."

"Or maybe you've watched too many horror movies," Piper suggested. "It's really me, Becks. I just have a whole new way at looking at the world now." She dropped down into my dad's favorite chair, sprawling like she owned the place. "We were being superstitious, frightened little gerbils last night. Running away from the best thing that could ever happen to us because we didn't understand it."

I gaped at her. "So the best thing that ever happened to Mrs. Pinter next door was to have her head sliced off?" I shuddered and tried to push the memory of last night's horror into a back corner.

Piper snorted. "Not everyone is capable of expanding their horizons." She looked over her shoulder at Luke. "You might want to stay inside all night, every night, sport. You'd be doomed out there." She turned back to me and cocked her head. "You, on the other hand, have potential."

"What the hell are you talking about? What happened to you?"

"Last night, while you were busy checking on the old lady next door, I peeked out the front window and saw our mutual friend standing outside the house, watching."

"Our mutual friend?" I asked, but then realized who she meant before she explained. "You mean Aleric."

"That's the one," she agreed.

"Who the hell is Aleric?" Luke asked. I could barely hear him over Bob's ferocious barking.

"The guy I'm dumping you for," Piper said, fanning her face. "He is so incredibly hot. Don't you agree, Becks?"

The Piper I had known had dumped a lot of guys, but always gently and always in private. She knew the importance of letting them have their pride, and she'd never deliberately hurt anyone. Very much unlike the person who sat in my house right now.

Luke hid the pain he must have been feeling behind a mask of stoicism. He'd been pretty frustrated with Piper lately, but I believed he truly loved her.

"I think you're not yourself, and we shouldn't take anything you say too seriously," I said.

"Ah, denial," Piper mocked. "Gotta love it. I was in denial myself, last night. Till I saw Aleric standing out there. When he motioned for me to come out, I just *knew* it was the right thing to do, that it would change my life." She closed her eyes, her cheeks flushed pink, as she drew in a deep breath through her nose, looking for all the world like she was sniffing the world's most delicious chocolate cake, savoring the moment before she dove in.

She opened her eyes again, and with a start of surprise I realized she didn't look exactly like the Piper I remembered after all. Instead of Piper's storm-cloud-gray eyes, she had eyes the color of emeralds in the sunlight. Eyes just like Aleric's. My hand tightened on the gun, and I just barely resisted raising it. Maybe my crazy-sounding theories had been right. Maybe this wasn't really Piper after all.

"It was *amazing*, Becks," Piper said, and those eyes took on a distant, dreamy expression. "It's a different world out there. A world where you can do anything you want and there's no one to tell you you shouldn't or try to make you feel guilty for it. It's like I've been living in some cramped little cage all my life and someone's finally opened the door."

"What are you *talking* about?" I asked, unable to comprehend what she was saying. "It's a world where potholes come alive and bite cars. Where nice little old ladies get their heads chopped off."

"You're getting hung up on the details," Piper said with a dismissive wave. "The night isn't for everyone, and people like that old bat and your dad and the Boy Wonder here aren't welcome. But *you* would be. Just think how much fun we would have together if we didn't have to follow anyone's stupid rules! You can be free, just like me. All you have to do is let go."

Luke's eyes met mine across the room, and he looked as lost and confused as I felt. I didn't know what had happened to Piper when she'd run off into the night, but it had made her almost unrecognizable. Something had changed within her, something so fundamental that Bob had sensed it long before we did.

"You're crazy," I said, but it was a lame-ass response, which she didn't dignify with an answer.

"We should get you to a doctor," Luke said. "You need help." I could see he wanted to go to her, despite the cruel things she'd said. Thanks to Bob, that wasn't an option.

Piper rose to her feet, and I reflexively raised the gun and took a step back. It felt completely surreal to stand there holding a gun on my best friend. If she'd been remotely herself, she would have been shocked or hurt or scared. Instead, those green eyes—eyes that didn't belong in Piper's face—glittered with amusement.

"Relax," she said, smiling indulgently at me. "I'm not here to hurt anyone. Not tonight, at least. I just came to give you the pitch."

"The pitch?" I repeated stupidly.

"Yeah. The sales pitch. Come with me. I promise you, it'll be the most fun you've ever had in your life, more fun than you can even *imagine* having." Her face sobered for the first time since she had set foot in the house. "Trust me, if you decide to fight it, you're in for a shitload of misery. Come with me tonight, and you won't have to suffer one little bit."

"If you think I'm setting foot outside this house, you're nuttier than a peanut butter factory," I responded.

Piper stared at me intently, one hip cocked to the side while she rubbed her chin in what I supposed was thought. Then she glanced over at Luke and Bob. "I suppose if I tried to drag you out by force, your boys there would object."

"Lay a hand on her, and I'll let Bob go," Luke warned. He sounded like he meant it. I'd never seen him look so furious before.

"Is that any way to talk to the girl you gave your cherry to?" Piper mocked.

Luke flushed red as a beet, and I winced in sympathetic embarrassment. That was so *not* something I wanted to know. Assuming it was even true.

He rose to his feet and took a couple of steps closer to Piper, bracing himself against Bob's lunge. "Get out," he told her. "I don't care what you look like or what you sound like. You're not Piper."

She gave a throaty laugh while still managing to keep a respectful distance from Bob's snapping jaws. She turned back to me.

"Enjoy him while he lasts," she said with a wink. "*I* certainly don't have any use for him anymore, and he's tolerably good, if a little unimaginative, in bed. But I want you out there with me." She jerked a thumb in the direction of the front door. "I used to think I had to apologize for what I wanted, or had to wait for someone to give it to me. I know better now. I can *take* whatever I want, and I don't give a shit whether you or anyone else disapproves. Someday soon, you'll be one with the night, just like me, and you'll understand."

I had the brief thought that maybe I should try to stop her as she sauntered to the front door. Maybe if Luke and I could restrain her, we could get her to a good psychiatrist in the morning, and she could be deprogrammed, or whatever it was she needed done.

In the end, I let her leave. It's a decision I will regret for the rest of my life.

# CHAPTER EIGHTEEN

Luke and I never did get around to going to bed that night. We were both too upset by our encounter with the new, not-improved Piper, and we ended up sitting and talking until after midnight. After that we watched an old movie on TV, and we both fell asleep on the couch long before the movie was over. Dad came home at some point and shooed us both upstairs, but I was still half-asleep and collapsed on my bed fully clothed.

The predictable result of our late night was that we were both exhausted the next night, our eyelids getting heavy not that long after dinner. I don't know about Luke, but I was tense and ready for Piper to make another appearance. It's no fun being exhausted and jumpy at the same time.

I made it to ten thirty before the call of my bed became too strong to resist. As soon as I told Luke I was going to bed, he yawned hugely and said he would do the same. We climbed the stairs together and then said what felt like an awkward good night in the hall. I watched out of the corner of my eye as Luke slipped into the guest room.

My dad's bedroom was on the third floor, and my sister had been gone for five years. I was used to having the second floor all to myself, and it was strangely unnerving to hear the occasional footstep or rustle from the neighboring room.

I felt incredibly conscious of Luke's presence as I took off my clothes. Luke was just behind that wall, and he was getting undressed too. The thought made my whole body flush with heat.

"You shouldn't be thinking about him that way," I told myself in a stern undertone.

His relationship with Piper was in shambles, but he wasn't any more available today than he'd ever been. It was always possible that Piper would snap out of it—at least I *hoped* it was possible—and even if she didn't, she and Luke hadn't exactly made a clean break. I should think about him exactly the way my dad did, as a neighbor and friend who was staying here so that neither of our parents had to worry about us being alone in the night. I should certainly *not* be imagining him taking off his shirt right next door.

Funny how telling myself *not* to think about something had exactly the opposite effect.

I hurried to change into my pj's, feeling strangely vulnerable standing around in my bedroom in nothing but my panties. Maybe Luke was thinking the same kind of impure thoughts next door.

I rolled my eyes at myself as I shoved my legs into a pair of soft flannel pajama bottoms. Usually I'd wear them with a clingy sleep tank, but when I pulled it on and glanced at myself in the mirror I immediately changed my mind. The way the tank strained across my chest made me feel like an entrant in a wet T-shirt contest. Not fit for public consumption.

Not that I had any reason to think Luke would see me in it. We were going to bed, and by the time I left my room in the morning I planned to be fully dressed.

Bob started barking.

Oh no, not again!

I heard Luke's door slam and felt the vibration of his footsteps on the floorboards. I had just enough presence of mind to grab a T-shirt and yank it on over my head as I hurried to see what was going on.

Luke was standing right outside my door when I opened it. He was wearing a thin white T-shirt and a pair of ratty gym shorts. Even with my adrenaline spiking through the roof I couldn't stop myself from wondering if that was what he usually wore to bed or if it was something he'd cobbled together because he usually didn't wear pajamas.

"You might want to get the gun," Luke said, causing me to want to sink through the floor in embarrassment. My priorities were seriously screwed. I'd been more worried about Luke seeing me in that stupid tank top than about protecting us both from whatever was outside.

I grabbed the gun, which I had stashed in a drawer in my nightstand, and together Luke and I went into the study, where we hoped to catch a glimpse of whatever had set Bob off.

I can't say I was surprised to see Piper standing out there in the street, but I was both surprised and unnerved to see that this time she had company. There were about a dozen other people out there with her, all with green eyes, and all carrying small paper bags. I didn't want to know what that was all about, although I had the sneaking suspicion I would find out all too soon.

"Damn it," Luke said under his breath. "I have to learn to shoot. I hate feeling so helpless. You can teach me, can't you?"

I made a noncommittal noise. There was no way my dad

would let Luke carry a gun around in the house. He'd seen far too many accidental shootings in his life to let a novice carry, and he would consider Luke a novice for a long time, even if he started hanging out at the range for six hours a day. Besides, I had a gun and knew how to shoot it, and I still felt pretty damn helpless.

Piper noticed us watching through the window and waved cheerfully. "It's time to come out and play, Becks," she yelled. "You know you want to."

I answered eloquently by flipping her the bird, because I didn't trust myself to speak. The only thing I wanted was for her and her friends to go away, but of course they didn't.

"Suit yourself!" Piper yelled, then threw something at the window.

Luke and I both leaped backward instinctively, but whatever it was hit the window with a splat. It was quickly followed by another splat. And another. And another.

"Seriously?" Luke said with a shake of his head. "They're egging the house?"

I hadn't immediately recognized the sound, but of course that was what it was. Luke stepped closer to the window to take a quick peek out.

"Looks like a couple of them have spray paint," he told me.

A hint of sulfur in the air told me the eggs they were throwing at the house were rotten. Of course. I bit my lip.

"Should I go out and try to scare them off?" I asked, brandishing the gun. But I already knew the answer to my own question.

"There are too many of them," Luke said. "The last thing we want to do is open the door."

Outside, Piper and her friends were having a blast, laughing and cheering at the mess they were making. Downstairs, Bob was barking his head off.

"I guess getting some sleep tonight is out of the question," I said with a resigned sigh. I was too wired to feel sleepy anymore, but I felt the heaviness of exhaustion in my limbs. I entertained the brief thought of opening the window and firing a couple of shots, but it wasn't worth it. I wasn't going to shoot people to stop them from egging my house, and I was sure Piper knew that.

"Yeah," Luke agreed. "Probably the best thing to do right now is try to ignore them. Letting Piper know she's getting to us will only encourage her. Wanna go watch another movie?"

My first reaction was to look at him as if he was crazy. How the hell were we going to be able to watch a movie with all this noise and commotion? But then I had to acknowledge that we didn't have a whole lot of options. Standing here in the dark in the study was already getting old, and if we watched a movie we could at least *pretend* we were ignoring Piper and her friends.

And so we went downstairs in our bare feet and pajamas and turned the TV to some movie we had no interest in and couldn't hear anyway. Someone out there had a portable stereo, because when they ran out of eggs to pelt the house with, they started blasting awful heavy metal full of screeching and wailing.

I crossed my arms over my chest and shivered. I was dressed to cuddle under my sheets and blanket, and I debated running back up to my room to grab a sweatshirt. Even with all the noise and chaos outside, I was still painfully aware that I was sitting next to Luke wearing my pj's and no bra. Maybe, instead of grabbing a sweatshirt, I should go get dressed.

But Luke was sitting pretty close to me on the couch, his arm draped casually across the back, behind me. He wasn't touching me, but it was like his body was a magnetic field and I was made of iron. Even reminding myself how unavailable he was, I couldn't motivate myself to get up, to lose this almost-contact.

A little while later the sound of approaching sirens pierced the noise from outside, and the heavy metal went silent.

"See you tomorrow!" Piper shouted.

She and her new friends ran away before the police cars arrived.


My dad is the most awesome police commissioner Philadelphia has ever had, and I don't think I'm being totally biased when I say that. I wouldn't have been surprised if the city had turned into some kind of lawless war zone, considering what was happening at night, but my dad—admittedly with a lot of help—was keeping things running. I honestly don't know how he was managing it when our police department was so overwhelmed, but he was keeping the peace, even though the problems kept mounting.

Despite extensive testing, the CDC had yet to find any evidence of disease in their volunteer subjects, but the federal government had no intention of lifting the quarantine. Every road leading out of the city was blockaded, the train stations were all closed, and the airport, too. Schools were closed indefinitely, as were many businesses. Most stores and restaurants—those that could get supplies, at least—stayed open during the daylight hours, but having to close in time for the four o'clock curfew meant they weren't making a whole lot of money.

During the daylight hours the city was relatively peaceful, thanks in part to the significant increase in the police presence. There were protests against the quarantine, of course, but they were civilized and orderly, without the rioting and chaos the doomsayers kept predicting. People were frustrated and scared and desperate for answers—who could blame them?—but so far no one seemed to think violence was the answer.

The nights, however, were a different story altogether.

The city changed more and more every time the sun went down, those changes becoming less and less subtle until *everyone* in the city could see them—and yet still no one could capture anything on camera. Statues rose from their places and roamed the city streets, thirsty for blood and violence. The facades of some buildings appeared to be made up of yellowing bones or reptilian scales, chain-link fences sprouted teeth, parking meters turned into fanged heads on sticks, door knockers turned into grotesque gargoyles . . .

I didn't see most of these changes with my own eyes, because I wouldn't dream of setting foot outside once the sun went down. But I heard about them from my dad and from the news, and some of them I could even see through the windows of my nice, safe home. There was a big metal vent on the roof of the dry cleaner across the street, and I saw it change into something that resembled a sea serpent, then snatch a perching pigeon in its jaws.

The changes were always external. The insides of houses and businesses retained their mundane daytime forms even while their outsides morphed. That was the good news—it seemed that as long as you stayed inside, the magic couldn't touch you. Its creations might scratch at your door or tap on your windows to terrify you, but they couldn't seem to get in.

The bad news was that a lot of the people who disappeared over those first couple of nights turned up again, changed like Piper. They took to the streets the moment the sun went down, and they were as deadly as any of the magical constructs. Whatever conscience they had had as ordinary human beings had clearly died. They traveled in packs, and unlike the constructs, they had no problem with going inside. They broke into stores and took what they wanted. They broke into houses and brutalized the inhabitants, invariably leaving them dead. They formed human blockades to stop ambulances and emergency vehicles from getting to where they were needed. The media started referring to them as the Nightstruck, and the name stuck.

Even with all the help the National Guard could give them, the police force was stretched thin as thin can be at night. They mostly left the magical mayhem alone—how do you stop something like a ten-foot-tall bronze statue with fangs from going wherever the hell it wants, whenever it wants?—but they did their best to protect homes and businesses from the packs of Nightstruck.

It was a dangerous job, more like combat in a war zone than ordinary police duty. Despite their best precautions, officers were killed and injured every single night, so that every day the force was just that much thinner. My dad was lucky if he got home four hours a day, and though he blew me off every time I tried to mention it, he clearly wasn't eating well. I could see with my own two eyes that he was losing weight, his pants getting baggy even when he cinched his belt up tight.

Luke's mom was on an almost permanent night shift at the hospital, so he spent more time at my house than at his own.

On the rare nights when she was home, Bob and I went over there, keeping our safety in numbers.

Within the course of a week, living life under quarantine, under siege, had begun to feel almost normal. I no longer felt quite as awkward around Luke, though I was uncomfortably aware that my crush on him was not going away. If anything, it was growing worse as I got to know him better and realized that, aside from his good looks, he had a seemingly endless list of good qualities. Smart. Nice. Helpful. Uncomplaining. Funny.

You get the picture. I was crushing on him big time, but I wasn't willing to do anything about it—even if I'd known how to let him know I liked him without embarrassing myself to death. Besides, I still held out hope that something would happen to turn all the Nightstruck—including Piper—back to their normal selves, in which case Luke was still taken.

Of course, one could argue that my hope of Piper returning to normal was more of a pipe dream than a true hope. Trailed by a group of other Nightstruck, most of whom looked like they might have been homeless before the night got its claws into them, she stopped by to torment us just about every night. Bob always gave us plenty of warning she was coming, and then she'd start knocking on the door and shouting, telling me to come out and join her. I felt no inclination to open the door for her again, so, like the unseen creature that had attacked the house while she and I were in it, she made a circuit, trying all of the windows. Every night she found them all locked, and even if she hadn't she wouldn't have been able to get in. The house had been broken into a couple of times when I was a kid, so Dad had had decorative iron grilles installed over all the first-floor windows. Even if someone broke out the glass, they would have no room to crawl in.

After the first couple of nights, Piper's night friends got bored with the exercise and stopped coming, but Piper brought a new friend instead. A small bronze goat, about knee-high to her, which clip-clopped along by her side, metallic hooves giving off the occasional spark.

As with most of the city's statues, Billy the goat didn't look like his daytime self when he stepped off his plinth and started roaming the streets. Ordinarily he stood in a plaza in Rittenhouse Square, and my mom and dad have pictures of both me and Beth playing around his feet and even riding him like a horse when we were little. In the day, he was a perfectly ordinary goat, with a pair of small, almost harmless-looking horns. At night, when he went roaming, his horns doubled in length and came to insidiously sharp points. Curved, wicked-looking claws jutted out all around his hooves, and there was a ridge of spines down the center of his back. And his various horns, spines, and claws were almost always spotted with fresh blood.

Piper seemed to have adopted the damn thing as some kind of pet. More disturbing yet, she could get it to follow orders. Like the time she had it spend an hour repeatedly butting that metal head against our front door. I was afraid the door would come crashing down. I suspected the goat wouldn't be able to come inside even if it broke the door, but I knew Bob would feel honor-bound to attack, and the goat would probably gut him. I also knew that there would be nothing keeping *Piper* from coming in, even if the goat didn't. So I once again had Luke sit at the table with Bob straining at the end of his leash while I waited in agonized tension in front of the door, my gun at the ready. There was no way I would actually shoot Piper, but I hoped she wouldn't know that and would keep her distance.

In the end, all my worries were for nothing. The goat battered the wood of our door all to hell, letting in plenty of arctic blasts, but it turned out the door had metal reinforcement in the middle, and that was too much for the goat to break through. Instead, we had to listen to the impact of its metal head with the metal door. By the time it and Piper wandered away for the night, both Luke and I had pounding headaches from all the noise.

After that, Dad decided we needed to fortify all the second- and third-story windows, just in case. They were all sturdy casement windows, but the panes were bigger than those on the first floor, and it wasn't impossible to imagine someone being able to crawl through if the glass was broken out.

He was so exhausted he could barely see straight, and yet he spent most of a day installing towel rods across the windows to serve as bars, because getting someone to install real bars or grilles would take forever. He also nailed some plywood over the holes Billy had left in the front door. He was *supposed* to be taking some time off to get some rest, but when I suggested that maybe Luke and I could take care of things, he blew me off. He was still feeling bad that he wasn't home with me every night, and fortifying our house seemed to ease his conscience.

He was stretching himself too thin, and everyone but him could see it. It was all I could do not to wrench the hammer out of his hand when he hit his thumb while trying to patch the front door.

"I'll be fine, Becks," he said as he shook his hand and waited for the pain to ease. At least he hadn't broken any bones.

Shortly after he finished installing all those towel rods—which were noticeably crooked—his cell phone rang, and he got into a heated conversation with someone he kept calling Sir. I suspected it was the mayor, and it turned out I was right. Over my dad's protests, he'd been ordered to take the night off and try to get eight full hours of sleep. Thank God. I didn't like the idea of my dad getting into a car and driving to work when he was so tired he couldn't see straight.

"You're going to bed and wearing earplugs as soon as you finish dinner," I informed him.

"Yes, Mother," he said with a weary smile.

I then did something I hadn't done in . . . well, forever, it seemed. I gave my dad a spontaneous hug.

"I love you," I told him, squeezing hard. I knew my mom was still giving him hell about not having gotten me out of the city before the quarantine hit. I also knew she kept badgering him to somehow use his connections to find a way to sneak me out—like I should be given special treatment because I was the police commissioner's daughter. Even if he'd found a way, I'd have refused to go. I didn't like dealing with our city at night, but the idea that I should be allowed to leave when no one else was went against everything I believed in.

Anyway, I knew my dad was hearing criticism and general nastiness from every side, every day, and I knew he was trying his hardest. He deserved to be reminded that, even though we'd fought a lot lately, I did still love and appreciate him.

"I love you, too, Becks," he said, his voice suspiciously hoarse. "And I'm sorry I've left you alone so much."

"Don't be. You're doing your job. I get that." Even if my mom didn't. She and my dad had loved each other once, but I think even before the marriage went sour, the current situation would have had them at each other's throats.

Our moment of father–daughter bonding ended when Luke rapped on the back door, just in time for the evening curfew, but I think my father felt better about things because of it. My mom has the guilt trip down to an art form, and he's pretty susceptible to it.

Even though my dad was home, Luke would still be spending the night at our place, because his mother was on yet another night shift at the hospital. As usual, I made dinner. Both Dad and Luke offered, but Dad was supposed to be on R & R and Luke was still a guest in our house, so I considered the cooking to be my responsibility.

The fact that Luke wasn't shy about showing his appreciation of my cooking skills had nothing to do with it. At least I told myself that, despite the glow of satisfaction in my belly every time he told me how great dinner was. Liking his praise so much sometimes made me feel a little needy, but hell, I'm only human. Being noticed and appreciated by someone you have a crush on can make for a nice little high, especially when you're living in a time so full of lows.

That night, the lows started as soon as dinner was cleared. Dad was halfway up the stairs to his bedroom when Bob suddenly went stiff and bristly.

"Not again," Luke groaned, and I silently agreed with him.

It was probably overly optimistic of me to think we might have a night of peace after Piper's failed attempt to break in, but I'd hoped for it anyway. I'd hoped Dad could fall into bed right after dinner and sleep undisturbed until morning—

something I doubted he'd be able to do if the house was under siege, even if he felt sure our defenses would hold.

Bob was snarling but not yet in full mad-dog mode, when there was an ear-piercing scream from outside. That set Bob off full tilt and made my stomach curdle. There was a crashing sound, like a bottle being broken, and then another scream. I could tell the person screaming was female, but that was all. I remembered what had happened to Mrs. Pinter, remembered finding her head propped against the side of the house across the way, and my knees went a little weak.

Luke reached over and took my hand, and I held on gratefully as we both stood there, frozen to the floor in the dining room. Most of me didn't want to know what was going on outside. But another tiny part couldn't stand the not knowing, couldn't stop trying to piece together whatever clues could be found in the sounds that were now obviously approaching our house.

There were multiple voices, many of them laughing and raucous, taking obvious pleasure in the girl's screaming. And when Bob had to pause in his barking to draw a breath, I was sure I heard the metallic clip-clop of the goat's hooves.

Moments later, my dad descended the stairs at a brisk pace. His service weapon was tucked into a shoulder holster. He was carrying the SIG in one hand and a pump-action shotgun—something I hadn't even known he owned—in his other. He handed me the SIG.

"Get upstairs, both of you," he told Luke and me.

My dad had an unmistakable aura of command, and Luke responded to that command just like any of my dad's underlings would. He started toward the stairs, tugging on my hand when I didn't immediately follow.

There was another scream from outside.

"What are you going to do?" I asked my dad, hoping against hope he wouldn't say what I thought—no, what I *knew*—he was going to say. The shotgun was not the weapon he'd choose to use inside our house unless absolutely necessary.

"I'm an officer of the law," he told me. "There's a crime being committed right outside my door." He shrugged helplessly.

I shook my head, even as Luke tugged on my hand a little more urgently. My dad was the police commissioner. He was supposed to be way past the point when he actively put his life on the line. He was supposed to be safe.

"Don't go out there," I begged him. I knew it was an argument I was never going to win, knew that my dad was incapable of staying safely shut up inside while someone was being hurt practically on his doorstep. But if he was too tired to handle a hammer without hitting himself, then he was in no shape to handle whatever was happening outside.

"I have to, Becks," he said simply, then looked over my head at Luke. "No matter what happens, you do not let her come after me. Understand?" He was using his command tone again, and once more Luke responded to it.

"Yes, sir," Luke said. I wondered if he would have saluted if he weren't holding my hand. "Come on, Becket," he said quietly into my ear. "You know a losing battle when you see one."

My heart was pounding, and my chest felt tight with fear. I couldn't tell how many people were out there, except that Dad would be badly outnumbered. The shotgun might intimidate the Nightstruck—they were still only human, despite whatever had happened to them—but it would have no effect on the goat or any other magical construct that might be out there. A sense of foreboding just about overwhelmed me, but the screaming intensified, and my dad wasn't about to entertain any debate.

"Go upstairs," he ordered once more, then strode toward the door, shotgun at the ready.

# CHAPTER NINETEEN

Luke and I ran up to my dad's study and looked out the window at the spectacle that was being staged—quite deliberately, I'm sure—in front of the house. A group of eight or ten Nightstruck mingled about in the narrow street, right under a streetlamp, so we had no trouble seeing them. They had a pretty girl about my age surrounded. Her clothes were torn, and she was bleeding from a split lip and a nasty gash on her forehead. Her sobs were loud and panicked enough to carry over Bob's barking, and she kept whirling frantically around, trying not to let anyone come up behind her.

Piper and the goat were both there. The goat seemed larger than I remembered, and let's just say that it was very obviously male. It threaded its way through the mob, none of whom reacted to my dad's shouted orders to stop what they were doing.

The girl tried to skitter away as the goat approached, but all she managed to do was throw herself into the grip of a couple of the other Nightstruck. They shoved her back into the center of their circle. The goat rose up on two legs, and I thought it was going to gore her with its horns, but apparently that horror wasn't enough for the creatures of the night. Instead, the goat wrapped its front legs around her thigh and started humping her leg like a horny dog. Which would have been grotesque enough without all the goat's various spines and horns.

The girl screamed and wrenched herself away. I gasped and covered my mouth when I saw the long, deep slashes in her thigh, slashes that were quickly turning her jeans red with blood.

Luke made an attempt to draw me away from the window, but we'd spent enough time together by now that the attempt was halfhearted. He knew there was no way to stop me from watching, short of tackling me to the floor and sitting on me. He settled for taking my left hand in his—leaving my gun hand free—and giving me a squeeze.

If I ended up having to shoot, I would need both hands, but for now I was grateful to have the anchor of his touch. Dread coursed through me, and I might have drowned in it if I didn't have his hand to hold on to.

There was a deafening boom as my dad fired the shotgun. He was still standing right on our doorstep, I guess, because I couldn't see him even when I pressed myself as close to the window as the motley array of towel rods would allow. One thing I did know was that he hadn't fired the shotgun *at* the Nightstruck, because none of them went down. I supposed he couldn't, when they had an innocent victim in their midst. Shotguns are not precision weapons.

Most of the Nightstruck turned to look, as if they'd noticed my dad for the first time. Piper, however, was looking straight up at me, making eye contact through the window. She was smirking and confident, not remotely rattled by the shotgun blast. She crooked a finger at me, beckoning, but I sincerely doubted she expected me to respond.

Dad pumped the shotgun loudly, and I finally caught a glimpse of him as he advanced toward the gathered Night-struck. Thanks to the injured victim, he still couldn't afford to shoot. I didn't know if the Nightstruck had enough brains or sense of self-preservation to figure that out.

For a moment it looked like they were going to call his bluff, like they were all going to stand there like statues until he was close enough that they could grab him. I willed the victim to make a run for it while her captors were distracted, but she had collapsed to the pavement and curled up in fetal position—maybe from pure terror, or maybe because the goat had hurt her so much she couldn't stand.

Dad bellowed at the street people to back away or he'd shoot, and he finally seemed to get through to them. The circle surrounding the girl dissolved as the Nightstruck slowly, casually backed away. All except Piper and the goat, who stood side by side.

"Don't think I won't shoot you, Piper," my dad called. "Back the hell up."

"Here's the problem, Mr. Walker," she responded, with no hint of concern. "If you shoot me, you might shoot the poor, innocent victim you're trying to save." She smiled. "You could put the shotgun down and go for your handgun, but there are kind of a lot of us, so that might not be a good idea."

"She can probably survive a few stray pellets," my dad said as he continued to inch closer. The rest of the Nightstruck continued to back up, but Piper just stood there like she thought she was invincible. "I'm sure she *can't* survive whatever you've got planned for her, so I'll just have to take my chances."

I bit my lip and squeezed Luke's hand so tight I was probably hurting him, but he didn't complain. If Dad could get close enough, he could direct the spray of pellets so that they wouldn't hit the victim—it takes distance for them to fan out and scatter, which is why sawed-off shotguns are illegal. I wondered if Piper knew that was what he was up to.

"Back away, Piper," I prayed under my breath. I knew the person standing out there in the dark was no longer the Piper I knew, was no longer my best friend. I also knew the chances of her coming back to herself were slim. But the thought of seeing her die right in front of me—at my father's hands, no less—was too terrible to contemplate.

"And what do you plan to do about Billy here?" Piper inquired, giving the goat a very careful pat on the head, avoiding the spines. "The shotgun won't be much use against him."

That was my concern, too, and I stood in agonized tension, thinking the goat might charge at any moment. But it kept standing quietly at Piper's side. It seemed to me almost like the two of them were waiting for something.

I wrenched my gaze away, quickly looking down the street behind my dad, sure someone or something was sneaking up on him, but there was nothing. When I looked back at my dad, he was almost close enough to have a relatively safe shot. He'd already fired a warning shot, and I didn't know how many shells his shotgun held. If the Nightstruck decided to take their chances and rush him . . .

I didn't want to follow that line of thought.

Piper, the goat, and the injured victim were on the sidewalk across the narrow street from our house. Dad had been approaching them on a shallow diagonal, slowly inching his way across the street. He was now only a few steps from the curb. If he continued on his current line, he would have to step over a storm drain to get onto the opposite sidewalk.

My eyes caught on the innocuous-looking storm drain. It hadn't undergone any strange nighttime transformation, and it looked for all the world like a normal storm drain, and yet something about it—and about Piper's air of waiting—made the hair on the back of my neck rise. I wanted to yell at my dad to go around the damn thing, but I was afraid of what might happen if I distracted him when he was getting this close to Piper and the goat.

I should have taken that chance. I should have yelled. And because I didn't, I'll have to live with the what-ifs for the rest of my life.

My dad is not a small guy, and he cast a sizable shadow as he crossed under the halo of light from the streetlamp. That shadow fell over the storm drain, making its depths all but invisible in the darkness, so I couldn't see exactly what happened next. All I saw was an indistinct whisper of movement, and then my dad cried out in surprise.

One leg slid out from under him, and he fell awkwardly on his butt, barely having the presence of mind to hold on to the shotgun. Before he had a chance to react, something unseen yanked on his leg. His foot and lower calf disappeared into the storm drain, and he had to let go of the shotgun to fight the pull.

"Daddy!" I yelled, the scream ripping out of my throat as I wrenched my hand from Luke's and grabbed hold of one of the towel rods over the window in a death grip. Luke was yelling, too, but I could barely hear him over the pounding of the blood in my ears.

Dad wedged his free foot and both his hands against the curb as his other leg was pulled farther into the drain. There was no way he could fit into that opening, but then, he didn't have to for bad things to happen.

The Nightstruck were closing in again. Piper sauntered forward and picked up the shotgun. Whatever was pulling my dad into the storm drain kept him from fighting her for it. His face was red and contorted with the strain of fighting the pull, his teeth bared in a feral grimace.

"You should have left us alone, Mr. Walker," Piper said loudly, but she was still looking up at me, evil green eyes boring into me. "You're not meant for the night. It's Becket we want, not you."

"Let him go!" I shouted, banging on the window with the flat of my hand.

Piper smiled at me. "Come out and get him!"

Dad wrenched his body sideways so he could look up at the window while still bracing himself against the pull. "Don't let her out of the house, Luke!" he yelled. "Keep her safe!"

Beside me, Luke started cursing, and I had the sense of him looking all around as if trying to find a weapon or some other way he could help. But I was the only one who had any chance of stopping this.

"Open the window for me," I ordered Luke as I double-checked to make sure my gun was ready to fire.

I was worried he wouldn't do it, that he would somehow feel that was disobeying my dad's command to keep me safe, but he didn't hesitate. He unlocked the window and shoved it open so I could take aim. The towel rods were annoying, but I could work around them.

"Let him go!" I shouted again, pointing the gun at Piper.

Still smiling, she took a quick step backward and let another of the Nightstruck—a bearded, filthy, older man who had no doubt been homeless before the night took him—stand between me and her. He wasn't big enough to cover her completely, but if I fired I would be much more likely to hit him than Piper. Which didn't matter to me in the least.

At least, not in theory. I gritted my teeth, and my finger tightened on the trigger, but I hesitated to fire. The only thing I'd ever fired at before was targets on a shooting range. I'd never even gone hunting, never shot anything that was alive. If the homeless guy were charging at me with murder in his eyes, I probably wouldn't have hesitated. But he was just standing there, no threat to me, and showing no sign of being a threat to my father.

Just over the homeless guy's shoulder, I could see Piper's lips twist in one of those smirks I was starting to hate more than anything in the world.

The goat suddenly reared up on its hind legs, then lowered its head and leaped forward. Its horns slammed into my dad's shoulder, and though he was a brave man, he couldn't help screaming in pain. When the goat backed up, its horns and the spines on its head were dripping with my father's blood. Maybe it had broken some bones, too, because my dad's arm went entirely limp. Without the use of his arm, he wasn't able to fully brace himself anymore. He screamed again as his leg was pulled all the way into the storm drain, as far as it would go, until his body slammed against the curb.

I no longer cared about the humanity of the homeless guy who had formed a human shield in front of Piper.

I pulled the trigger, but my eyes were blurry with tears and my hands were far from steady. My dad had told me once that even the best-trained, most experienced police officers miss more often than they hit, in the heat of battle. Your body's fight-or-flight response shuts down your fine motor skills and makes it physically impossible for most people to shoot straight. I was no exception to that rule.

My first shot went completely wild, and I was so panicky I immediately squeezed off a second that was even wilder. Piper kept smirking, and the rest of the Nightstruck were completely unintimidated.

My higher reasoning kicked in and reminded me there were more Nightstruck out there than I had ammo for, and that they weren't going to give me time to get another mag and reload. I had to make every shot count.

The goat rammed my dad again, this time in the opposite shoulder. His scream almost made me pull the trigger again by reflex, but I fought the need, fought to steady my hands and to breathe evenly. It was a fight I was doomed to lose.

My third shot was better, winging the homeless guy in the shoulder. His only reaction to the hit was a mild flinch, and he remained parked exactly where he was.

The goat backed up and took yet another shot at my dad, this time at his exposed leg. There was no scream this time, just a groan. Blood soaked both his shirt and his pants and pooled in the gutter. If I didn't stop this soon, he wasn't going to make it.

"I have to go down there," I said. "I have to be able to move to get a clear shot."

"No way," Luke said, looming behind me. "That's exactly what they want."

Intellectually, I knew that. And I knew giving them what they wanted was a terrible idea. But I couldn't just stand there and do nothing while they killed my father.

"Come on, Becks," Piper called. "It doesn't have to be like this. Just come out and talk to me. I won't hurt you. I promise."

Like the promise of this stranger meant anything!

I tore my eyes away from the horror outside my window and turned my most imploring look on Luke. "You have to let me go out there. I can't stop them from here."

I tried to step around him, but he moved to block me, grabbing my shoulders and giving them a little shake. His eyes were glassy, and his every muscle was clenched with strain. But he didn't budge.

"You can't stop them out there, either," he said hoarsely. "I'm not going to let you throw your life away."

There was a horrible, cracking sound of impact, and I whirled around to look out the window once more. The goat had taken another shot at my dad's exposed leg, which now lay bent at a crooked angle.

Dad wasn't moving, and Luke wasn't about to let me go outside. Even if I could convince him to let me go, by the time I talked him into it, ran downstairs, got all the locks open, and went outside, the goat and the Nightstruck would have finished Dad off.

There was nothing constructive I could do. And so I started shooting again, even though it was hopeless.

I finally took down the homeless guy with a shot that was aimed for his torso but that hit him in the neck. His blood splashed all over Piper, streaking her too-blond hair, and he fell to the pavement, clutching his throat as blood spilled out from between his fingers.

Another of the Nightstruck stepped forward to shield Piper.

I emptied my clip as the goat continued to brutalize my dad, until his entire body was bloody and torn and broken and there was no way he was still alive.

With my eight shots, I managed to kill one Nightstruck and

wound two more, which is better shooting than it sounds like. But it wasn't enough.

When the bullets ran out, the Nightstruck calmly collected the unconscious—or maybe even dead—girl they'd been tormenting earlier. It took two of them to extract my dad's body from the drain. I fell to my knees and made some horrible choking sound when I realized they were going to take him away. Luke knelt beside me and wrapped his arms around me. He tried to turn my face away from the window, but I resisted. I didn't want to see, and yet I couldn't stop myself from looking.

Piper continued to stare at me the whole time, and there was no hint of regret or apology on her face.

"Come with me, and all the pain will go away," she called, but she didn't sound like she expected me to take her up on it. She shook her head. "We'll talk again when you've had time to think about the situation."

My whole body shook with a sob, and though I knew the gun was empty, I kept pulling the trigger anyway, over and over again, as the Nightstruck took my father's body away.

# CHAPTER TWENTY

I don't want to talk about the next few days. I don't remember them all that well anyway, which is a blessing. There was a lot of crying involved, of course, interspersed with periods of dull numbness and disbelief. The worst part was having to tell my mom and my sister what had happened. I knew none of it was my fault, and yet it was hard to remember that, when I listened to them cry. The what-if games had begun in my mind, and no amount of logic could stop them.

Thanks to the quarantine, I couldn't go live with my surviving family, none of whom lived in the Philly area. Dad's second in command came over to the house and talked over my options with me. In ordinary circumstances, a girl like me with no family to take her in would move into the foster care system, but thanks to the situation, the foster care system was strained to the breaking point and needed all its resources for the many younger kids who couldn't get by without an adult guardian. At seventeen, I was capable of taking care of myself.

Luke's mom offered to serve as my unofficial guardian, and with my okay, that was more than enough for the authorities. My own mother wasn't so okay with it, and she was pursuing legal action in hopes of forcing the government to either let me out of the quarantine area or let her in.

Yeah, good luck with that, Mom.

Luke and his mom were great, and were the only reason I stayed reasonably sane during those first few awful days. Despite the hospital's desperate need, she stayed home from work for several nights, treating me like the broken thing I was. She moved me into their guest room and even took Bob in, despite being allergic to dogs.

Neither my mom nor my dad was the coddling type, both believing in self-sufficiency above all else, but Luke's mom was a more nurturing sort, a natural-born caregiver. She never once told me not to cry, nor would she let me do anything for myself. I wasn't allowed to cook, or help her and Luke with the housework, or even run to the grocery store for a quick errand, at least not for the first few days. Which I'm sure was just as well. If I'd gone to the store for milk, I probably would have stood in front of the dairy case for hours in an agony of indecision over whether to pick whole or two percent. I just wasn't all that functional.

I knew I was starting to get a bit better the morning I offered to walk Bob—which Luke had taken on as his own personal chore—and Luke's mom actually let me. Luke came along, but he insisted it was just to keep me company, not to keep an eye on me in case I had a breakdown.

I had begun the long, slow recovery process. Dr. Gilliam told me gravely that I would never "get over" my dad's death. She had lost her mother ten years ago, and she said sometimes the pain of it would sneak up on her and take her by surprise, even now.

"But it does get easier," she assured me with a sad smile.

"Time can't fully heal the wound, but you'll figure out how to live with it. We all have to go through this at some point in our lives."

It's not like I hadn't known I would in all likelihood outlive both of my parents. That was just the natural way of things. But I'd never let myself think about it, always thought it was some terribly distant eventuality. Even when my dad was still in the field, his life in potential danger every day, I'd never truly believed anything would happen to him, no matter how much my mom worried.

Reality could be one hell of a bitch.

It was four long days and three even longer nights after my dad's death when Dr. Gilliam decided she had to go back to work. I was still prone to sudden, unexpected crying jags, but I was at least getting to the point that I could occasionally think about something other than the horrible, aching loss. And the situation out in the city wasn't getting any better. There were casualties every single night, and every emergency room in the city was flooded the moment the sun set. It didn't help matters that the nights were still getting longer.

When Dr. Gilliam told me she was going back to work, I told her I wanted to go back to my house to spend the night. I appreciated her care more than I could say, but even though my home was only across the way from the Gilliam house, I was feeling homesick. I wanted to sleep in my own bed, in my own room, even though being in that empty house was sure to give me painful reminders of what I had lost.

I thought she might argue with me, but she didn't. I guess she understood. Luke and Bob came with me, of course, and if I closed off some shutters in my mind here and there I could almost convince myself Dad was off at work and would be back before the night was out.

The new routine became very much like the old one, with Luke and Bob and me staying at my house when his mom was at work and at his house when she was home. The only thing that was different—aside from my dad's absence—was that Piper and her friends no longer stopped by to torment me. I kept expecting that bone-chilling moment when my early warning system (aka Bob) went on alert, but for a little over a week after my dad's death nothing happened. No Nightstruck called to me, no metal goats rammed my door, no unseen, malevolent creatures tried my windows.

I wouldn't say either Luke or I had relaxed our guard much. I had found where Dad stashed the ammo for the SIG. I'd also found an old, worn ankle holster, so I didn't have to carry the gun around in my hand when I moved from room to room. It was designed for a bigger, male ankle, and even at its smallest size it was a little loose, but I preferred that slight discomfort to the risk of absently leaving the gun in one room and discovering I needed it in another. We checked the windows and the security of our impromptu bars over them every night, and we entered a state of heightened awareness as soon as the sun dipped below the horizon and what was now being called the Transition happened.

But even though we were nominally prepared for it, it still felt like a blow below the belt when one night, during dinner, Bob leaped to his feet and charged the front door. Both Luke and I pushed our chairs back from the table, and I grabbed the gun out of its holster and double-checked it. Piper had said she'd be back, had said we'd "talk later," but the thought of seeing her again almost made me throw up.

Luke and I stood at the ready in the middle of the living room, though what exactly we were at the ready for, I don't know. There was a metallic squeak I recognized as the sound of the mail slot being pushed in, and that sick feeling in my stomach worsened exponentially.

"Bob, come here!" I shouted, with little hope that he would obey. As well trained as he was, I think the creatures of the night short-circuited all that training and threw him into the land of blind instinct. Maybe he would have obeyed if the command had come from my dad instead of from me.

I was already running toward the door, planning to physically haul Bob away from danger, but I wasn't fast enough. Bob let out a high-pitched yelp that practically made my heart stop beating. He scrambled backward away from the door, and I could see the tip of something sharp and pointy withdrawing through the mail slot. With a whimper of pain, he flopped down on the floor and started licking the top of his leg.

I was crying and so angry I was shaking as I approached my brave, heroic dog, terrified that he was about to die in the line of duty.

"Careful," Luke warned, though he made no attempt to stop me. "Wounded animal."

It's true that wounded animals can be unpredictable, but I couldn't be bothered to care about that. I knelt at Bob's side and shuddered in relief when I saw that the wound, though bloody, was in his shoulder, not his chest. It obviously hurt, but it didn't look life threatening.

The mail slot creaked again, and I saw a pair of brilliant green eyes watching me through the opening. Bob growled and tried to stand up, but I held on to his collar.

"Your dog will be fine," said a male voice, and I finally realized those green eyes belonged to Aleric. "I was careful not to hurt him too much."

Bob's growl deepened, and he lurched to his feet despite my effort to keep him down.

"Luke, will you get his leash, please?" I asked without looking. Blood trickled down Bob's leg, but even with the wound I was sure he was stronger than me—especially when I could only hold on with one hand because of the gun—and I couldn't let Aleric take another poke at him.

Apparently Luke was the proactive type, because before I'd finished the sentence he was there at my side, leash in hand. He clipped the leash on Bob's collar and gave a little tug.

"Come on, Bob," Luke said, patting his leg encouragingly. "Let's go have a Milk-Bone, okay, buddy?" Luke leaned close so he didn't have to shout. "I'm going to take him upstairs. I'll be right back."

I felt safer having Bob close by, but with him already hurt and me waving a gun around, Luke probably had the right idea. I nodded reluctantly, and Luke gave Bob's leash a tug.

Luke and Bob had definitely bonded during the time we'd spent together, and though Bob resisted being led away, he didn't resist as hard as he could have. I pointed my gun at the mail slot, but Aleric's eyes had disappeared and the metal flap was closed. I wished that meant he was gone, but of course I knew better.

"Don't think I won't shoot you through the door," I yelled, though in all honesty, it wasn't something I saw myself doing. Aleric was obviously one of the Nightstruck, and that automatically made him a bad guy. However, he hadn't done anything to me, hadn't been there on the night my dad was killed, and I didn't feel justified shooting him in cold blood.

"That might be a bad idea," Aleric said. "There are metal reinforcements in the door, aren't there? You wouldn't want to hit one of those reinforcements and have the bullet ricochet."

Unfortunately, he was right. Firing through the door would be a dumb idea. It was just as well I hadn't really planned on doing it.

"Let me make it easier for you," he said.

The first of the dead bolts on our door turned with a click, and I gasped. There was the sound of keys clinking together, then the second dead bolt turned.

My mouth hung open and I started to shake. Apparently Aleric had my dad's keys.

"Don't worry," Aleric said as the doorknob began to turn. "I'm not here to hurt you. I won't even cross your threshold. I just want to talk face-to-face."

The door swung slowly open, letting in a blast of chill air. *Pull the trigger,* I urged myself, but I stood frozen, almost unable to move. Bob was barking himself hoarse, but the sound came from a distance now as Luke dragged him up the stairs. I considered yelling for Luke to let him go, but didn't. My every instinct said Aleric was out of Bob's league.

My finger tightened on the trigger as the opening door revealed Aleric standing there, tucking a ring of keys into the front pocket of his tight black jeans. It was freezing out, but his bomber jacket was hanging open, revealing a green T-shirt that matched his eyes. On the pavement at his feet lay the fireplace poker he'd used to jab Bob. There was blood on its sharpened tip.

As he'd promised, he made no attempt to cross the threshold, and the moment Dad's keys were tucked away, he held both his hands out to his sides in a gesture of surrender. Despite my fear, despite my anger at him for hurting Bob, I found I couldn't shoot someone who was just standing there in front of me and going out of his way to show he was no threat. Even remembering the consequences of failing to shoot immediately on the night of my dad's death couldn't motivate me to pull the trigger.

"Why do you have my dad's keys?" I asked, still pointing the gun and trying to find the will to shoot.

"Piper gave them to me," he answered. "I thought it was time you and I talk, but I didn't think you'd open the door for me."

"I have nothing to talk to you about!"

He arched an eyebrow. "You sure about that? Sure you don't have any questions you'd like to ask me? Because I'm willing to give you some answers."

I snorted. "Like I would believe anything you said."

To my immense relief, I heard the slam of the study door upstairs, followed by the pounding of Luke's feet on the stairs as he ran back to me. I was armed and dangerous, and Aleric showed no sign of attacking me, but I didn't want to face him alone.

Aleric shrugged. "You'll never know until you try, now will you?"

I was skeptical. I was afraid this was some kind of trick. I was afraid I'd already made a huge mistake by not pulling the trigger.

But I had to admit I was also curious. No one really understood what had happened to the Nightstruck, why they had changed so dramatically. I couldn't trust anything Aleric said, but it was possible I might learn something of interest, something that might help restore the Nightstruck to their old selves.

"Fine," I said. "I'll play your game. But if I even think you're about to set foot in this house, I'll blow you away."

"Don't worry," Aleric said. He smiled, and for once there was no particular malice behind it. "I physically *can't* come into your house."

He looked at something over my shoulder and laughed. I turned my head just slightly and saw that Luke had armed himself with a fireplace poker of his own. It wasn't sharpened, like the one Aleric had stabbed Bob with, but Luke was more than big and strong enough to make it into a formidable weapon. Why Aleric found it funny was beyond me. Luke's a really nice guy, but the look on his face right now would have scared the shit out of anyone sane.

"Let me guess," Luke said, holding the poker like a baseball bat and looking ready to swing for the fences. "This must be that Aleric guy Piper was going on about." He looked so angry I feared for a moment he would go into testosterone overload and attack, but he wasn't completely out of his mind and knew better than to step in front of my gun.

"And you must be the Boy Wonder," Aleric said. "Pleased to make your acquaintance." He gave a silly little bow, eyes fixed on Luke's face to take in his reaction. I suspected that, thanks to Piper, Aleric would know all too well how to push Luke's buttons, so I tried to draw Aleric's attention back to myself.

"What did you mean when you said you can't come into the

house?" I asked. "The Nightstruck break into people's houses every night."

Aleric let his hands fall slowly back to his sides, but he kept his fingers splayed open so I could see he wasn't reaching for anything or making any threatening gesture. "If I were one of the Nightstruck, then yes, I would be able to come into your house. But I'm not."

"That makes no sense. If you're not Nightstruck, what are you?"

He frowned and cocked his head for a moment. "I'm not exactly sure what to call myself. I am one of a kind, and that's not ego talking."

"Explain."

"I'm basically like those things you call magical constructs."

I looked him up and down quickly. "You don't look like any statue I've ever seen in the city."

"I said I'm *basically* like those things, not that I'm *exactly* like one. They are inanimate objects, given a semblance of life by magic. I am actually alive in and of myself. I'm just not human." He gestured toward my gun with his chin. "That would have no effect on me because I don't have internal organs you can damage."

That elicited another snort from me. "Yeah, right. I'm just going to lower my weapon and give up because you said so."

"Go ahead and shoot me if you don't believe me. That'll prove I'm telling the truth. I won't hold it against you."

I glanced over at Luke. There was cold anger and resolve in his face, but when our eyes met I saw a hint of uncertainty. He didn't know what to make of Aleric any more than I did.

"You seriously want me to shoot you?" I asked, more because

I was stalling to give myself time to process than because I wanted an answer.

"I don't care one way or another," Aleric said. "Just making a helpful suggestion."

"Shoot him in the leg," Luke suggested. "As long as you don't kill him, you'll be able to live with yourself if it turns out he's bluffing, right?"

I gave Luke a grateful nod. It was the perfect idea. I lowered my aim from Aleric's chest to his thigh, then hesitated just a beat to make sure he wasn't going to object. My aim was steady, my hands not shaking. I swallowed hard and squeezed the trigger.

Aleric didn't even flinch. I thought I had to have missed, as impossible as that seemed from this range. But even if I had missed, Aleric would have at least flinched if he'd been lying about his invulnerability.

Just to be sure, I raised the gun to his chest again and pulled the trigger a second time. And again he just stood there patiently, unaffected.

Reluctantly, I lowered the gun. I hoped he was telling the truth about not being able to come inside. If my gun didn't hurt him, then I didn't suppose Luke's fireplace poker would be any more effective. We had no way to defend ourselves.

"Satisfied?" Aleric asked with a quirk of his eyebrow and a jaunty smile that grated on my raw nerves.

"That's not the word I'd use," I answered, shivering in the cold that was pouring through my open door. "What is it you want with me, anyway?"

His eyes widened in mock surprise. "Isn't that obvious? I want you to come out."

"But *why*? Why me, I mean?"

He pursed his lips, and once again I had the feeling that he was searching for an answer, like I was somehow asking him questions he wasn't expecting. "Because you're special to me. Because we share a bond."

"Bullshit! I don't even know you, and I don't want to."

"The bond is there, whether you like it or not. I am blood of your blood, as it were."

I felt momentarily dizzy and had to put a hand on the wall to steady myself. Blood of my blood.

"Becket?" Luke asked with concern. He touched my shoulder lightly. "Are you all right?"

I looked into Aleric's eyes, at those electric green eyes that couldn't exist in the natural world. Eyes I had first seen in the nearly invisible face of the not-baby I had tried to save. A creature I had bled onto, thanks to the hidden pin that had pricked me.

Blood has significance in folktales the world over, and though the magic that had taken over our nights was like no folktale I'd ever heard, it wasn't hard to believe that blood was the key. That pin had been in the not-baby's blanket for a reason. I remembered my thought that the creature's eyes sparked with triumph when my blood hit it.

Luke's hand tightened on my shoulder, the concern on his face deepening. "Talk to me, Becket. What's wrong?"

How could I possibly answer that?

"She's putting the pieces together," Aleric answered for me. "Figuring out who and what I am."

"B-But . . ." I stammered, then took a deep breath to try to pull myself together. "But that . . . *thing* . . . burst into a million little bits and blew away."

Aleric nodded. "And so it did, spreading the seeds of magic

all through the city. But your blood remained, rich with the magic it had absorbed, and I am what it produced. I might almost claim you as my mother."

"You're lying," I said, without conviction.

"You know I'm not. You brought me into this world."

Luke gave my shoulder a little shake. "Hey, don't let this guy get to you. He . . . *it* is just trying to get into your head."

"Like calls to like," Aleric said. "Blood calls to blood. Come with me, and I can take all your pain away. You'll be free of mourning and fear and loss. Anything you want can be yours. All you have to do is take it."

My heart thumped loud and hard against my breastbone.

Luke stepped in front of me, shielding me from Aleric's view and brandishing the fireplace poker. "You leave her alone," he snarled. "She's not coming with you, so get the hell out of here."

Aleric laughed. "You couldn't stop me from taking Piper. Hell, you didn't even *try*. What makes you think you have any say in this?"

I couldn't see Luke's face, because he had his back to me, but I could see the red flush that crept up the back of his neck. It hadn't occurred to me that he felt guilty about what had happened to Piper, that he might consider it was somehow his fault he wasn't with her on the night she succumbed.

Aleric clearly had a knack for finding people's weak spots. I moved forward to stand by Luke's side, hoping to present a united front.

"Don't let this guy get to you," I said quietly, and Luke smiled ever so slightly to hear his own words echoed back at him.

"It's so precious how the two of you defend each other," Aleric said. He fixed me with a piercing stare. "I think you'll find that changes when it sinks in that you're directly responsible for opening the door between our worlds. Every death and every loss can be laid squarely at your feet. The only way to escape what you've done is to come with me. One day, I'll be king of this world,, and you'll be my queen."

"You turned my best friend into a monster, and she killed my father right in front of me. You're delusional if you think I'm coming anywhere near you."

Aleric shrugged. "Piper would have turned, with or without me. The night magic finds fertile ground in the weak and the selfish, and her nature left her vulnerable. Only the night can take that pain away from you, can make you whole again. Come with me. There is nothing for you here but misery. I can—"

Nothing but misery? Of course there was nothing but misery! Because Aleric had *made* it that way.

My hand rose with no conscious order from my brain, and I squeezed the trigger, emptying the gun into Aleric's chest despite knowing it would have no effect. He just stood there with a condescending smile and took it.

When the gun clicked on empty, Luke strode past me and slammed the door in Aleric's face.

"You're through listening to him," he said, turning all the locks.

I sat down on the floor with a thump, my legs too jelly-like to hold me. I should never have taken Aleric's bait in the first place, should have done exactly what Luke just did and slammed the door. Aleric might be able to open it again, but it would have been hard to have a conversation while we fought over the door.

Luke and I both waited in silence for Aleric to start unlocking the door again. But with Luke standing there at the ready, there was no way Aleric could get all the locks open at the same time.

"It's only going to get worse," Aleric called. "The Night Makers are coming, with or without your help. Fight me if you must, but in the end you'll find that I'm right."

# CHAPTER TWENTY-ONE

Luke sat me on the couch and wrapped a blanket around my shoulders. As if he wasn't being awesome enough already, he also made me a cup of cocoa and brought Bob back downstairs to cuddle up next to me. Bob's wound had stopped bleeding, and from what I could see through his fur, it was relatively shallow. I'd still take him to the vet and have it looked at in the morning, but at least it didn't seem to be bothering him much.

I held my cocoa in my right hand, taking cautious sips, while with my other hand I scratched behind Bob's ears and earned his undying love. Luke sat on Bob's other side and patted his flank.

"Guess we'll have to find some way to block the mail slot," he commented. "I'm sure that asshole and his friends could have done a lot worse."

I nodded but couldn't find my voice. I kept hearing Aleric saying *Blood of your blood* over and over in my mind. Whatever that not-baby was, my blood had somehow triggered its dispersal, had triggered the evil magic that had taken hold of our city. Thousands had died already, and no one had any clue how to stop what was happening.

And it was all because of me.

Luke reached over Bob and put his hand on my shoulder. "Stop that," he said gently.

"Stop what?"

He gave me a knowing look. "Just because Aleric said it, that doesn't mean it's true." If he had any doubts, he did a great job of keeping them hidden.

"He told the truth about the bullets not being able to hurt him."

Luke looked distinctly unimpressed. "So he told the truth about something you could verify yourself. That doesn't mean he told the truth about anything else."

"Remember how I told you that baby thing had weirdly green eyes? I didn't make the connection at first, but those eyes looked exactly like Aleric's, just on a smaller scale."

"All of the Nightstruck have the weird green eyes," he reminded me. "It doesn't mean anything."

I put my cocoa down and crossed my arms over my chest, clutching the blanket tighter. The heater was doing its best to counteract the effects of having the door wide open for so long, but it would take a while for the living room to get up to a comfortable temperature again. Though I suspected much of my own chill was coming from the inside.

"Just because we don't want to believe what he said, it doesn't make it not true." My voice was little more than a whisper. I was afraid I'd start crying if I spoke any louder.

Luke rose to his feet and snapped his fingers at Bob. "Move over, buddy," he said.

Bob raised his head just slightly, and his look said, *Really? You think that's going to work?*

But Luke was no idiot, and he'd come prepared. He reached

into the pocket of his jeans and pulled out a Milk-Bone. Suddenly, Bob was a lot more interested in what Luke had to say. His ears perked, his tail wagging.

"I read you like a book," Luke said to him, then put the Milk-Bone down on the far cushion of the couch. And just like that, Bob had moved over as commanded, allowing Luke to sit next to me. Bob gave him a reproachful look, as if offended by the dastardly trick, but he got over it quickly and made himself comfortable on Luke's other side.

To my surprise, Luke put his arm around me, pulling my body close against his. I knew it was supposed to be a comforting gesture, not a romantic one, but the feel of his arm around my shoulders, the warmth of his body against mine, filled my senses, almost enough to drive my misery away.

"Even if he's telling the truth," Luke said, "you have nothing to feel bad about."

That brought my misery back to full strength in a heartbeat. "Nothing to feel bad about?" I cried, trying to pull away. Luke's firm arm wouldn't let me. "If he's telling the truth, every awful thing that's happened since that night is all because of me. My father *died* because of me! And there's worse to come." The tears were rising in my throat, hard though I tried to hold them back. Maybe if I hadn't let Aleric get to me so much, I could have questioned him some more, gotten him to explain who or what the Night Makers were—and what might happen if they came. But I hadn't been in the right frame of mind to ask rational questions, and I wouldn't have trusted the answers anyway.

"It's not because of you," Luke said, giving my shoulders a squeeze for emphasis. "You tried to save the life of a helpless baby. What were you supposed to do? Walk away and let it die?"

"I *knew* there was something wrong," I protested. "Bob tried to tell me, and my instincts tried to tell me, and—"

"And what kind of person would have believed those instincts and let the baby lie there abandoned in the cold?" he persisted.

I couldn't answer that. It was easy to say I should have walked away when I knew the consequences of trying to help. But without the twenty-twenty hindsight, was there any chance I'd have let my instincts trump my common sense and compassion?

"I'll tell you what kind of person," Luke said more softly. "A heartless, selfish, cowardly scumbag of a person. Not the kind of person you would want to be."

He put his other arm around me and pulled me into a hug. A hug I needed more desperately than light, than food, than air. I forgot all my normal self-consciousness, clinging to him, pressing my face against his shoulder as the tears shook me and he held me and stroked my hair.

I didn't cry for long. I'd cried so much over the past week that it was like my body couldn't take any more. As wretched as I still felt, the tears dried up and my breath evened out. I had the vague feeling that I should pull away, now that the crying jag had run its course, but it felt so good to have Luke's arms around me. I couldn't force myself to end it a second earlier than necessary.

"You're one of the most amazing people I know," Luke said softly. "Don't let Aleric or Piper or anyone else convince you otherwise."

Luke thought I was amazing? Pleasure chased some of the chill from my body, though I hardly felt deserving of the praise. No matter what Luke said, I knew Aleric had been telling me the truth, that I had somehow let the magic into our world and was directly responsible for everything that had happened since. That was the opposite of amazing.

I was still cuddled up against Luke's chest, and he was showing no sign that he planned to let go anytime soon. I told myself I should take the initiative and sit up straight, put some distance between us. But that was when his fingers started skimming over my shoulder.

It was a light, tentative caress, but it definitely did not feel like a gesture of comfort. My breath hitched in my throat and my pulse fluttered.

Surely I was misinterpreting things. Luke was just holding a damsel in distress and trying to make her feel better. I was reading things into that soft movement of his fingers, things that couldn't possibly be there. If Luke were interested in me in *that* way, he'd have shown it long before now.

Whatever the meaning of that gentle touch, I didn't have the willpower to pull away while he was doing it. I lay still, almost frozen in his arms, willing him to keep doing it, practically holding my breath. He stirred beside me, turning his body slightly more toward me, and I felt a brief pressure on the top of my head.

Did he just kiss me?

No way. That must have been his chin brushing the top of my head as he changed position. He just hadn't been able to avoid my head because it was resting against his shoulder.

But it hadn't felt like a chin. A chin was hard and bony, and that was not at all what I'd felt pressing into my hair.

Maybe he'd thought it was just another reassuring gesture. Maybe his mom had kissed the top of his head when he was a little kid, and he thought that was what you did when you wanted to comfort someone.

It wasn't that I didn't *want* it to be something more. It was just that I was terrified of getting my hopes up—or making a fool of myself. We spent every night cooped up in the same house together, and if I acted like he was coming on to me and I was wrong, I didn't know how I could bear the humiliation of it.

There was that pressure on my head again. It lasted longer this time, long enough for me to hyperanalyze the sensation and determine that yes, that was a kiss.

Luke's fingers moved slowly from my shoulder to the bare skin of my neck, and goose bumps erupted all over my body. His touch skimmed up to my face, his hand deliciously warm against my chilled skin.

I could bend, twist, and otherwise contort the kiss on the top of the head into a gesture of comfort, but there was no way to misinterpret this as anything but a caress. I swallowed hard, hardly daring to believe this was happening—and almost panicked with the realization that I had no idea what to do. The sum total of my experience with boys was an uncomfortable date at my junior prom with the son of one of my dad's friends. We hadn't known each other, and it turned out we were both equally shy, which made for stilted, awkward conversation. We'd kissed when he dropped me off at home, but only because we thought we ought to, not because we particularly wanted to.

Luke cupped my chin and gently tipped my face up toward his. His eyes were huge and dark, and there was an intensity in them I'd never seen before. There was no question that he was going to kiss me, and not on the top of the head this time, and I fought a swell of panic. He was used to kissing Piper, who had never been shy and never lacked confidence. She also had considerable experience by the time she and Luke started dating. There was no way I could measure up to that standard, no way I could set myself up for a comparison with Piper and come out the winner.

There was also no way I was going to pass up the opportunity to kiss Luke, no matter how potentially complicated it would make things between us in the future.

The first brush of his lips against mine was surprisingly tentative. He'd always seemed to me like a good match for Piper in the confidence department. He wasn't as much of an extrovert as she was, but I'd never seen much in the way of self-consciousness.

*Stop thinking about Piper!* I commanded myself.

Luke deepened the kiss, his lips stroking more firmly, his mouth open. I drank it all in: the warmth and softness of his lips, the scent of his skin, the gentle rasp of his five o'clock shadow. Technically I didn't really know what I was doing, but it was like a dance, and I was happy to follow where Luke led.

When Luke's tongue brushed against the seam of my lips, I obediently opened my mouth wider. The first touch of his tongue inside my mouth was so strange, so foreign, that it almost knocked me out of the moment. I don't know what I'd expected a tongue to feel like—to be honest, hadn't ever given it any thought—but it wasn't like this.

If it had been anyone but Luke, I might have balked at the unfamiliarity of that sensation. I wouldn't necessarily have stopped, it's just that I might have felt the need for a little time to mentally regroup and readjust my expectations. But I wasn't about to risk losing this moment with him, not when I couldn't help fearing it was the only moment we would ever have. I kept expecting him to pull away, to come to his senses and remember that I was his neighbor, the girl he'd never had any interest in.

It didn't take long for me to adjust to the sensation of Luke's tongue in my mouth. Not long at all. In a second or two, I was kissing him back with equal enthusiasm, if not with the same skill. He didn't seem to mind, endlessly patient with my awkward fumblings.

We made out for what felt like somewhere between two seconds and forever, until I no longer felt like I was clueless and out of my league, until I forgot my fear that I would pale in comparison to Piper, until I practically forgot the rest of the world existed.

Unfortunately, the rest of the world *did* exist, in all of its current craziness. Our kiss was interrupted by a burst of raucous laughter right outside the front window. Luke broke away from me lightning quick, grabbing hold of Bob's collar before the injured dog could leap from the couch and charge at the front door. Bob barked and tried to struggle away from Luke's grip, but Luke was practically lying on top of him, holding him down, keeping him away from the potential danger of that mail slot. It was a good thing he'd won Bob over already or he might have had his face bitten off.

Lips still tingling from the glory of the kiss, I held my breath and once more pulled the gun from my ankle holster. But apparently this group of Nightstruck was just passing through, not stopping by to torment me. They were loud, and from the sound of it, they were idly smashing things as they went by, but they kept moving.

I didn't relax and put the gun away until the last echoes of their voices faded into the distance.

"I'd better clear the table," I said, standing up and pretending not to see Luke's puzzled frown. Guess that wasn't the kind of thing he was used to a girl saying to him after a nice make out session, but the interruption had brought all of my self-consciousness rushing back. I didn't know what to make of him kissing me like that. Was it just one of those things that happens in the heat of the moment? Was he already regretting it, wondering what he'd been thinking? I'd just lost my father, and he'd basically just lost Piper, and people tend to act impulsively when they're in that kind of emotional turmoil. If that was why Luke had kissed me, I didn't want to face reality. Not yet.

So I acted like Ms. Fifties Housewife instead, taking longer than necessary to clear the dishes we'd abandoned on the dining room table when Aleric had come calling. When Luke tried to help, I brushed him off with a false, perky smile. And when that busywork was done, I decided I was in need of a long, hot shower, which gave me the excuse to flee to my bedroom and be alone.

Was I being an abject coward? Yes. But knowing that wasn't enough to make me go back downstairs.

# CHAPTER TWENTY-TWO

I had feared that the kiss would make things awkward between Luke and me, and I was right. I'm pretty sure it was all my fault, that I was being a neurotic train wreck about the whole thing, but I couldn't shake the suspicion that the kiss had been some kind of mistake on Luke's part. That he'd just done it because he felt sorry for me, or because we had both been scared by Aleric's visit, or just because he was your stereotypical guy and I'd been available. It was a suspicion I didn't want to have confirmed, so anytime Luke tried to talk to me about it or ask me what was wrong, I changed the subject so fast I gave myself whiplash.

I missed Piper—*my* Piper, not the creature she'd become—so badly it hurt like a physical pain. She was the only person I could even imagine talking to about the emotional jumble I couldn't seem to deal with. She'd always been the one I talked to about girl stuff, about my thoughts and feelings and fears. She'd been there for me during the terrible last few months of my parents' marriage, when our house had been like a verbal war zone and I felt like a helpless witness, watching the two people I loved most in the world tearing each other apart. How I wished she could be there for me now.

Though I don't suppose I'd have been able to talk this particular dilemma over with her anyway, seeing as Luke was her boyfriend. If Piper were still in the picture, none of this would have happened in the first place and I wouldn't have anything to be confused about.

The quarantine dragged on, though the government's assertion that the city's madness was the result of some contagious disease grew increasingly absurd. With my dad gone, I no longer had a way to get inside information about what was *really* going on, but there was no way the government hadn't sent people in hazmat suits into the city at night. Surely those people had seen what the rest of us were seeing, and the hazmat suits would prove it wasn't some disease or hallucinogen. But the quarantine stayed in effect anyway, and people who tried to sneak out were arrested and thrown in jail.

The continued quarantine meant there was little to no chance I would be able to make my planned trip to Boston to spend Thanksgiving with my mom and sister. Unlike me, Luke had family who lived within the city limits, and Dr. Gilliam didn't so much ask me to join them for Thanksgiving as assume I would. Sitting in on some other family's Thanksgiving dinner was an incredibly unappealing option. However, my other option was to spend the day alone in my house, which sucked even more.

I wished the dinner were happening at Dr. Gilliam's place, so that if I found it unbearable I could slip home. Unfortunately, her father and her stepmother would be hosting us in their condo down by the Delaware River.

"We'll all spend the night there," Dr. Gilliam told me. "That way we won't have to worry about trying to get home before curfew."

"But I can't leave Bob home alone all night!" I protested, thinking I'd found a way out of going, and wondering if that was a victory or not.

Dr. Gilliam smiled. "Of course not. Bob's invited, too. My folks have a black Lab who'd be delighted to make his acquaintance."

I doubted Bob would be similarly delighted. He wasn't particularly aggressive with other dogs, as long as they weren't aggressive with him, but he was . . . let's just call it standoffish.

"We'll be careful about introducing them," Dr. Gilliam assured me. "If it seems like they won't get along, we'll separate them. It'll be fine; you'll see. And I'm sure he'll forgive you for uprooting him when you give him his own turkey dinner."

I had to admit, a turkey dinner would be a big hit with Bob. So apparently I was going to have Thanksgiving dinner and spend the night at a stranger's house. It was going to be one hell of a tough day, full of memories of my dad. I was going to have a hard time thinking of things to be thankful for. But when I called and told my mom about it, she burst into tears and said how very happy she was that I wouldn't have to spend the holiday alone, and I realized that in spite of my ambivalence, I was pretty glad about that, too.

Thanks to my family being scattered all over the country—and out of it, because of one aunt and set of cousins who live in England—the biggest family gathering I'd ever been to had been no more than eight people, counting me and my folks. Luke had warned me that his family was a big one, and when we arrived at his grandparents' condo, I found he'd been telling nothing but the truth. There were fifteen people, most of whom were in his parents' generation. There were a couple of bratty boys, aged four and six, and one cousin named Marlene, who was sixteen, but that was it for young folk. Which was actually kind of fine with me, because it made it easier not to be overly social.

Sometimes I felt fine, if a little removed. But other times grief snuck up on me and smacked me hard in the face. More than once I felt like I was going to lose it and go off on a crying jag right in front of all these strangers.

What struck me hardest was watching Dr. Gilliam interact with her father. There was such affection and mutual respect between them, and I was achingly aware that I would never have a chance to relate to my own father like that, as one adult to another. I would never know how our relationship would have evolved when I left the nest and when the immediate aftermath of the divorce had blown over. That hurt so much that I had to duck into the bathroom to have a good cry a couple of times.

Both times, I'd slipped away in what I thought was an unobtrusive fashion, and both times, when I stepped out of the bathroom, Luke was there waiting for me. The awkwardness was still there between us, but I didn't have the willpower to refuse the hugs he offered me.

If Thanksgiving was this bad, I hated to think what Christmas would be like. Even if the government finally lifted the quarantine—which I flat-out didn't believe would happen— and I got to spend that holiday with my own family, the sense of loss would still cling to me.

No, I wasn't in the most thankful state of mind, and I probably came off as dull and standoffish. A few of the adults tried to engage me in conversation, but though I tried my best, words were hard to find and those conversations died before they were born. The only person I felt even mildly myself around—other than Luke and his mom—was Luke's cousin Marlene, but that was because she kind of reminded me of Piper, with her bubbly nature and her amazing facility for carrying on one-sided conversations.

Despite the gloom that hovered over me, I found that I couldn't help liking Marlene. She was charmingly unconventional, a combination of jock and artist. She was into rowing and volleyball, but she was also an avid painter and had apparently painted the portrait of her grandparents that hung over the mantelpiece of the gas fireplace. I know practically nothing about art, but I thought the painting was damn good and couldn't help being impressed. Marlene sat to my left at dinner and kept up an effortless stream of chatter, despite my own reticence.

"She started talking when she was in the womb," Luke teased, "and hasn't shut up since."

I leaned back out of the line of fire as Marlene tossed a crumbly bit of roll at him, something the three of us found more amusing than the adults did.

The condo was a pretty good size, considering this was Center City Philadelphia, but it still required a creative use of resources to find places for fifteen people to sleep. There was a lot of bed sharing going on, and Marlene and I had a couple of air mattresses packed into a study that was barely big enough to hold them. Bob, who'd tolerated the attentions of Missy the black Lab throughout the day, had apparently had enough and decided to join us, squeezing into the space under the desk and curling into a contented ball.

Marlene and I changed into our pj's, and I wondered what the chances were that I'd be able to sleep tonight. My body felt exhausted, and emotionally I was running on empty, but I feared what would happen when I closed my eyes. Today had been hard, but at least there'd been distractions. Those were all gone now—or at least, so I thought.

"Luke told me what happened to your dad," Marlene said, sitting cross-legged on her air mattress.

I froze, strangely startled. For all the talking Marlene had done today, the topics of conversation had never been serious. She'd told a lot of stories, most of which were funny, and she'd talked about books and TV shows and movies. I envied her facility with small talk and wasn't prepared for her suddenly grave tone.

"Are you tired enough to sleep yet," she continued, "or do you want to stay up awhile?"

My throat tightened and I shrugged. I wouldn't have been able to get words out even if I could think of any.

"I've never lost anyone like that myself," Marlene said, "but my best friend lost her mom in a drunk-driving accident last year. I know she's kind of a mess on holidays, so I imagine it's tough on you, too."

I let out a shuddering sigh. "You could say that." I tried to return Marlene's kind smile, but I doubted I did a very convincing job of it.

"If you don't want to talk, that's fine. I just wanted you to know that you *can* talk if you want to."

For all the time I'd spent lately wishing I had someone my own age to talk to—someone other than Luke, who came with other complications—Marlene was still basically a stranger to

245

me, and I wasn't inclined to open my heart to her. However, I wasn't inclined to lie down and be alone with my thoughts, either, and I wished I were better with small talk.

"Thanks," I said. "But I don't think talking about it is going to help right now."

"Like I said, that's fine." She flashed me another smile, and I could see no hint of hurt or irritation in her. "But we don't have to talk about gloomy stuff if you don't want to. If I'm being annoying and you just want me to shut up and let you sleep, let me know. I promise I won't take it personally."

"You're not being annoying," I hastened to assure her. "I just kind of suck at small talk."

Marlene laughed and waved off my concern. "I talk enough for three people. At least that's what my folks say. I'm always happy to have an audience that actually listens to me."

I laughed, despite the heaviness in my heart.

"You're a hell of a lot easier to talk to than Luke's *last* girlfriend," Marlene continued with a roll of her eyes. "I mean, I talk a lot, I know, but it's not always about myself. I actually find other people interesting too."

I didn't know which part of that statement to react to first. When my dad had bad-mouthed Piper, I'd always been quick to leap to her defense, but my feelings for her were such a jumbled mess right now I couldn't even tell if I *wanted* to defend her. So I tackled the easier subject first.

"I'm not Luke's girlfriend." I could feel the heat rising in my cheeks, knew Marlene would have no trouble seeing my easy blush. But one kiss—okay, a whole bunch of kisses, but all in the space of just a few minutes—didn't make me into Luke's girlfriend. "We're just friends and neighbors is all."

Marlene raised an eyebrow and cocked her head. "Oh really?" she asked, with infinite skepticism.

The heat in my face intensified. "Really." I *wanted* to be Luke's girlfriend, but even if I could convince myself that he was genuinely interested in me that way, there was still the issue of Piper. Obviously, he didn't want her the way she was now, but I would still feel like I was betraying my best friend if I took advantage of what had happened to her to steal her boyfriend.

"I've known Cousin Luke since we were both in diapers," Marlene said. "I've never seen him look at a 'friend' the way he looks at you."

I blinked in surprise at that. I'd never noticed Luke looking at me in any special way. I wouldn't have been surprised if Marlene had caught *me* looking at *him* like some love-struck puppy, but not the other way around.

"He's still technically with Piper," I said, but it sounded lame even to me.

"Even if Piper hadn't gone off the deep end, there was no way they were going to be together much longer. Luke was too loyal to dump her, but believe me, he was getting tired of some of the shit she pulled."

Marlene was obviously another entry on the short list of people who didn't like Piper. The pre-night Piper, that is. There wasn't much to like about what Piper had become now.

Marlene gave me a long, speculative look that made me want to squirm. Then she said, "I'll tell you a secret, but you have to promise you won't tell Luke I told you. He'd kill me."

It sounded like this secret was one that wasn't hers to tell, and if I were being honorable I'd have urged her not to share it. If Luke had secrets, that was his business, not mine. But there's a difference between knowing the right thing to do and actually doing it.

"I won't say a word," I promised.

"Pinkie swear, cross your heart, hope to die, all that stuff?"

I laughed at her earnestness. "Absolutely."

She leaned forward conspiratorially and lowered her voice as if she thought someone might be listening in. "Luke always really liked Piper, and they had fun together and all, but she was never really the one he wanted."

"Huh?"

"He's had a crush on you for, like, forever."

"What?" I squeaked, sure I must have heard her wrong.

"I kept telling him he should ask you out if he liked you so much, but he was convinced you weren't interested. He said you would barely give him the time of day and that you avoided him whenever you could. I always suspected that didn't mean what he thought it meant, but he thought it would be too awkward if he asked you out and you said no, what with you living so close and seeing so much of each other."

I hate to think what color my face had turned by now. My mom had always warned me that some people who don't know better confuse shyness for aloofness or unfriendliness. But somehow it had never occurred to me that Luke might have interpreted my shyness around him as meaning I wasn't interested.

"No way," I said, fighting against the warmth of hope that tried to kindle in my belly. "You're just making this up. Trying to play matchmaker or something." Or maybe distract me from the misery of my first Thanksgiving without my dad.

Marlene snorted. "If I didn't already know he was interested, there wouldn't be much point in playing matchmaker.

It's not like he's going to go out with someone just because I told him to. We're close, but we're not *that* close."

I shook my head in helpless denial.

"Piper made it easy for him," Marlene continued. "She gave him plenty of evidence she was interested, so asking her out was zero risk. He's a really good guy, but like most guys his ego can be surprisingly fragile sometimes."

I swallowed hard, remembering how he had kissed me, how natural and right it had felt. I'd been telling myself it was an act of pity, a heat-of-the-moment impulse he surely regretted, but maybe it wasn't *his* fragile ego that was at issue here.

"I'm sorry if telling you all that makes things more complicated for you," Marlene said, a furrow of concern between her brows. "Maybe I should have kept my big mouth shut. But as you may have noticed, keeping my mouth shut isn't one of my strong suits."

I laughed weakly. "Don't apologize. I'm glad you told me. I just . . . need some time to rethink everything. I always thought *he* wasn't interested in *me*. But even if we're both interested, it's still complicated."

"Because of Piper."

"Yeah."

We both fell silent.

The condo was on the twentieth floor of an impressively tall building, and the study had a nice view of the Delaware, with no other tall buildings in sight, so neither Marlene nor I had thought to close the blinds. There was a sudden loud tapping sound on the window that made both of us jump and gasp.

Bob catapulted out of his den beneath the desk, snarling and jumping at the window. It was too dark out to see much of anything, but there was a flurry of tapping sounds, and a shadow crossed the window, skittering downward. The tapping sound continued, fading away as the whatever-it-was made its way down the building, presumably heading for the sidewalk.

It was always possible it had been just some random night construct having fun with the people in the building, tapping at windows and generally terrorizing them. It might have had nothing to do with me at all.

But I couldn't help the creeping suspicion that something had been sent there for me. That it had been watching me. *Spying* on me. And the thought that it might have overheard that particular conversation and might report it back to Piper or Aleric wasn't comfortable at all.

# CHAPTER TWENTY-THREE

Marlene was fast asleep and Bob was snoring so loudly I was surprised he hadn't awakened the whole household. It was after two in the morning, and I had yet to come close to finding peace and falling asleep. My eyes were gritty and my whole body felt about fifty percent heavier than usual, but my mind didn't care how tired my body was.

Marlene had been quick to dismiss the sounds at our window as just another episode of the city's night madness, but I couldn't shake the feeling that that creature had been here specifically for me. Maybe I was being paranoid or egocentric—I really, really hoped I was—but I doubted it. As far as I could tell from the news, the madness in the night was impersonal, the constructs and the Nightstruck attacking anyone who had the bad luck to cross their paths, rather than targeting individuals. But Piper—and Aleric, too—wanted me in particular. I hadn't seen Piper since the night she and her new friends lured my dad out to his death, but I was under no illusion that she was through with me.

My overnight bag was wedged between the head of my air bed and the wall, my dirty clothes sitting rolled up on top of it. If it had been any farther away, I might not have heard the ding of a text message coming through over Bob's persistent snoring.

There was no one who would legitimately send me a text at two in the morning. Which meant I should ignore it, on the assumption that it had to be a wrong number. Maybe if I were even a tiny bit closer to sleep I would have, but instead I dug my phone out of my bag and squinted at the message in the darkness.

I'll call in 5. Answer, or U won't have house 2 go home 2.

I shuddered and hugged myself. I didn't recognize the number, but I knew it had to be Piper. If she wanted to make a call or send a text, she would simply steal someone's cell phone. I wondered if the phone's true owner was still alive.

I wondered, but if the answer was no, I didn't want to know.

It goes without saying that I had no desire to talk to Piper. Ever again, unless she came back to herself. But she was not a construct, and that meant she could get into my house if she could find a way around all the locks, which I had of course changed since learning Aleric had Dad's keys. Hell, even if she couldn't find a way in, she could probably find a way to burn the house down from the outside. It wouldn't matter to her that she'd probably take out the entire row of houses in the process.

Not wanting to risk being responsible for another horror, I slipped quietly out of my bed and tiptoed out of the study. There were people sleeping in every room of the house except the bathrooms, so I made my way to the nearest one and prayed it wouldn't be occupied.

I was in luck—the bathroom was empty. I slipped inside and

locked the door, then turned on the light and squinted in the sudden brightness. I would have to keep my voice down, no matter what Piper said, or the people sleeping in the living room would hear me.

I didn't want to sit on the commode, so instead I sat on the floor with my back resting against the wall. I stared at my phone, which I had put in silent mode, and tried to control my dread. Just the *thought* of hearing Piper's voice was enough to make me shudder. Even if somehow, through some miracle, she could be restored to herself, could become the pre-night Piper again, I doubted I could ever be her friend again. Maybe that wasn't fair of me; maybe she was just a victim of the night and shouldn't be held responsible for her actions. But fairness didn't much matter. Technically it was the goat that had killed my father, but it was Piper who had arranged it all, and I would never, ever forgive her for that.

My phone lit up and buzzed, and I had to close my eyes to stave off a wave of nausea. I didn't know how I could manage having a conversation with Piper right now, but I couldn't let her take my house away from me. Not that I could stop her, if she had other demands I couldn't meet or if she just wanted to do it to hurt me.

I answered but couldn't force myself to speak, just sat there silently with my heart thumping so loudly I felt like I was walking through the giant beating heart at the Franklin Institute. It was a display meant to teach kids about how the heart worked, but it had always freaked me out.

"Hey there, Becks," Piper said in a cheerful, upbeat voice that made me want to reach through the phone and strangle her. "Did you have a nice Thanksgiving?" I still couldn't find my voice, but as usual that didn't bother Piper. "I hear you had a lovely dinner with my boyfriend and his family. Luke loves them to death, I know, but I was never what you call impressed. Especially with that Cousin Marlene of his." I could almost hear the eye-roll. "Impossible to get a word in edgewise around that one."

It was a lovely irony to hear Piper complaining that someone else talked too much, but I had the feeling she expected me to comment on it, so I didn't. I didn't want to give her the slightest shred of satisfaction. I'd answered her call because I felt that I had to, but so far I saw no reason I actually had to talk to her.

Piper let out a huge, dramatic sigh. "Okay, okay. I know you're mad at me. And I know this had to have been a really hard day for you. First Thanksgiving without your dad and all."

It was all I could do to maintain my stony silence, and my teeth ground together so hard it made my head ache. But again, there was no need to give her the satisfaction.

"I'm telling you, Becks, you have no idea how much better you'll feel if you just let it all go. Being out in the night, being part of it . . . Well, words can't describe how awesome it is. It would be awesome even if your everyday life was all roses and sunshine, but when your life sucks like it does now . . ." Another big sigh. "You're torturing yourself, clinging to the past, for no reason."

"I'm not torturing myself!" I protested, unable to hold the words back. "*You're* the one who's torturing me." A sob stole any other words I might have said, and I hated myself for not being able to stay in control.

"I know that's how it looks from where you stand, Becks," Piper said, and if I didn't know better I would have sworn there was a hint of sympathy in her voice. "It's tough love in the extreme, but I'm really trying to help you. You belong out here. You deserve a life without cares or worries or responsibilities. A life steeped in magic and power and just plain fun. That's what I want for you, and as far as I can tell, the only way to get it for you is to make it impossible for you to tolerate the day."

I laughed bitterly. "Yeah, right. You killed my father in a selfless act of charity."

I could hear Piper's smile in her voice. "I never said it was selfless. I love my new life, but I don't want to give up all my friends to have it. Some of them have to go because they're not suited to it."

"Like Luke you mean?" I asked. I remembered she had told me once before that Luke would not be welcome, but I hadn't thought much about what that might mean.

"Yeah, he's a no-go. Too much of a goody-goody for this kind of life."

It was against my better judgment to engage Piper in conversation, but I had to admit I had a lot of questions about the night world and about what had happened to the people who were lost to it. Whether I could trust Piper's answers or not was a whole other question.

"So what am I, some kind of bad girl?" I asked, genuinely curious why Piper and Aleric seemed to think I was a good candidate to join them.

"It's not that you're a bad girl," Piper said. "It's just that you have the potential to be one. If you'd been raised by different parents, or maybe even if you'd just gone to a different school, you'd be a very different person right now. You have the makings of a hell-raiser, even if so far you've managed to shout all those feelings down."

"That's ridiculous," I argued, but I wasn't so sure. I'd been on a very different road back in the days when I was in middle school, tormented by my peers, called Becky the Brain by everyone I knew, and reviled for it. My parents had left me in that school for two long years after the bullying began, because they thought sending me to a private school would make them into snobs. I had been so very angry, at the bullies, at the school that couldn't—or wouldn't—stop them, and at my parents, who couldn't see past their personal prejudices to realize keeping me there was a terrible idea.

If I'd stayed at that school, if the world had continued to add more fuel to the anger that had been building inside me . . .

"Tell yourself it's ridiculous, if it makes you feel better," Piper said. "It's not my fault you don't like the answer to your question."

*It doesn't matter,* I told myself. *You are who you are now, not who you might have been.* But I knew my mind would circle back to the subject again and again and again.

"Why was it so important to you that I pick up the phone?" I asked. "Just so you could have some more fun poking sticks at me?"

"I'm not poking sticks at you," Piper said, with exasperation in her voice. "Like I said, I'm trying to help you. Trying to get you to the place where you feel better and all of this shit stops hurting so much."

I wondered if she was aware of her own hypocrisy, then decided it wouldn't matter if she was. She'd say anything, do anything, to get what she wanted. And apparently what she wanted was me.

"But it's obvious you aren't convinced yet," Piper continued. "You seem to like Marlene. How terrible would you feel if something happened to her and it was all because you were too selfish to do the right thing and give yourself up?"

My hand clenched on the phone, and my heart gave a nasty thump. "Don't you dare—"

"But maybe you'd be okay as long as you still had Luke. I wouldn't want you to put too much faith in the bullshit Marlene was feeding you. Luke was all mine, and would have been mine as long as I wanted him. He's into you now because he's on the rebound, and because, hey, you're available. I know you know all that, but I bet you still have hopes that you and he will, like, get married and have babies and live happily ever after or some such shit."

"I'm hanging up now," I said through gritted teeth, but I didn't actually do it.

"I'm going to take out everyone you care about," Piper said. "I'm glad you've met Luke's family, because that'll give me a nice pool of victims to choose from. One by one, I'll take them away from you, until you have no one left. Let's see how many losses your conscience can take before you realize you really have no choice.

"Call this number and let me know when you're ready to give in. And try to remember that, no matter how much it hurts, everything I'm doing is for your own good. I'm still your friend, and I'll be here for you whenever you're ready."

In the end, it was Piper who hung up.

# CHAPTER TWENTY-FOUR

I didn't get a whole lot of sleep after getting off the phone with Piper, so when Dr. Gilliam drove me back to my house, I practically fell asleep in the car. We had to drive most of the way across Center City to get home, and it looked nothing like any other Black Friday in my life. The sun didn't rise till around seven these days, so there were no early-morning sales to bring people out in droves. Stores were open—most of them at least—but there were very few customers visible through their windows.

The city's maintenance workers did their best, but there was no keeping up with the destruction and mess the Nightstruck and the constructs caused when the sun was down. Broken glass littered the streets and sidewalks, piles of litter blew in the breeze, and graffiti—much of it obscene—was everywhere.

Piper's call, my lack of sleep, and the dismal sight of the city combined to sink my mood to an all-time low, and I couldn't wait to get home and close myself in my room for a little alone time. There are times when you want to talk about your problems and times when you want to hide from them. This was the latter.

It wasn't as hard to park on the streets these days as it used to be, so Dr. Gilliam was able to find a spot right in front of her house. She invited me to spend the day with her and Luke, as I usually did when she wasn't at work, but I pleaded exhaustion and said I just wanted to go home and sleep for a few hours.

Luke was too much of a gentleman to let me carry my own bag, so he took my overnight bag and I took Bob and we crossed to my house through the courtyard.

A nasty surprise awaited me. When we turned the corner onto the patio right outside my back door, we found a tall ladder propped against the wall and a sprinkling of broken glass below it. With a sinking feeling in the pit of my stomach, I looked up.

Someone had broken the glass out of one of the windows on the second floor. I didn't know what had happened to the towel rack bars my dad had installed, but they weren't there anymore. I supposed they weren't all that hard to get around, as long as you didn't have to worry about a vicious German shepherd getting in your face or about the neighbors calling the police.

Under ordinary circumstances, I would have immediately backed away and called the police myself. As the daughter of the police commissioner, I certainly knew better than to enter a house when there was such clear evidence it had been broken into. However, I knew exactly who had broken that window, who had invaded my home, and it wasn't anyone who could still be hanging around now, in the daylight. I didn't know where the Nightstruck disappeared to during the day—no one did—but for sure it wasn't my house.

I took out my keys with a shaking hand. Luke laid a hand on my shoulder.

"That's probably not a great idea, Becks," he said.

Even in the midst of my growing rage and dread, I felt a little hint of warmth at hearing him call me by the nickname. Only close friends and family called me Becks, and I couldn't remember ever hearing Luke do it before.

"We both know who did it and that they're not hanging around," I said, twitching away from his hand while trying not to be rude about it.

"Yeah, but we don't know that no one else took advantage of the opportunity to go in," Luke argued.

Technically he was right. But I figured most of the burglars and thieves in our city had been subsumed by the night already and weren't likely hanging out in my house. Also, the police department had more than enough on their plates already without wasting their time on what was probably nothing.

"We have Bob," I reminded him as I unlocked my back door. I took a deep breath to steady myself, not knowing what horror to expect, before pushing the door open and stepping inside. Not surprisingly, Luke stayed right on my heels.

The good news was that we didn't find any blood or dead bodies. The bad news was . . . well, everything else.

Piper and her night-dwelling friends had been thorough. Every stick of furniture in the house was broken. Every cushion and pillow and bed was gutted. Every wall—and in some places even the ceiling—was covered in foul graffiti. Every dish and mirror and knickknack was smashed, every piece of electronic equipment spilling its wiry metal guts.

She'd ransacked my room and my dad's room, shredding every stitch of clothing. She'd torn pages out of all the books and had even torn up the cute kiddie pictures my sister and I had drawn. Dad said he was storing them so he could trot them out to embarrass us if ever we brought home a boyfriend. He even followed through on that threat with Beth once. I remembered, because my mom had picked a fight about it, irritated with him because Beth was irritated.

As if all that wasn't enough, the place reeked of spilled booze, cigarette smoke, pot, and urine.

Luke tried to coax me away, but I wasn't willing to leave until I'd taken full stock of the damage that had been done. Maybe it was like poking at a sore tooth and I should have stopped, but I couldn't bear not knowing.

Except for what I was wearing and the change of clothes in my overnight bag, everything I owned was destroyed. The house itself might be salvageable—I'd have to have someone come look at it and see—but everything inside it was irreparably ruined.

"Let's go," Luke said gently when we had explored every room. He took my arm and guided me toward the staircase. "My mom and I will take care of calling someone to come clean this up. You've been through enough without having to deal with that."

I followed him willingly enough, too numb to argue, even though I thought I should. It had been my choice last night not to give in to Piper's demands, and it was up to me to deal with the consequences of that choice.

I knew I was in bad shape, because I didn't even feel tempted to cry. Not when I saw the house, not when Luke and I hurried back to his place to tell his mom what had happened. Not when Dr. Gilliam hugged me and assured me everything was going to be all right. Not even when they finally left me alone in the guest room to get some rest while they made calls on my behalf.

. . .

The rest of Black Friday wasn't much better. I probably should have gone out and done some shopping so I at least had a few possessions to my name, but I was too dispirited to manage it. I finally broke through the tear barrier when I had to call my mom and tell her what had happened to the house. Dr. Gilliam had done some research for me while I was moping in the guest room and had determined that it would cost something around an arm and a leg to repair the damage to the house, although of course none of the contractors she talked to would come right out and give an estimate sight unseen.

Whatever the total bill turned out to be, it would be way more than I could take care of myself. I was getting by using a credit card on my mom's account, but I wouldn't be able to use it for the repairs, and I wouldn't have access to any of Dad's money until the will had gone through probate, which was going to take forever, thanks to the death toll and the shortened workdays. Mom was going to have to handle paying for the repairs from a distance.

My mom was warmer and more nurturing on that call than I'd ever known her to be before, and I desperately wanted to cuddle up in her arms and let her take care of everything. Dr. Gilliam was being great, and I was incredibly thankful I had her, but she wasn't my mom. I felt like a little girl again, and not in a good way. I cried ugly while clinging to the phone like it was a lifeline.

After that ordeal was over and I had at least marginally calmed myself, I thought again about the call I'd had with Piper last night.

I felt robbed and violated by what Piper had done to my house, but she'd threatened to do far, far worse if I didn't give in. She'd threatened Luke and his whole family, and I knew the threats weren't idle. For as long as I resisted, Luke and his family would be in grave danger, and that was a hard concept to live with.

I couldn't, in good conscience, keep the threat to myself, so I told Dr. Gilliam about Piper's call. I had no idea where I would go if she decided I was too hot to handle, and I didn't know if my going somewhere else would in any way help, but I offered.

"You're not going anywhere," Dr. Gilliam told me firmly.

"But if me being here puts you all in danger—"

"What's the alternative?" she interrupted. "Piper didn't threaten to hurt us because you were with us, she threatened to hurt us because she thought it would hurt you. That's not going to change if you go somewhere else."

"Maybe I should just give in," I said. It was the first time I'd allowed myself even to think that, but if I were the good, unselfish person I liked to think I was, shouldn't I do everything in my power to protect those I cared about? Those who were in danger only because of me?

"Never!" Dr. Gilliam said, taking my shoulders and giving them a little shake. I had never seen her look so fierce. "You don't deal with bullies by giving in to them. That just makes them demand more." Her expression softened. "None of this is your fault, Becket."

But of course it *was*. I hadn't told her about my conversation with Aleric, about my realization that I had unwittingly invited this evil into our city. I might not have done anything wrong, but that didn't mean it wasn't my fault.

"Do you really think it would help anything if you ran out and became one of the Nightstruck?" Dr. Gilliam persisted. "You've seen more than enough of them, of what they do. Is that what you want to be?"

"Of course not!" I snapped, then reeled my temper back in. Piper had said that if I joined the Nightstruck, the pain would all go away. I'd stop grieving for my dad, I'd stop being scared, I'd stop worrying about other people. Maybe there was just a tiny kernel of temptation buried beneath a truckload of denial.

"We'll take extra precautions," Dr. Gilliam promised me. "But sacrificing you is not an option."

I bit my lip and nodded my agreement. If I could have been sure Luke and the rest of his family would be safe if I gave in, then I might have put more consideration into actually giving myself up. But who knew what would happen to me if the night got its hooks in me? I thought I was a pretty good, nice person, but the night would take all of that away from me. Piper had been a pretty good person—if not exactly perfect—before the night took her, and look at what she had become! Who was to say I wouldn't be a threat to Luke and his family myself, just as Piper was a threat to me?

No, I was just going to have to live with the guilt of being a danger to Luke and his family. And hope Piper didn't manage to make it exponentially worse before someone somewhere figured out how to return the city to normal.


Luke's mom was home for the entire Thanksgiving weekend, and though she was obviously glad for the rest—like my dad, she'd been working so hard the strain was showing on her—I could tell she also felt guilty about taking any time off. I'm sure if she hadn't been ordered to stay home she would have been out working every night, just as she had been practically every night since the quarantine began.

On Monday night she went back to work. It was the first

time Luke and I were going to spend any significant time alone together since Marlene's startling revelations. Revelations that Piper had denied, of course, but under the circumstances, I was far more likely to take Marlene's word than Piper's.

If Marlene was telling the truth and Luke had been into me all along, did that change anything? Surely it at least meant that I should stop questioning his motivation in kissing me the other night. Surely it meant it hadn't been out of pity or anything like that.

With school on an indefinite hiatus, and with me being unable to leave the house once the sun set, there was very little to do in the evenings. If I were home by myself, I probably would have spent hours with my nose buried in a book, but it seemed rude to do that and just ignore Luke in his own home. Not that I was capable of ignoring Luke when Marlene's words kept swirling around in my head. I was painfully aware of him at all times.

I was desperate for distractions, afraid I was acting totally weird and giving my turmoil away. I wanted to ask Luke if what Marlene had said was true, but I couldn't think of a subtle way to sneak the question in, and I didn't have it in me to just blurt it out. When you came right down to it, I had way too much self-doubt to believe a guy like him could be into me, kiss or no kiss.

We spent some time after dinner playing video games, but I stink at them in the best of circumstances. Apparently I stink even more when I'm distracted. My reflexes were too slow, and I couldn't seem to remember which control did what. Luke gave no sign that my ineptness bothered him, but he couldn't be having a whole lot of fun with the nonexistent level of competition I was giving him.

"Why don't you just play and I watch," I suggested, after

crashing and burning within about five seconds of starting a racing game set to its easiest level. I put my controller down on the coffee table and willed myself to start acting more normal. Any minute now he was going to ask me what was the matter, and I was probably going to blush so red I glowed.

Luke tossed his own controller aside. "I'm kind of sick of all my games anyway," he said, getting up to turn off his PlayStation. "I'm ready for Christmas and a new batch."

I think he was just saying that for my benefit, but I wished he would keep playing. Surely if he was playing a game, I'd be able to fade gracefully into the background. After everything Luke and I had been through together, I had finally started to feel at least mildly comfortable around him, but Marlene's revelation had turned me right back into the tongue-tied, self-conscious idiot I'd been at the start.

And then, after he'd turned the console off, came the moment I'd been dreading. Luke sat next to me on the couch, cocked his head, and asked the Question.

"Is something wrong? Other than the obvious, I mean. You seem . . . I don't know, distracted."

I forced a smile that I'm sure looked completely fake. "I'm fine," I lied, but the heat in my cheeks meant I had not a chance of convincing him.

Luke looked down at his hands, a worried expression on his face. "I screwed everything up the other night, didn't I?"

"Huh?" I genuinely had no idea what he was talking about. I was too absorbed in my own turmoil to consider the possibility that he might be having some of his own.

"I shouldn't have kissed you," he said, and I recoiled. Since he was looking at his hands, he didn't see my reaction. Which was just as well, because I'm sure I was turning even redder than I'd been already, and my eyes might have been getting a little shiny.

Luke regretted kissing me. So much for Marlene's story of unrequited love. It shouldn't hurt so much, not compared to everything else I'd been through lately, but the pain of rejection took my breath away. How stupid and naïve had I been to think he'd want *me* after he'd had Piper?

"I didn't mean to make things all awkward and complicated between us," Luke continued, and he finally turned his head to look at me. When he got a glance at my face, his eyes went wide with alarm. He reached out and took my hand, which was clenched into a white-knuckled fist as I tried to reel in all my raging emotions. I couldn't have forced a word out of my throat if I'd tried.

"Shit," Luke said. "I'm screwing things up again." I shook my head in denial. "Yes I am," he said, squeezing my hand. Then he took a deep breath. "I'm sorry I made things awkward. I assumed that was because I kissed you and it made you uncomfortable. I'm not actually sorry I kissed you."

"You're not?" I asked in a breathless whisper. A fragile hint of hope sparked in my chest. Hope had been in short supply lately, and I hardly dared allow it into my life.

Luke reached up and brushed the fingers of his free hand down my cheek. "Not if you're not."

My throat was still all tight and achy. I swallowed hard to try to push the lump down and moved a little closer to him on the couch so I could let him know without words how not sorry I was.

He leaned into me, eyes locked with mine. My heart did a happy little skip. I'd gone from gloomy to giddy in no time flat. When his lips brushed tentatively across mine, all coherent thought fled my mind, replaced by sensation and awareness.

There was tension in that first kiss, as if he couldn't quite believe that I had no objection, but the little sigh that escaped my lips clued him in fast enough. He gathered me into his arms, holding me close, sharing the delicious warmth of his body as he deepened the kiss. It felt so good it left my senses reeling, as every nerve in my body came tingling to life all at once.

The rest of the world ceased to exist. All the pain, all the fear, all the stress—they all fell away as I lost myself in the press of his lips, the stroke of his tongue, the caress of his hands. I had wanted this for so long, dreamed about this for so long, but had never really believed it would happen.

Hope crept around the barriers I had built to protect myself. Hope that maybe, somehow, things weren't as awful as they seemed, that my capacity for happiness hadn't been completely destroyed. Hope that there was a future, one that was infinitely brighter than the miserable present.

Bob interrupted our kiss before it had a chance to get too hot and heavy, his cold wet nose nudging at us in an uncharacteristic demand for attention.

"Not now, Bob," I said, trying to push him away. He whined softly and pawed at my leg, making himself impossible to ignore.

Luke sighed softly, but instead of getting irritated, he reached out and scratched behind Bob's ear. "Poor guy. There's been an awful lot of change in your life and you don't have the benefit of understanding what it's all about."

I was super disappointed that we weren't kissing anymore, but I swear I could feel my heart swelling. There was something about Luke showing compassion for my dog that just made me want to burst.

Luke put his arm around me and settled me close by his side. Bob tried to wriggle his head in between us, but Luke's compassion didn't go quite that far. Bob had to settle for laying his head on our legs and looking up at us with sad, soulful eyes.

"Why do I have a feeling we're being played?" I grumbled, but the sad dog eyes were a weapon I'd never been able to resist.

Bob sighed in bliss when we both began scratching his ears. We shared a little smile that warmed me from the inside out. My pulse was still pattering from the kissing, and I very much wanted to do more of it. But there was something surprisingly romantic and intimate about snuggling on the couch with him like this, even if we did have a furry chaperone. I wasn't sure if a couple of hot kisses made me Luke's official girlfriend, but I was pretty sure the way he was holding me did. For the moment, at least, that was all that mattered.

# CHAPTER TWENTY-FIVE

Luke's mom usually came home from her megashift at about eight A.M. It had become my habit to fix her a light meal, either breakfast or some leftovers from the night before, so that she could get something nutritious into her system before crashing for the day and then repeating the whole process the next night. It's not like I'm a wannabe chef or anything, despite the amount of cooking I'd been doing lately; it was just that there was so little I could do to repay the Gilliams for everything they were doing for me, being my surrogate family and even giving me a home when Piper had trashed my own. It felt like the least I could do.

I had set up to make omelets as soon as Dr. Gilliam got home, having beaten the eggs, chopped up some onions, sliced some mushrooms, and grated some cheese. Everything was ready so that I could get started the instant she came in the door. She would be exhausted and longing for her bed, so if I kept her waiting too long she'd skip the meal, as I'd learned from experience.

As I said, usually she got home around eight o'clock, having left the hospital the instant the Transition swept over the city. There was some variation, of course. Sometimes she had traffic or roadblocks to contend with, or she had a patient she couldn't leave immediately. So I wasn't particularly surprised or worried when eight o'clock came and went without her appearing.

"Let me text her and see how long she thinks she'll be," Luke said, but he got no answer when he tried. Also not particularly alarming. If she was with a patient, she very likely wouldn't answer the text until she was done.

But whether it was intrinsically alarming or not, I think both Luke and I were alarmed anyway. How could we not be, when we both had Piper's threat hanging over our heads? We told each other there was nothing to worry about, each trying to soothe the other, but I don't think my reassurances were any more convincing to Luke than his were to me.

It was almost 8:45 when we both finally heard the sound of a key in the lock. The relief that flooded me was so strong you'd have thought I'd just gotten a stay of execution. If I had had to deal with Dr. Gilliam getting killed by the Nightstruck because of me, I honestly didn't know how I could have borne the guilt.

My relief was short-lived. The moment Dr. Gilliam walked in the door, the blood drained from my face and Luke made an incoherent sound of dismay.

"Neither of you panic," Dr. Gilliam said, her voice sounding raw and exhausted. "I'm going to be fine."

Her eye was blackened, her lip was swollen, and there was a sizable bandage on her forehead. Her left arm was in a sling, and her stiff, uncomfortable-looking walk spoke of further injuries we couldn't see.

"What happened?" Luke choked out. He looked like he wanted to hug her but was afraid he might hurt her. I didn't blame him.

Dr. Gilliam's eyes shifted briefly to me, then away. That quick, furtive glance filled me with dread. Whatever had happened to her had to do with me. I was sure of it.

"Why don't we all sit down," she said, dropping into the recliner with a groan and a sigh.

Luke and I sat on the sofa facing her, neither one of us relaxing into the cushions. Bob sensed the tension in the room and came over to rest his head on my legs. I obediently started scratching behind his ears. I know petting dogs is supposed to help lower blood pressure, but there wasn't much hope of that working here.

"What happened?" Luke asked again, more grimly this time.

Dr. Gilliam grimaced and looked at me. "I almost talked myself into lying about this to try to spare you. I hope I'm doing the right thing by telling the truth."

"So it was about me?" I asked, my voice going weak. A comforting lie might have been nice, but I wasn't sure I'd have believed it anyway. Maybe Dr. Gilliam realized that.

She nodded. "The Nightstruck kidnapped a man and his daughter. They beat him up and stabbed him, then promised they would let his daughter go unharmed if he came into the emergency room and got me outside somehow.

"There's a lot of security in the hospital these days, of course, but it's almost all focused on keeping the Nightstruck out, not on keeping anyone in. The guy jumped me and knocked me out." She pointed at the bandage on her forehead. "He carried me outside and handed me over. The only reason I survived is that one of the nurses saw him carrying me out and called security. They were able to chase the Nightstruck away, but as you can see, I'm a little worse for the experience. Still, I'm going to be fine. Nothing's broken, and I'm alive."

"Well, then, I guess everything's okay," I said bitterly, my hands balling into fists in my lap. Bob wasn't happy that I stopped petting him and stuck his cold, wet nose against one of those fists. "Stop it, Bob!" I snapped, jerking my hand away. He gave me a reproachful look, but he stopped nosing my hand and lay down at my feet.

"Becket, honey, I know you feel like this is all your fault, but I promise you it isn't. If Piper wasn't fixated on you, she'd probably be fixated on Luke instead. Our family would be vulnerable no matter what."

But I knew she was wrong. It was clear that Piper had lost all interest in Luke the moment she'd been Nightstruck. He was literally too good for her. So if it weren't for me, the Gilliams would be in no special danger.

Not to mention that I was directly responsible for the magic that had entered our city. There was no power on earth that could convince me this wasn't my fault.

Now if only there were something I could do about it. . . .

"Don't you for one heartbeat consider giving yourself up!" Dr. Gilliam said. "That is not an option. Understand?"

I nodded, because I *did* understand. I didn't know what I would turn into, what I would be like, if I was Nightstruck. The Gilliams were all I had left in this city, and I didn't think my long-standing crush on Luke would go away if I changed. Piper's obsession with me showed me exactly how toxic strong connections could become.

I guess my silent nod wasn't very convincing.

"I can't tell you how much it would hurt me if you gave

yourself up when you're under my protection," Dr. Gilliam said. "I promised your mother I'd take care of you. If I have to worry about you running off into the night while I'm gone, then I'm going to have to stop going to work."

"I won't run off into the night," I promised, mentally crossing my fingers, because I wanted to keep all my options open.

I couldn't help noticing that Luke hadn't said a word throughout this discussion. He didn't join in with his mother's pleas, he didn't tell me it wasn't my fault. He didn't even make any comforting gestures, like patting me on the back or holding my hand. Things he'd done easily and often before. I slanted a glance at him and saw that he was looking down and slightly away from me, as if hiding his face and the feelings it might reveal. You would never guess that just last night we'd been cuddled together on this very same couch, kissing.

I couldn't blame him. Not when his mother had been beaten up and almost killed because of me. But oh God, did it ever hurt. I wanted to think this was a temporary setback, that in a few hours—or maybe a few days—he'd find a way to overlook my role in his mom getting hurt, but I found I had no more optimism left in me. In one lightning-swift strike, Piper had taken Luke away from me, just when I'd finally allowed myself to hope he was mine.

I was more alone than I'd ever been.


I hit rock bottom that night. I hadn't thought I could sink any lower than I had right after my dad died, but I'd been wrong. Back then, in the good old days, I hadn't known that I was directly responsible for letting the night magic into the city. Grief is a horrible, miserable emotion, but it becomes downright toxic when you add guilt into the mixture.

I couldn't go on like this. As careful as Dr. Gilliam and Luke and the rest of their family might be, I had no doubt that Piper and the Nightstruck would get to them eventually. I was already drowning in guilt, and it was only going to get worse. Unless I did something about it.

But what could I do? I'd already determined that giving myself up wasn't an acceptable option. I supposed if I killed myself, that might be enough to make Piper lose interest in the Gilliams, but as low as I felt, I didn't feel *that* low. Besides, I couldn't do that to my mom and my sister. They'd already lost my dad—and I knew my mom was hurting pretty bad about that, despite the divorce and the hard feelings—and they didn't need me making things worse. And let's not even talk about what it would do to Dr. Gilliam and Luke, who were bound to feel responsible.

For the first few hours of that night, those were the only two options I could imagine, and they swirled around in my mind on an endless loop. Again and again I rejected them and ordered myself to come up with something better, but my own emotions kept getting in the way, overwhelming me and derailing any potential new chains of thought.

It wasn't until I finally lay down and tried to go to sleep that I realized there was a third alternative. One that made me break out in a cold sweat and made everything inside me recoil.

The Gilliams weren't in danger because of *me*. They were in danger because of *Piper*. And the one sure way to get them out of danger was to get rid of Piper.

I sat up in bed and hugged my knees to my chest, shivering and sweating, both at once.

It was an absurd thought.

Twice before I'd been faced with the prospect of shooting a fellow human being, and twice before I had balked. Sure, I'd pulled the trigger eventually, but it took the extraordinarily extenuating circumstances of my dad being killed before my eyes and of Aleric swearing the bullets wouldn't hurt him before I'd been able to do it. And these had all been strangers.

Was I honestly thinking of shooting Piper, my one-time best friend, in cold blood?

I tried to imagine what it would feel like to hold a gun on her, to pull the trigger, and my entire being cried out in horror and refusal. She had turned into a monster, but except for the green eyes and the awful hair, she still looked like the Piper I used to know. The girl who had never been put off by my shyness, who had such a gift for making me laugh, who had listened to me patiently when I'd complained about my parents' troubled marriage. That girl had had a lot of flaws, I won't deny it, but I'd loved her like a sister.

Realistically, I didn't hold out much hope that Piper or any of the rest of the Nightstruck could be restored to their original selves. They'd been changed by magic, and that was something completely out of human reach. I guess that meant I didn't hold out much hope that the city itself would go back to normal, either. Everyone liked to talk about the changes as if they were temporary, but I doubt I was the only one who feared this might be the "new normal."

But though logic told me it wasn't realistic, there would always be a part of me that would stubbornly cling to hope. Which meant there was part of me that thought Piper could be saved—unless, of course, I killed her, in which case that hope would die with her.

I took a few deep breaths in a vain effort to calm my racing pulse.

There was no way I could do this. No way. I was contemplating cold-blooded *murder*, for God's sake!

*Murder of someone who murdered your dad,* I reminded myself. *Murder of someone who's already tried to kill Dr. Gilliam once, and who you know is going to try to kill everyone you care about.*

If Piper were out of the picture, then Luke and Dr. Gilliam and the rest of the family would be safe. Well, as safe as anyone could be in this city.

My shaking stilled, though I was still sweating and my stomach seemed to be turning backflips inside me. I swallowed hard a couple of times to keep my gorge down.

For all my angst, for all my resistance, for all of my doubts, I'd known as soon as the idea had popped into my head that I had found the one and only viable solution to the problem of Piper. The one and only way to stop her from picking off anybody and everybody I had left.

The prospect was daunting in the extreme. I doubted it would be hard to get to Piper—all I had to do was call the cell phone she had stolen and tell her I was ready to give up. I had no doubt she'd believe me, believe my capitulation was a direct result of the attack on Dr. Gilliam. She would meet me, and I would take my gun with me and shoot her dead. In theory, at least.

But meeting her would mean going outside at night. There were nasty constructs and packs of Nightstruck roaming the streets, and they might not care that I was only stepping outside to turn myself in. I might be sending myself on a suicide mission. Worse, I had no idea what made ordinary people turn

Nightstruck, and there was always a chance that whatever it was might happen to me before I was able to carry out my plan. It obviously took more than just stepping outside during the night, because I'd done that on the night poor Mrs. Pinter was killed and I hadn't been swept away. But without knowing what triggered the change, it would be hard to avoid it happening.

By going after Piper, I'd be taking all the same risks. But at least, with my plan, they were risks rather than certainties. And the likelihood that the Gilliams would be safe as a result was a lot higher.

I slipped out of bed and began quietly getting dressed. Because of her injuries, Dr. Gilliam was not at work tonight, which meant I was going to have to sneak out of the house. I knew she would try to stop me if she had any clue what I was planning. Hell, what sane person *wouldn't* try to stop me? I could hardly believe what I was doing, and I almost talked myself out of it about a hundred times. But then I pictured Luke being restrained by some unseen creature while the demonic goat gored him, and I knew I couldn't just let that happen, that I was the only one who could stop it.

Steeling myself against the terrible images that kept flashing through my mind, I placed a call to Piper.


Bob raised his head and wagged his tail weakly as I crept through the living room toward the front door. He was still half asleep, and I hoped he would ignore me and drift back off. Instead, he yawned hugely, lurched to his feet, and trotted over to me. No doubt he thought it was time for his morning walk, although he hadn't been out in the dark for ages and there was still more than an hour left before sunrise.

I didn't know why Piper had set our rendezvous so close to dawn. When I'd called her, I'd hoped it would all be over, one way or another, by now, but she'd said she couldn't possibly make it until six thirty. I didn't ask what was keeping her so busy that she couldn't come meet me. I didn't want to know.

"Go back to sleep, Bob," I whispered, making a shooing motion toward his dog bed.

He just stood there, giving me hopeful eyes, waiting patiently for me to do his bidding. Anxiety tightened my chest, and I hoped the Gilliams would take good care of my dog if something happened to me. This scheme of mine was seeming crazier by the minute.

I'd spent the long hours of restless waiting writing a rambling explanation and farewell to Dr. Gilliam and Luke, as well as one for my mother and one for my sister. I didn't want to disappear on them without a trace, wanted them to have at least a little hint of closure if I didn't come back. I also wanted to be sure no one saw those letters unless absolutely necessary, so I handwrote them, hoping I'd be back home in time to scoop them up and destroy them before anyone read them.

I patted Bob's head and told him to stay. He made a high, thin whining sound when I walked away, and I wasn't sure if he was complaining about not getting his walk or if he was just worried about the crackling tension he sensed in me. At least he stayed put. He was still ultrasensitive to the Nightstruck and the constructs, and the last thing I wanted was for him to catch a glimpse of something and go berserk while I was trying to sneak out.

I put on my warmest coat and hat, sticking the gun in the coat's pocket. I put a box of ammo in the other, though I figured if I needed the extra ammo I was already doomed. Trying to stifle the practical part of my mind that told me this was the stupidest plan in the history of the universe, I opened the door and stepped out into the freezing night air.

Stepping outside felt like something momentous, but in reality the street was deserted, so nothing happened. I closed and locked the door behind me, then stuck my hands in my coat pockets in a vain attempt to keep them warm.

Piper had refused to meet me right outside the house and had told me I had to come to Rittenhouse Square, to the place where Billy the goat stood during the day. It was only a few blocks—a short walk, under ordinary circumstances. But these were not ordinary circumstances.

I forced myself to start moving forward, one foot in front of the other, getting my first good look at the changes that had taken place during the night.

Everything was at least marginally familiar, the buildings all the same size and approximately the same shape. But that was where the resemblance to the day ended. I looked over my shoulder at the Gilliam house, which seemed perfectly normal and ordinary on the inside. On the outside, however, it was a nightmare come to life. Instead of being made of brick, as it was in the day, the house's facade was constructed entirely of bones, some bright white in the moonlight, some yellow with age, some coated with dirt. Where the door knocker should have been, a naked skull leered out at me.

I shivered and told myself to keep moving, and I tried to give myself tunnel vision, to only look at the pavement before me so I wouldn't have to see my surroundings. However, I was also afraid that I would be attacked at any moment, and that made tunnel vision impossible.

The streetlamps had all turned into gallows, the nooses

swaying in a nonexistent breeze. The street signs looked fairly normal, until you read the words on them and realized they were encouraging acts of violence. The parking meters had eyes, and those eyes followed my every move. A toothy pothole cruised up and down Walnut Street like a shark awaiting unwary victims.

I passed a shop that I knew flew an American flag during the day. Apparently the shopkeeper didn't take the flag in at night like he was supposed to, and the thing had turned into a long, sinuous tongue that tried to lick me as I went by. I shuddered and hurried my steps.

Sirens wailed in the distance, almost comforting evidence that I was still in the world I knew, that there were people out there who dared to travel these streets at night. The occasional sound of gunfire revealed what a struggle those people faced as they tried to fight off the depredations of the Nightstruck.

I didn't see any Nightstruck, and at first I didn't see any constructs, either. Then, when I was about halfway to the square, I saw what I thought was a decorative trash can. I gave it a second look because it wasn't the normal city trash can and in fact looked much more like the kind that were in the square itself. Instead of being solid and blocky, the trash cans in the square are circular and made out of strips of metal. The strips flare at the top, creating an almost flowerlike opening.

Anyway, there was no reason for one of those trash cans to be sitting on the sidewalk on Walnut Street, and the thing was missing its requisite trash bag anyway. The hair on the back of my neck stood up, and I came to a sudden halt when what were supposed to be metal strips moved, the flared tops all turning like heads to look at me.

They turned like heads because they *were* heads. Snake

heads, to be exact. They hissed at me in unison, and the hydralike construct rose on stubby metal legs and trundled toward me.

I stood frozen to the sidewalk, staring in wide-eyed horror. I'm not one of those girls who runs screaming at the very thought of a snake. But this was far worse than an actual snake, and my gun would be useless against it.

*It's got short, stubby legs,* I told myself. *You can outrun it.*

It was between me and the square, so I would have to run past it instead of away from it, which was not a prospect I relished. Still, it was better than standing here waiting for it to reach me, so I darted forward, crossing the street at a diagonal to get as far away from it as possible.

I got past it easily enough, but I heard those stubby little legs clinking against the sidewalk as it pursued me. I ran as fast as I could, the cold air burning my throat and lungs. The construct kept up easily, and when I glanced over my shoulder I saw that it was only about a body length behind me, heads hissing and snapping at me.

One thing I have never been is an athlete. Adrenaline was giving me an extra boost, but I wasn't used to running, and though I kept pumping my arms and legs as hard as I could, I knew I was slowing down. I expected to feel the bite of those snakes' metal fangs at any moment, but though I didn't turn to check, it didn't sound like the construct was gaining on me.

Still I kept running, my pace getting slower and slower. And still the construct didn't gain on me. Was it possible the thing was getting tired just like I was? Or was it maybe closer to dawn than I thought and the magic that animated it was fading? But that couldn't be, because there was no hint of light in the sky.

Eventually I couldn't run anymore, and I came to a panting halt. I whirled around with my gun in hand, knowing it wouldn't hurt the construct but having no better way to defend myself.

To my surprise, the construct came to a halt as well, stopping when I was just out of reach of the closest snake heads. Its legs bent so that its bottom was resting on the sidewalk, for all the world like it was sitting down and waiting to see what I would do next.

Keeping my gun pointed at it, I took a couple of steps backward. It followed, then sat again when it was just out of reach. I then tried taking a couple of steps to my right, and again it mirrored my motion. I couldn't step any closer without being in striking range of the snakes, so that was an experiment I didn't try. I *did* try a quicker move to the side, intending to try to dart past it and go back the way I'd come.

I wasn't entirely surprised when the construct moved way quicker than seemed possible, to block my way.

It wasn't here to hurt me. It was here to herd me toward Piper. Maybe she thought I'd get cold feet and change my mind about meeting her.

I blew out a deep breath, searching for courage. There was no turning back now. But that didn't matter, because there was no way I was going to change my mind. I knew what I had to do.

I couldn't stand the idea of having the construct at my back, so for a little while I progressed toward the square in a weird sideways walk-shuffle-hop that was both slow and tiring, after my frantic run. I finally decided to bite the bullet and walk normally, my shoulders tight with strain, my entire body tensed for an attack from behind. But the construct kept its distance, herding me inexorably to my fate.

# CHAPTER TWENTY-SIX

During the day, Rittenhouse Square is a lovely, popular city park. Benches line the paths, and even in the winter the place is alive with greenery from trees and grass and bushes. At this time of year, the trees and streetlamps would usually be glittering with pretty white Christmas lights, but I supposed there was no point in putting up lights only the Nightstruck would see.

The square is usually bordered by short ornamental iron fencing, but in the night that fencing had tripled in height and was topped with knife-sharp spikes. There would be no entering from anything but one of the paved paths—not that I'd been planning on hopping the fence anyway.

I made my way around the square until I reached the entrance that was closest to the little plaza where Billy the goat made his daytime home. The city streets were scary enough at night, but the square was somehow even scarier. I couldn't help wondering if some of its other sculptures—like, say, the lion—had come to life in viciously altered form just like Billy. And, of course, I was worried there were more trash can hydras in there.

The hydra that had been following me hissed and snapped,

perhaps impatient with my hesitation. I triple-checked my gun to make sure it was ready to shoot. I wondered if I should just hold it in my hand as I marched into the square, but a gust of icy wind convinced me that was a bad idea. I doubted Piper being Nightstruck would make her any more punctual, and there was no point freezing my fingers off—maybe making them so numb it would affect my shooting.

That said, I doubted my ability to do a quick draw when I had to fumble around my coat pocket to find the gun, and I might just as easily shoot my own foot before I got the gun out. So I compromised, sticking both the gun and my hand in the pocket, fingers wrapped around the butt and the finger guard.

Another hiss from the hydra got me moving again, and I passed through the entrance into the square. The hydra didn't follow me, instead parking itself firmly in the middle of the path behind me, blocking the exit. I wondered if the other exits were similarly blocked and decided I had to assume the answer was yes.

The night magic didn't seem to affect living things, so the plants and the trees all looked the same. The park benches where people loved to sit and eat their lunches on a lovely day, however, had enlarged and now sprouted rows of teeth. They resembled nothing so much as Venus flytraps, waiting for an unwary insect to take their bait.

Out of curiosity—or a desire to stall—I felt around my left coat pocket and found what was left of a pack of gum. I tossed it at one of the benches And even though I'd expected it, I still jumped and screamed when the jaws slammed shut with an eardrum-shattering bang. I hoped the damn things were as sedentary as they looked.

Billy was normally situated on a plinth in the middle of a

small circular plaza relatively close to the edge of the square. With all the streetlamps turning into gallows, there was barely any light in the square, and I moved slowly, hoping my eyes would adjust. The glow from all the high-rises surrounding the square at least meant it wasn't pitch black. However, it was still dark enough that it would make shooting from any distance a challenge. I would have to get close enough to Piper that I couldn't miss.

I wasn't surprised that Billy wasn't on his plinth. Nor was I surprised that Piper wasn't there waiting for me. But I wasn't sure how I could bear to stand there alone in the dark, waiting for her to show up. I could barely see anything farther than about fifteen feet away from me, and I was chillingly aware of just how many bad things lurked in the darkness.

Still, it wasn't like I had a choice anymore. And with dawn now less than an hour away, there was only so long Piper could keep me waiting.

There was a semicircular stone bench in the plaza, and to all appearances it hadn't been changed by the night. I briefly considered sitting down, then decided I didn't trust appearances. Just because I didn't see any changes, it didn't mean the bench was harmless. I was probably too restless and nervous to sit anyway.

I saw no sign of any living creature, but I knew I was not alone. The square was alive with sounds, all of which came from somewhere beyond my limited range of sight. Many of them were the metal-on-brick sound of constructs walking on the paths. I could tell from the pattern of sound that some of them walked on four feet and some on two, but though I occasionally caught a shadowed glimpse of movement in the distance, I never saw anything clearly.

None of this did my nerves much good. Every time I heard a sound I jumped and whirled, wishing I could have a wall at my back so that there was at least one direction no one and nothing could sneak up on me from.

Thanks to the arctic blasts of wind, I couldn't feel my ears or my nose, and my cheeks were burning from the cold. I stamped my feet in a vain attempt to keep them from going numb, and I paced around the circle to stay as warm as humanly possible. I checked my watch approximately every thirty seconds, but, astoundingly, that didn't make Piper show up any quicker. If I weren't convinced that the various constructs in the square wouldn't allow it, I might have chickened out and left.

Finally, after what felt like forever, I heard a little *click-click-click* sound that was all too familiar: the sound of Billy's metal hooves trotting along the pavement. I turned toward the sound, straining both eyes and ears for any sign of Piper. I thought I heard the quiet thump of a human footstep, but Billy's clicks were too loud for me to be sure. I canted my body so whoever or whatever was approaching couldn't see my right side, then carefully eased the gun out of my coat pocket. I kept my arm down so that my leg blocked the gun from sight, holding my breath and waiting. I was shivering from cold and nerves, and in my heart of hearts I still wasn't sure I'd actually be able to go through with my plan.

Billy, in his almost demonic night incarnation, was the first to appear out of the darkness. Memories flashed through my mind, memories I had managed to keep mostly suppressed because I was unable to face them. I heard the sickening crunch of my father's bones as Billy rammed him, saw the blood that dripped off those horns and spines, felt the crushing sense of helplessness I'd suffered as I'd watched.

My shaking hand rose of its own volition, and for a moment I wasn't sure I was really present in my own body. My mind knew with perfect clarity that I should keep the gun hidden until Piper was close enough to shoot, that it was possible she'd flee if she realized what I was planning to do. My mind also knew that a bullet couldn't hurt a magical construct made entirely of metal. But my body seemed to be a little fuzzy on the facts.

I took aim at the goat, which came to a stop and just stood there staring at me, its head cocked to one side like a curious dog. My finger tightened on the trigger, and I'm pretty sure I'd have squeezed it all the way if Piper hadn't made an appearance just then.

She looked terrible, her clothing torn and dirty, her hair sticking out at all angles. There was a smear of darkened blood on the ratty peacoat she wore unbuttoned over ill-fitting camo pants. But for all the ugliness of her outward appearance, there was a healthy glow to her skin and she had obviously gained some weight, which looked good on her. She looked like a street person with an unusually healthy and plentiful diet.

"I wouldn't recommend shooting at Billy," Piper said cheerfully. "Who knows where the bullet would end up after it bounced off?"

Her words reminded me that it wasn't Billy I was here to shoot. If it were, I wouldn't be such an emotional wreck.

I shifted my aim and willed myself to pull the trigger the moment I had Piper squarely in my sights. I knew that the more I thought about it, the less likely I was to go through with it.

Piper's eyebrows arched in surprise when I pointed the gun at her, but she didn't look overly concerned. "It'll be kind of hard for me to initiate you into the night if you shoot me. And it would be bad manners."

My hands shook and my aim wavered. All I had to do was pull that damn trigger and Luke and his family would be out of danger. I had brought that danger upon them, and it was my responsibility to save them from it.

So why wasn't I doing what I had to do?

"Come on now, Becks," Piper said. "We both know you're not going to shoot me. You may have an inner bad girl just dying to come out, but she's not *that* bad. My inner bad girl was much closer to the surface, and even I had to become one with the night before I could actually *kill* someone. So let's cut the bullshit, okay? If you're still pissed at me when you're one of us, then you can go ahead and kill me. You won't even feel bad about it." She shrugged as if it hardly mattered to her.

I knew better than to listen to her, and I especially knew better than to talk to her, but that didn't stop me. "I thought it was going to be all unicorns and fairies after I changed, so why would I still be pissed at you?"

Piper laughed. "Unicorns and fairies? That's not what I said, Becks. I said you would feel a whole lot better and that you'd stop hurting. Big difference. Believe me, you can still feel angry. I know, because I'm feeling just a bit irritated that you're standing there holding a gun on me." She grinned hugely. "But anger can be a real rush sometimes. The only thing that sucks about anger is having to keep it in because no one lets you express it. That's what changes when you join the night. No one's going to tell you you shouldn't be angry or that you shouldn't act on what you feel."

"And how would I do that, exactly? Join up, I mean." Yes, I was stalling, still fighting to make myself do the right thing. But if I was going to stand there in a welter of indecision, I might as well see if I could get any information out of Piper. Maybe she would say something that could help others in Philadelphia avoid becoming like her.

Piper crossed her arms over her chest. "Put down the gun, and I'll show you. It doesn't hurt or anything. I promise."

My arms were getting tired from holding the gun out in front of me, and my hands were going numb from the cold. If I aimed for Piper's torso, I could probably hit her without having to try too hard, but I wasn't any closer to pulling the trigger now than I had been when she'd first appeared.

I had already failed, though I didn't yet want to admit it to myself. My only chance had been to fire the moment Piper first came into view. Before I had a chance to think. Before I had a chance to see her, hear her, remember what she had once been. No matter how bitchy she was being now, no matter what my recent memories, I couldn't forget the girl who was my best friend, and that meant I couldn't shoot.

Shuddering, I lowered the gun, though I wasn't about to drop it as Piper had commanded. Maybe I didn't have the guts to shoot her, but that didn't mean I was going to join up, and I had a feeling she might object when she realized that.

"Good job, Piper," said a voice behind me.

I shrieked and pulled the trigger reflexively as I whirled around. I was lucky I didn't shoot my foot off.

Aleric stood in the plaza behind me. Unlike Piper, he didn't look like he'd been sleeping in the streets or Dumpster diving. His jeans were torn at the knee, but the tears looked like they were factory made, and his black leather bomber jacket looked so shiny and new I was surprised there weren't tags hanging off of it. He'd apparently raided a salon and used a ton of product to get that overly neat bed-head look, and if it weren't for the color of his eyes and the aura of cruelty that clung to him, I'd have thought him the hottest guy I'd ever seen.

Aleric smiled, apparently amused by my wild gunshot and startled cat impersonation. I wasn't comfortable having either him or Piper at my back, so I took a few hasty steps to the side so that I could keep them both in my line of sight. I didn't know at first who to point the gun at, but I'd already seen that shooting Aleric was pointless, so I decided on Piper.

"Gee thanks, Al," she said. "I'd just gotten her to put the gun *down*."

Aleric ignored her as if she weren't even there. "You surprise me, Becket," he said. "After everything Piper has done, after everything she's threatened to do, you still can't shoot her?"

"Hey!" Piper protested. "Are you *trying* to get me killed here?"

Aleric still ignored her, all of his attention focused on me. I thought maybe he was about to jump me, but he just stood there, looking at me in a way that made me feel like worms were squirming around under my skin.

Piper took a step toward me while I was distracted by Aleric, but I quickly snapped back to attention and yelled, "Stop, or I'll shoot!"

My voice and my hands were shaking so much I didn't think I sounded very threatening, but Piper stopped and held her hands up. If she had kept moving toward me, I think I might have found the courage to pull the trigger, but of course she wasn't going to make things that easy for me.

Aleric sauntered over to the stone bench I'd declined to sit on earlier, leaning his butt against its back and looking back and forth between me and Piper. He sure looked like he was enjoying himself, the corners of his mouth lifted in a faint smile, his eyes sparkling.

"You know she arranged for the attack on your surrogate mother last night, right?" Aleric asked. "It was her idea to hold that little girl as hostage. And of course she never had any intention of letting the child live, whether its father succeeded or not."

"Aleric?" Piper asked, and for the first time since she'd been Nightstruck, I heard uncertainty in her voice. "What are you doing?"

His green eyes seemed almost to glow in the darkness, and though my gun was pointed in Piper's direction, I couldn't tear my gaze away from his.

"Your will is admirably strong," Aleric said. "She killed your father right before your eyes. She trashed your home. She tried to kill your boyfriend's mother. And the next time she tries, she'll succeed. She won't kill Luke right away—she'll leave him for last, because after he's dead the other deaths won't hurt you so much."

My eyes filmed with tears and my ears started buzzing. These were all the reasons that I'd convinced myself I had to kill Piper in the first place. He was telling me nothing I didn't know, nothing I could argue with. Killing another human being was unequivocally wrong. But letting Luke and his family get killed because of me was wrong, too, and I could stop it.

Piper said something I couldn't hear over the buzzing in my ears.

"I was there on the night she killed your father," Aleric said, his eyes still boring into me. "You could have saved him, you know. If you'd fired the gun the moment you had a chance, then Piper would have died and lost control of Billy."

I shook my head in denial, but my throat was too tight and my breath too short to protest. The constructs didn't need anyone ordering them about to be vicious. Why would Billy have backed off when my father was a helpless, trapped victim?

And yet, as illogical as it was, I couldn't help the way my insides cringed at the memory and at Aleric's words. *It's your fault,* an evil voice whispered in my mind. *Your fault, and your responsibility to fix it, no matter what it takes.*

"Did you keep count of the number of times Billy struck your father?" Aleric asked. "Did you ever ask yourself how much of it he was conscious for? The pain he must have suffered. . . . Do you remember the sound of him screaming?"

"Shut up!" I screeched. It wasn't just my hands and arms that were shaking now; it was my entire body. I was drenched in sweat despite the cold, and I could hardly get enough oxygen into my lungs. Every detail of that terrible night was burned into my memory forever. Most of the time, I was able to shove the memories away into a dark corner, but not tonight. Not with Aleric hammering at me.

"All because Piper wanted you to come play with her," Aleric finished, with some satisfaction.

He'd poked and prodded and pushed me to the breaking point, but I like to think I wouldn't have gone over without the final, unbearable nail he drove into my coffin.

A scream split the night. A scream of terror and pain. A

scream I could not fail to recognize. The scream of my father dying while I stood at the window and watched.

I didn't decide to pull the trigger. It just happened.

And there was another, entirely different scream.

# CHAPTER TWENTY-SEVEN

My nose stung with the acrid scent of burnt gun-
powder, and my ears rang. Piper's eyes were wide
and startled, her mouth open in shock as she looked down at
herself.

The bullet had hit in the center of her torso, right around
the base of her sternum. She clapped both hands to the wound,
and blood overflowed her fingers, steaming in the frigid
air.

The gun dropped from my nerveless fingers, and I stifled a
sob with both hands as I blinked to clear the tears that were
blurring my vision.

I'd done it. I'd shot her. Shot Piper, my best friend.

She shuddered and staggered, her knees visibly shaking as
she tried to stay on her feet. She turned her gaze not to me,
but to Aleric.

"Why?" she asked, then made a little sound of pain as her
knees gave out and she dropped to the pavement on her butt.
She was still staring at Aleric in shocked disbelief.

"I lied," Aleric said, with no hint of regret in his voice. "She
wasn't fully primed to become one of us yet. She needed another push." He looked at me, his face glowing with satisfac-

tion and the thrill of victory. "Think about this, Becket: Why did you shoot her?"

I wouldn't have answered him even if I'd been capable of speech. There wasn't a whole lot of light, but I could see that Piper's coat was getting drenched with blood despite her attempts to stanch the flow. I could also see that her face was ghostly pale and that her eyes were no longer that unsettling, inhuman shade of green.

"Did you shoot her when I pointed out she was a threat to those around you, as you planned?" Aleric continued. "Nope. That wasn't it. When did you pull the trigger, Becket?"

"Shut up!" I snapped. I found my feet moving me forward, toward Piper, who looked so pale and shocked and frightened. I had no idea if that bullet wound was fatal or not, my knowledge of anatomy not precise enough to know if I'd hit anything vital, but I knew it didn't look good. And although I couldn't help being glad to see Piper's eyes turn back to normal, I also couldn't help thinking that was a bad sign.

"You didn't shoot in some noble, selfless act of sacrifice. No, you pulled that trigger when I reminded you what happened to your father. You killed Piper not to save the lives of others, but in anger, in fury, as revenge for what she'd done. There's nothing even remotely noble about that."

"Shut the hell up, Aleric!" Piper said. Her eyes met mine, and I saw nothing in them except the old Piper, the Piper who'd been my best friend for years. "Run, Becket," she urged. "Get inside." Her face twisted in a grimace of pain.

I'd been so numb I hadn't even noticed my feet moving, but now I dropped down to my knees beside her, putting my hand over hers and pushing. "Put pressure on it," I said in a raspy whisper. "That's what you're supposed to do, right?"

Piper shook her head and made a weak effort to pull away. The effort cost her, and she groaned. "Forget about me," she said when she could find her voice again. "You have to get inside. Now!" She sagged down to the pavement, hands still pressed to the wound as she curled her body around it.

"We have to get you to a hospital," I said. Ignoring the blood that now coated my hands, I felt around in my coat pockets, searching for my cell phone. It might take longer than Piper had, to get an emergency crew over here, but I had to try.

"Forget me!" Piper said more sharply. She reached out and grabbed my wrist just as my fingers touched my cell phone. "Get inside. Hurry. You can't be outside during the Transition. Not in the state you're in."

"Huh?"

"The Transition. It's like a riptide. When the sun comes up and the magic recedes, it pulls at you if you're vulnerable. Usually you'd be strong enough to resist, but not now. Not after this. You'll be Nightstruck for sure."

"Would that be so terrible?" Aleric asked. He was standing nearby, looking down at the two of us, with a gloating smile on his face. "If you join us, you won't feel the least bit bad about having shot and killed your best friend in a fit of anger."

I'd left the gun where I'd dropped it, otherwise I might have fired off a couple of shots at him right then. They wouldn't have hurt him, but at least it would have given me a hint of an outlet for some of the rage and horror that were building inside me.

"Run," Piper said, more weakly. "Go. Leave me. You can't help me, and you don't have much time. Dawn's coming."

She blinked rapidly and her breath hitched. Then her eyes slid closed and her hands went limp.

"Piper!" I sobbed, touching her shoulder but not daring to shake her for fear I'd hurt her worse. "Stay awake! Please!"

I knew she wasn't dead. Not yet, at least. But the pool of blood that had formed beneath her continued to grow larger. It was too much blood. Even if I could get paramedics here at the snap of my fingers, Piper was doomed. I'd suspected as much the moment the green had faded from her eyes, could think of no reason why the night might let her go except that she was of no use to it anymore.

A sob tore from my throat, and I stifled it with my blood-coated hand. I had come here to kill Piper, but I realized now that I had never truly expected to succeed. Deep down I'd been convinced I wouldn't be able to pull the trigger, and I'd never really considered what I'd have to live with if I did it.

But only if the night didn't take me.

If I wanted the pain to go away, if I wanted to escape the guilt that was already choking me, all I had to do was sit here by Piper's side and wait.

What did I have to go home to? I was trapped in the city, cut off from my mother, my sister, my remaining family. My house was unlivable and would be for the foreseeable future. My father was dead. Luke couldn't forgive me for getting his mom hurt. And I had murdered my best friend. Why on earth would I want to go back to all that?

I was tempted. Very, very tempted.

But that was the coward's way out. I had allowed the magic in, had started the nightmare that had killed so many and would kill so many more. Aleric had been after me—mostly through Piper—from almost the very beginning. It wasn't because he liked me, and he hadn't chosen me at random.

There was a reason he wanted me to be Nightstruck, and that reason couldn't be anything good.

Was it possible that I had the means to undo the damage I had done? It was my blood that had triggered the magic's growth. Perhaps my blood could reverse it. And what better way was there to make sure that didn't happen than to manipulate me into the joining the night so that I'd no longer care about the suffering of my fellow human beings?

I staggered to my feet. I wasn't sure I believed my own arguments, but I *did* believe that Aleric very much wanted me to be a Nightstruck and that giving him what he wanted was a bad idea.

He smiled at me indulgently as I swayed and tried to regain my bearings.

"It's too late, Becket," he said. "You'll never get inside before Transition, and you're too broken to fight it."

"We'll see about that," I said. I dashed the tears from my eyes—no doubt getting streaks of blood all over my face—and started running for the exit. I thought Aleric would follow me, try to stop me, but he must have been very convinced I couldn't get inside in time, because he let me go.

I pulled out my phone as I ran, checking the time. I didn't know exactly when sunrise occurred, but I knew it was somewhere around seven. My heart seized when my phone told me it was 6:58. I had scant minutes, maybe even seconds, to find my way inside.

The hydra was still parked in the pathway, hissing and snapping. I didn't have time to figure out a way around it, so I just blew past, expecting to be bitten and maybe ensnared. I was pleasantly surprised when I hit the sidewalk unscathed.

There was no time to think or devise a plan. All I could do was make for the nearest building and try to get in.

The nearest building was a hotel. In the old days, there would have been polite doormen waiting at the glass entrance doors to let me in, but since the changes, those doors were barred and reinforced. The lights were on in the lobby, and I could see a pair of armed security guards lurking about, ready to jump into action at any sign of an attack.

I slammed into the bars and reached through to pound on the glass. "Help me!" I screamed. "Let me in!"

I can't imagine what those guards must have thought. I was out at night, hysterical, and covered in blood. They had to know I wasn't Nightstruck, because I didn't have the green eyes, but they had no idea what might be after me. They both drew their weapons and pointed them in my direction.

"Please!" I cried. "Just let me in!"

But I realized there would be no way I could talk them into opening those doors, not in the small amount of time I had left. Even if I could calm myself enough to make a coherent plea.

I turned to look behind me, and to my horror I saw a faint glow in the sky, a glow that was getting brighter by the moment. I had no time.

My phone was still in my hand, and I quickly typed out a text to Luke, hoping to at least give him and his mom some clue of what had happened to me.

*Became Nightstruck by being out during Transition. Love U.*

My skin was beginning to tingle strangely. I hit Send before I had a chance to change my mind or delete that last part. Facing almost directly east, I watched the sun rising over the city, saw the Transition taking over before my very eyes, saw the high-rises on the other side of the square lose their scaled, spiked, or otherwise unpleasant facades and turn back into normal buildings, saw the rows of gallows changing back into streetlamps.

Aleric stood at the very edge of the square, smiling at me and waving until the Transition hit. The iron fence around him shrank back to its usual height, and Aleric disappeared altogether.

Panting and terrified, I pressed my back against the bars, delaying the moment the Transition would hit me for as long as I possibly could. Piper said that ordinarily I'd be able to re-sist the pull, so I tried to calm myself, tried to ignore my best friend's blood on my hands.

"Don't think about it," I ordered myself. I told myself to think about flowers and puppies, about Marlene's contagious smile and Luke's intoxicating kiss. All the good things that would be forever gone from my life if I let the night take me. I had to fight it, had to hold on to myself no matter how much it hurt.

And then the first hint of dawn's light hit me. I saw a brutal montage. Billy, his spines and horns dripping with blood. My father's body lying broken and bleeding in the gutter. Piper col-lapsing to the pavement as blood poured from the place where I had shot her.

A paradoxical euphoria filled my body, chasing away the horrors one by one. The relief was indescribable, and I wept with it. It was like that first glorious sip of air when you've swum un-derwater too long. I knew that air was poisoned, knew I shouldn't let it into my lungs. I had promised myself I'd fight it.

But I breathed it in anyway, and everything changed.